THE COFFIN TRADER

THE COFFIN TRADER

EDITA A. PETRICK

Chapter 1

THE SILENT AMBULANCE passed her, heading east towards Rocky Hill. Lauren flicked on her signal to make the right-hand turn into the staff parking lot. The flashing light wasn't on either. An ambulance departing leisurely from the campus of Winthrop College meant...?

She finished turning and drove to her parking spot.

What did it mean? She knew damn well what a howling ambulance shooting down any street meant. The person inside needed medical help—fast. But the opposite scenario had to mean that the person inside no longer needed assistance. Who would drop dead of a heart attack at nine o'clock on a Saturday morning?

Most of the three thousand who comprised the college's student body would still be sleeping on Saturday morning, charging up for the traditional Saturday night club-hopping up in Hartford. And many of the college's two hundred faculty and staff would be doing the same, except for a dozen or so diehards who would sacrifice their weekend to come and talk to their computers, and search for new ways to sharpen the focus of their lecture material.

She realized that she should take her foot off the brake and finish parking. An idling car wasted gas.

Every Saturday, she had to use the east delivery entrance in the back of the Essex Hall. Walking to her office, she forgot all about the ambulance while she focused on a more pressing issue: would Errington fire her today? He would be in for sure; he used Saturdays to come up with new, imaginative ways to deliver bad news to his staff, like a grant cancellation or workspace reduction. Trying to shake off these worries, she swiped her security card. Once the light blinked green, she entered her password. Five minutes later, she had exhausted her memory and her patience, keying in every numerical sequence she remembered ever using, but the door wouldn't open. Bryce Culver, the head of campus security, insisted that staff change their passwords every month. She'd changed hers a couple of weeks ago at the end of September. The six-digit combination should have worked.

She dropped her hand with the security card and hung her head. She had three choices. One, she could take out her cell phone and call Errington, who would have come in at the crack of dawn. He'd not miss an opportunity like this to remind her that he had approved her doctoral thesis topic under duress; that he didn't believe the Connecticut waste management industry needed a new waste processing facility, and that the Department of Environmental Management expected its doctoral candidates to uphold their share of producing brilliant scientific papers even at the expense of their theses. She could also drive back home and spend the rest of the weekend perusing job ads in the Hartford Gazette. And finally, she might zip-up her windbreaker and walk around the building to try her luck at the seldom-used west delivery entrance.

"I'm spineless," she said, zipping up her navy blue windbreaker.

SHE WALKED WITH her head down, chin tucked against her chest. Even though the sun shone brightly, the October wind stung her cheeks. An arm appeared in front of her and literally bounced her back.

A stern voice said, "Just a moment, ma'am. I'm afraid I can't let you pass."

She stumbled backward, startled by the unexpected obstacle.

"What's going on...officer?" She took in the uniform, the polite but unyielding expression, the still-outstretched arm. Finally, she focused on the police car behind him.

"I'm afraid I can't let you pass," he repeated.

"I work here. What happened? What's all this...?" She motioned at the police cars.

"Excuse me," a man's voice said behind her.

She turned, wondering what had happened to merit the presence of what looked like half the Hartford police force. The man wore his black leather jacket zipped up, so he had to be a sensible person, and flashed his badge.

"Detective Terney, Hartford Police Department, Homicide," he said. "May I see some identification?"

"Homicide?" She looked back and forth between the policeman and the detective.

"ID please," he repeated, voice hardening.

"Sure, sure." She fumbled with the straps of her leather knapsack, trying to think what exactly homicide signified, especially back here at the little-used entrance.

He studied her driver's license and her college staff card for a long time.

"It's really me. I'm just not photogenic," she said. His scrutiny of her documents started to make her uncomfortable.

He didn't react to her sarcasm, didn't even lift his head, but said, "Please come with me, Dr. Sarasohn."

"I'm not a doctor yet," she said and saw him glance at her.

"Fine. Please come with me."

She knew it wouldn't affect him, but she made a face at him nevertheless and moved for the door.

"Up the stairs, to the second floor—and all the way to your office." he said.

She turned. "How do you know my office is on the second floor?"

He indicated the staircase with his eyes. "Keep moving. You'll see. I'll be right behind you."

She climbed the stairs, uncomfortable with his presence behind her, and once again found the door to the corridor thrown wide open, its steel panel pinned to the wall. Her office stood at the end. The crowd of blue uniforms clustered around her door.

"Mitch..." She stopped, her mouth turning dry. Cops holding convention around her door had to mean only one thing: Mitchell had decided to come in today too, and something must have happened to him.

"We've already checked. Your colleague, Mitchell Plow, is all right." She heard Terney say. "It wasn't him."

She breathed a sigh of relief and faced him. "Then who?"

He raised his brows. The action forced his mouth into a grimace. "I hoped you'd be able to tell us."

"What happened, Detective? Obviously, it happened in my office, so what's going on here?"

"Dr. Errington found the body of a young man in your office."

"Errington found a dead body...in *my* office?" A bubble of hilarity rose in her throat.

"Do you normally come to work on Saturdays?"

"Yes. Errington found a dead man..."

"Does your boss normally come to see you on Saturday mornings?"

"Yes...well, no, not really. He usually just phones to check if I came in. He must have wanted to tell me...something." At the last moment, she decided on vagueness instead of speaking her mind and saying that Errington probably came to either fire her or to deliver another ultimatum about publishing a paper, soon.

"So it's not normal for your boss to come see you on Saturday morning?"

"Look, Detective, it's neither normal nor abnormal. He does whatever strikes his fancy. He's my boss," she said edgily. "Did he know the man?"

"No. Your boss thought it might be one of your students."

She groaned. How typical of Errington to quickly shift the focus from himself to his staff.

"Your office has been trashed," Terney said. "Either the victim or his killer must have been looking for something."

"Oh great! So they've found my secret society files." She snickered, even though she knew that Terney might think her attitude mercenary. A young man found murdered in her office. In her place, Linda, or any other colleague, would be horrified. But none of them had been coming to work on Saturday these past couple of years, expecting to be lectured, patronized or fired. She couldn't tell Terney that the murder gave her an emotional reprieve, no matter how short lived it might be.

Terney kept staring at her, his forehead creased into a hard v-notched wrinkle. She said, "I don't keep anything valuable in my office, Detective, just my work. None of the mineral specimen in my collection is precious—not to a degree that they'd be worth something on the street. There are a few samples of gold-bearing sulfides and gneiss, but I'm talking samples here, not any viable amount of precious metal. I'm sure Mitch doesn't keep anything valuable either. His thesis is in shoreline protection. Mine is waste management, and both are environmental topics. There isn't anything from either of our research that's worth stealing—yet. I mean, if someone wanted to pirate research, Dr. Errington's office would be a much better bet than our cubbyhole."

"How about drugs?" Terney's frown refused to leave his face.

"No." She decided to be plain and terse.

"Mr. Plow?"

"No."

"How well do you know your colleague?"

"Well. If Mitch kept drugs in our office, I'd be the first to notice. You must have been in our office." She waited for his nod and continued, "So you know that in such cramped quarters, it's impossible to miss popping Aspirin, never mind doing drugs."

"Come." Suddenly, Terney's hand fastened on her upper arm, pulling her down the corridor.

"Is the man...the victim...?"

"The coroner's people have already removed the body. The forensics staff is still working. That'll take time. Your boss called 911 just after seven o'clock. What time do you normally come in on Saturdays?"

"Generally, nine o'clock. I'm not late, if that's what you mean."

"Why would your boss come looking for you that early in the morning?" he asked, nodding ahead and walking toward the group of cops, who parted ranks to let them through.

"He probably wasn't looking for me, at least not at that time. He probably went to my office to leave me a note...something that couldn't be sent through e-mail." She wondered if he'd figure out what kind of notes bosses usually didn't trust to e-mail, but delivered in person.

"A nasty note," he said. "Is your boss unhappy with your work here?"

"I don't write and publish brilliant research papers fast enough for his liking. Oh my God!" She leaned against the doorframe once she saw her office. An elephant couldn't have done more damage. Any which way she looked, crushed boxes, broken glass, and ripped paper lay strewn everywhere.

"Careful," Terney said and squeezed in beside her. "Like I said, the forensic staff will work here for a while, one at a time, I suspect. I'm afraid you won't be able to use this office for some time."

"Because of that." She motioned at the floor. The police must have first picked up all the shredded paper before drawing the outline of a body.

"That and the fact that I need you and Mr. Plow to go through everything that's in here and see if anything's missing."

"Where is Mitch?"

"We called his landlady. He's at his girlfriend's in Wethersfield. I want you and Mr. Plow to start going over everything as soon as possible."

She looked down and touched one of the mineral samples, a bed of amethyst crystals, with the tip of her boot. "I'm telling you,

Detective, Mitch and I had nothing of value to anyone but the two of us in here."

"You might have something that you don't consider valuable. However, the victim and his killer might have thought otherwise."

"Do you know the young man's identity?"

"We found his wallet in his jeans. Whoever killed him wasn't interested in the forty dollars he carried on him. According to his New York driver's license, his name is Oswaldo Gomez. Did you know him?"

"I'm not sure. I don't think so. I've been teaching here five years. A lot of kids come through my classes. I also teach a mineralogy and crystal identification class twice a week at the Heston Community Center in Hartford. Maybe if you showed me his picture..."

Terney dipped a hand in his pocket and brought out a plastic bag. He offered it to her. "According to his driver's license, he's twenty-four. If you've been teaching here five years, it's possible he might have been one of your students."

She peered at the plastic ID, trying to prod her mind into recognition. The stamp-sized picture looked clear and harsh, like all identification photographs. The victim must have been sixteen at the time judging by his pumpkin-round face, and shaved head with a single black braid hanging down his forehead, representing trademark of teenaged angst—and maybe a street gang affiliation. He had dark skin and could be Mexican, maybe Cuban, or he might have been from any of the countries she saw years ago as a twenty-year-old idealist with Greenpeace, where sun dried up the spilled blood at the same rate it dried up water.

His eyes, even from such a small picture, seemed to glare with hostility. How ironic that the photographer's camera had sucked out the anger and stamped it on a piece of plastic for all the cops who might be looking at it to see and feel. Last year, when she went to a photo kiosk to get passport photos, the attendant said not to smile. It wasn't permitted to smile anymore for photos that would appear on official documents. Cheer, just like goodwill toward men, became a thing of the past, a myth. She wondered if somewhere down the road, in the near future, official identification might be stamped with the person's genetic code and its brief interpretation: predisposed to violence—damaged goods.

She raised her head and leaned back. "I'm pretty sure he wasn't my student. I might have seen him somewhere, a mall or even on a street, but I don't know him."

"Would you be able to check your records?"

She looked around at the mess of papers strewn all over the floor. Did the police expect her to glue the pieces together? The overturned chair, and the slashed LCD monitor lying next to the computer were easy to pick up. Her smashed plastic file holders, and the broken glass from the framed diplomas and certificates that used to hang on the wall, could be swept in couple of hours. But the bits of paper....

With a sigh, she said, "Once I clean up, and if my hard drive's not damaged or if it can be at least restored, I'll take a look at my class lists to see if his name figured amongst my early students, but I don't think so."

"Why not?"

She smiled and tried not to show her discomfort. "He's a...well, I teach mostly first-year elective courses. Five years ago, Mr. Gomez would have been nineteen. He'd have been a sophomore, or even a junior."

"A lot of people start college at nineteen or even older," he said.

"Yeah, I know," she said, averting her eyes.

"You still haven't answered my question, Ms. Sarasohn."

"Look, Detective, I'm very sorry that a man is dead, and if I didn't show it...."

He interrupted her. "We're all different. We all deal differently with ugly things like murder and death. I'm not judging you. Answer my question."

"If Mr. Gomez would have been in one of my classes, I would have definitely remembered him. He'd have been one of my token ethnic students, if you know what I mean."

"Yes. I know exactly what you mean," he said, nodded, and handed her his business card. "If you manage to take a look at those class lists, I'd appreciate it if you'd give me a call. And if you can think of any connection, no matter how slim or improbable, don't hesitate to call me. Thanks for your cooperation." He put the plastic bag with the boy's license in his pocket and walked out the door.

Chapter 2

ON THE BOTTOM half of the front page, the Sunday edition of the Hartford Gazette carried the news about the body of a young man discovered in an office in Winthrop's administrative building. The police hadn't released the victim's name pending family notification. The two-inch column might be easily missed, even for the most detail-oriented reader.

Errington must have studied the Gazette with a magnifying glass, and afterward cut out the column and enlarged it with a photocopier. He came to see her Sunday afternoon. He thrust a sheet of paper at her and said, "See that? Just take a look at that, Ms. Sarasohn, and tell me why my staff would want to bring such shame on my department."

She knelt on the floor in the corridor, looking through boxes the police had brought out of her office and stacked along the wall. The sheet of paper touched the tip of her nose.

She rose, braced her back with her hands, stretched, and turned to face him. "Dr. Errington. So you came to see me—finally. I hoped Mitch came back with the pop. The fridge door must be stuck again. Is there any place the police can store these boxes other than here in the corridor?"

"Answer my question." His face, normally gaunt and clean-shaven, seemed puffy and sunburned, like someone who had fallen asleep in a tanning cubicle.

"Why didn't you come to see me yesterday? The police investigators stayed here for hours. I told Detective Terney what I know, which is nothing."

"He was killed in your office!" he said so forcefully that the two policemen flanking her office door leaned over and stared.

"Yes, and isn't that just like me, loaning my office out to killers. Do you think I should have charged rent?"

"Don't be impudent, you, you...I was the one who found the dead body!"

So that's what offended his tender sensibilities—the indignity of finding a corpse in her office.

"If you came to see me more often, sir, instead of using e-mail, you'd know that finding a dead body in my office is not a routine event." She knew her sarcasm would have little effect, but it felt good to stand up to him.

He threw down the photocopied column, made sounds as if he'd walked into a room full of smoke, and left. God, was there any relaxing technique that worked to clear the kind of tension that came out of confrontation with Errington?

She lowered her head in time to see Mitch appear around the corner, a can of pop in each hand.

She waved at him. "I have to go outside, take a walk...save some pop for me." One of the policemen asked her where she was headed. She repeated she needed a breath of fresh air, and he let her go.

By Monday, the media lurked everywhere on the campus. Bryce Culver posted guards at all the entrances to Essex Hall, but there was a forest of cameras trained at the building and anyone who entered or exited.

Errington cancelled all her Monday classes. He must have

immediately realized that such a foolhardy action might reflect poorly on him; instead, he assigned Mitch and Linda Moore, his assistant, to teach her classes for the rest of the week.

He came to see her in the staff lounge. "You need time off. Besides, the police will want to question you, so you have to be available," he said.

"I told the police everything. I don't know the victim or why he came to my office in the first place," she said, moving aside for the policeman to put down another box filled with broken glass, twisted picture frames, and damaged diplomas.

"Was he your boyfriend, or maybe someone you met in a night club?" Errington didn't listen to her. He always followed his agenda. If she didn't say what he wanted to hear, he wouldn't acknowledge her reply.

"Didn't you hear me?" She raised her voice and faced him, their Sunday confrontation still fresh in her memory. "I've never seen him before. I don't know how or why he came to my office."

"Perhaps an acquaintance or someone you knew from your hometown…"

"Dr. Errington!" She knew she stood in danger of being fired, but shouting became the only tool she had to get through to him.

Predictably, he took offence. "Don't shout at me, Ms. Sarasohn. I understand you're distraught, but that's no reason to shout at me. This disgrace—"

She cut him off. "Murder, there I said it. Not disgrace, not an accident but outright murder happened in my office. The victim's name is Oswaldo Gomez. The homicide detective had no problem believing anything I said, and I told him that I didn't know the victim, that he wasn't nor ever had been one of my students."

"How can you be sure?" He leaned forward, staring at her, his eyes widening as if she'd just materialized in front of him. She rubbed her forehead to gain time, because he seldom focused so quickly in their conversations. She also never figured out whether he really ignored her replies or whether it was his tactic to keep her off balance. His interest was not just sudden but acute. Did Errington worry about something else than *his* department's reputation?

"My computer's trashed, and Randy at the lab said he doesn't think he'll be able to salvage the hard drive. But the dean's secretary has all the class lists and she's also working today."

He recoiled with shock. "You didn't call Ms. Stong, did you?"

She nodded once, sharply. "Yes, I did, and I used that phone." She pointed at the wall-mounted telephone for the staff's use. "I told her exactly why I needed those class records."

"You didn't!" He pressed a hand against his chest.

She laughed. "Mitch came in on Saturday afternoon. He said the media van had already camped out in the parking lot. You brought me the enlarged column from the Sunday Gazette, and today, I had to call Bryce Culver just to park my car in my parking spot. It's all over Hartford. There's been a murder at Winthrop College. Actually, Amber said that the dean held a meeting with the president because the college has to issue a formal statement for the public and the media. Of course, the students' parents will want to know—"

"Enough!" He waved his hand in front of her. "I hoped to contain this *disgrace,* and I hoped that my staff would understand and act with sensitivity."

"Hasn't the dean called you yet?" She knew that's what Errington feared the most—having to account for the *disgrace* since the murder occurred in his department.

"I spoke with the dean on Saturday. He concurred that the issue had to be handled with sensitivity. I expected you to understand and behave accordingly."

"According to what? Today, Bryce helped me to avoid the media, and I spent the rest of Saturday and all of Sunday checking my trashed belongings to see if anything's missing. I talked to detective Terney, and he said he'd call me to go to Hartford and sign the statement once it's ready. That's all I've done."

"But you called Amber."

She laughed. "Amber invited me to lunch. She wanted to get all the juicy details on the murder in my office. I declined, and if that's not sensitivity and acting responsibly, I don't know what is. I needed those class records, not just this year's, but also all my previous class records."

"Did you ever have him as your student?"

"I just told you I don't know him. I've never seen him before. Oswaldo Gomez is a total stranger to me."

"Why would he come to see you in your office?" His tone of voice turned coldly speculative.

"I don't know, and you're assuming a hell of a lot. He might have just hid in my office if he thought someone threatened him. He just had to push the door since the lock doesn't work. He might have been heading for your office and got lost..."

Errington gasped, took a step back, turned around, and marched out of the lounge. She came to expect such theatrics from him. And maybe such drama was good psychology. Not knowing if she faced Dr. Jekyll or Mr. Hyde kept her in a constant state of apprehension—and confusion. However, this time there was something just a little...off in his performance. He shed the role and focused too quickly on the issue and the speaker. He really wanted to hear her answer, and that meant...? She sighed. She was in no shape to psychoanalyze Errington's latest performance. Maybe later.

She knew he couldn't fire her unless the police established some kind of link between her and Oswaldo Gomez, and there was no way that would happen. Had it occurred to Terney that Gomez might have simply used her office to hide if he thought someone had followed him? But to hide in a room stationed in a dead-end hall wasn't exactly smart. If the victim knew someone followed him, the natural thing would have been to head for the stairs, keep seeking an exit. Besides, if the victim barged through the door, he'd see a tiny office that couldn't possibly offer him a hiding place. In that case, he'd have shut the door and run down the corridor.

"Only I come in on Saturday, so he *must* have come to see me, after all," she whispered, chilled by the possibility that Gomez might have been looking for her. "But why...?"

"I've no idea." Mitch said behind her.

She looked up to find him handing her a can of pop.

He continued, "The fridge is almost empty. It's time to stock up on pop and bottled water. I saw Errington blast out of here. What did you tell him?"

She sighed, pulled the tab, and took a sip. "Nothing. I don't know anything. Are you going to be all right? I mean teaching my classes and yours."

"No problem. So he took you out...for how long?"

"A week, I think."

"Why don't you get some rest?"

She motioned at the cartons all around them. "I have to check and double-check that nothing's missing. Did you finish checking your stuff?"

"Yep. What little I keep here is still here, just in pieces. What if this guy, Gomez, wasn't coming to steal, but brought something?"

"Like what?"

"I don't know."

"Nobody brings anything to our office, Mitch—except for you and me."

"He has to be connected to you somehow."

"Why?" She glared at him. "Why can't he be connected to you? You share the office with me. Why is everyone assuming that the victim came to see me?"

"Because he came on Saturday. I never come here on weekends, not if I can help it."

"You've come before."

"Once, Lauren, only once, and you had to let me in. You're what my ancestors called 'habitué.'"

"I come to work on Saturday because Errington ordered me to do it. A habit's not an order, Mitch, and you're not French."

"My grandfather's name was Jean-Paul Sauvignon."

"You're Mitchell Plow."

"On my mother's side I'm connected to a great Gaul."

She shook her head. Mitchell Plow didn't have his PhD but he'd been hired to teach three first-year classes and two sophomore classes, so she figured he had to be the Director's new "darling boy." A month later, she wondered why, indeed, did Errington hire Mitch, since his doctoral thesis topic didn't have any teeth. It also wasn't "sexy" enough to bring glory to the Environmental Management Department. Reclamation of exhausted landscapes used to be a hot, popular topic—twenty years ago. And Mitch talked the way he dressed; simply and without political correctness. Whenever he tossed off his sweatshirt, her eyes stuck to a watch with a tacky purple and yellow fabric strap and a hula-dancer painted on its dial. His girlfriend, Jenny, a legal secretary, gave it to him last Christmas as a token of her appreciation for his romantic gift to her—a case of California Chablis.

"All right, Lord of Gaul," she said, trying not to smile. "I'm going to go through those class lists again, but first, I need a breath of fresh air."

"It's Monday, my dear colleague. Yesterday was all-clear, but today there's a crowd of media out there."

"A media car sat out there on Sunday too." She grimaced.

"Go have your electronic cigarette in the washroom. It's safer that way. Besides, it's just a pacifier anyway."

Chapter 3

S HE STAYED HOME on Tuesday, moving aimlessly between the three small rooms of her tiny bungalow, often stopping by the living room window to look out.

She told Mitch that Sunday, when she went out for a cigarette, a media car sat parked outside. It was mostly true. Except she saw the same car—a silver sedan—Sunday morning when she arrived on campus. It sat parked a few spaces over from her car. She decided to confront the driver and got out. The car reversed and left so quickly, the tires screeched. That night at home, she thought she saw the same sedan parked on the street. On Monday, she kept staring at every silver sedan in the parking lot and on the road. Since the media sat outside in full force, it was no use to try and spot "her" silver sedan and she gave up.

On Wednesday, she drove to Hartford. Gritting her teeth, she refused to look at passing cars. Three times she drove by the police headquarters on Conroy Street, and on the fourth pass, she kept driving until the cut-off to get on the Interstate. At the last moment, she made a right-hand turn, cruised the district until she found a coffee shop, and pulled into the parking lot.

Lauren used the payphone in the coffee shop to call. She hoped Terney would pick up the phone and not someone else. At the sound of his familiar voice, relief rushed through her.

"Terney speaking."

"Lieutenant, it's Lauren Sarasohn from Winthrop. Are you busy?"

"Always—but I can make time if necessary."

"I'm in Sagalyn's Coffee Shop, about two blocks from the...."

He interrupted. "I know where it is. Do you want me to come down there?"

"Yes. I'd like to buy you a cup of coffee."

"I'll be there in ten minutes." He hung up.

She bought a coffee and a homemade version of croissant, and chose a seat near the window. Terney took his time. She finished her croissant and coffee. It felt uncomfortable just sitting there, staring at the parking lot, so she went to get another coffee and one for Terney as well. By the time she returned to her seat, a blue Chevy pulled into the parking strip and Terney got out.

"Thank you," he said and sat down. He proceeded to fix his coffee. She made a mental note that he took two creams and two sugars. Such balance seemed to define him, and she suspected that whatever he did, he would seek to balance his thoughts and actions.

"Did you find any more information about the victim, Detective?" she asked. Suddenly, she wasn't so sure how to broach what bothered her.

He shook his head. "Nothing more than what we've already established. Definitely Cuban, a landed immigrant. His sister, Ellen McKinley, lives at 1365 Roper Drive—does it ring a bell?"

"No. Ellen McKinley isn't a Cuban name."

"She married a McKinley."

"So Gomez lived in Hartford?"

"He lived with his sister and brother-in-law until he finished high school. He left for New York, got a job as a bellhop at the

Carlyle and kept it until we found his body in your office. But you didn't call me to talk about the victim."

"I think someone's following me."

"A feeling or a fact?"

She hissed softly. She'd been asking herself the same thing—was it just her overwrought imagination or was it real?

"It might be just my nerves, but I left my house on Sunday and I think a silver sedan followed me. I made a right turn off Pilgrim Street into the parking lot, and the sedan continued going west. It stopped at the stop sign and made a left turn onto Clarke."

"Where would that take it?"

"Clarke is a dead-end street. It connects Spindler Hall with the Mason campus residence complex."

"So anyone heading south on Clarke would be heading for the campus residence complex?"

She nodded. "It might have been a parent or relative, visiting a student."

"You don't think so."

"Mitch and I spent Sunday sorting through the office debris. At three o'clock in the afternoon, my boss came to see me. Once he finished airing his worries about my professional conduct, I had to go outside to clear my head. That's when I noticed the silver sedan—again. It sat four parking spaces from my Volkswagen. The driver remained inside. My nerves are shot, but I got pissed off and walked towards the car. I crossed the median. The driver just zoomed out of there."

"Did you see it again?"

"That evening, I looked out my window. I went outside, but I guess by the time I walked down the driveway, the car must have left. Or I might have just been imagining things. I'm pretty stressed out these days."

"Stress usually makes us sharper. At least that's my experience," he said.

"Oswaldo Gomez wasn't my student, Detective. I don't know why he'd come to my office. I've got no idea who'd want to kill him. I've been struggling with these things for three days now. Why would anyone follow me? I don't have anything of interest to anyone, maybe not even to Errington," she finished, frustrated and angry that this had to happen now and to her. "I'm very sorry that a young man died. I'm not callous and self-absorbed, but my boss is the type who's always on the lookout for faults in others, and I'm his favorite scapegoat. He hired me, but I've always felt that he hired me precisely to have someone to blame for anything and everything. The rest of my colleagues are..." she trailed off, not knowing how to phrase it.

"Without vulnerabilities. They're able to either shrug off their boss' criticism or fight back. You don't. Why not?"

"I don't know." She sought escape in pretending to mix the un-dissolved sugar on the bottom of her coffee cup.

"Do you feel inferior to your colleagues because you haven't finished your Ph.D.?"

"I am inferior precisely because I don't have what they all have: the highest academic credentials. Only nine percent of the Winthrop teaching staff doesn't have a doctorate degree. Mitch and I probably account for most of that percentage."

"Would a doctorate title make you feel worthy and on par with the rest of your colleagues?"

Lauren started to say yes, but stopped. She didn't know. She told herself that those three tiny letters—Ph.D.— set her apart from the rest of her colleagues in Errington's department, and made all the world of difference. But even as she kept reinforcing that line of thought, a voice whispered that it was a crutch...that she chose to define herself in such one-dimensional terms.

"I don't know whether completing my doctorate would make anything better or not," she said. It was more honorable to confess ignorance than to feign indifference.

"I've done some checking," he said and rose. He strode over to the counter and brought back two more coffees with condiments. He continued, "At sixteen, you were the only high school student from Maine to serve as a page in the House of Representatives.

And while you lived at the residence hall, you spent the weekends and holidays with Aileen Summerville and her family, the Maine Senator who nominated you. She gave you a glowing recommendation. You fast-tracked through high school and entered Duke University, one of the top ten schools we have, on scholarship at seventeen. Your professors at the Nicholas School of the Environment had the highest praise for your—"

"What's your point?" she interrupted.

"My point is that you finished your Master's degree, spent six months in the position of a White House intern, where the President's Science Advisor took you under her wing, but you didn't use her clout to continue with your Ph.D. and marry such excellence to a political career. Instead, you joined Greenpeace, and spent the next four years living in tents or on dilapidated houseboats, trekking all over the globe to wherever the cause took you. You came back and Ms. Perez offered you a healthy grant if only you chose one of the topics on her agenda, but suddenly you turned shy and all but disappeared from the academic scene. What happened?"

"My mother died," she said flatly, seeking escape by looking at the door as if expecting someone else to join them.

He remained silent for a long time. Finally, he cleared his throat and said, "You make it sound as if she was the only one who loved you and supported your dreams and ambitions."

"If you checked my background, you know that's exactly the case. Why did you check my background, Detective? Am I a suspect?

"You keep assuring me that you're not connected to the victim."

"I'm not," she snapped back. "Did you also check out Mitch's background?"

"No one would come to your office looking for Mr. Plow on Saturday."

She rose.

"Sit down," he ordered. "I'm a policeman and I check backgrounds if I see a pressing need for it, not because I'm curious about your life. For twenty-five years you behaved in a certain way. But suddenly your behavior changed. I want to know why."

"I told you. My mother died," she mumbled. "I spent four years trekking all over the globe, getting experience that, if I chose to go into politics later on, would almost assure me success. And while I built ladders that would let me climb to the pinnacle of success, my mother was dying. I phoned home often and she never told me...never mentioned anything, not even once."

"It's not your fault your mother died. She'd have died no matter what you did or didn't do. Her doctors knew it, and she knew it. She made a choice not to tell you precisely because she wanted you to derive every advantage possible from your Greenpeace adventure."

She grimaced. "It wasn't an adventure."

"But that's what you now think. Now you see it as an adventure, an indulgence."

"If I'd stayed, gone to Duke or Harvard, I'd have been closer to her. I'd have known she was sick the moment she found out."

"You've spent a year in Florida, a cocktail waitress in Jacksonville, serving Margaritas on the beach or by the poolside. That's a pretty strange choice for an academic. To me, it sounds more like punishment or running."

"You don't understand. If I'd been closer to Mother, I would have noticed when she became sick, and that would have been time to use all those connections—"

He cut her off. "Dr. Hilton at Bangor is one of the best specialists in uterine cancer. He said it wasn't possible to operate. Your mother believed him. She died within three months of being diagnosed. Why can't you accept the fact that you couldn't have done anything, no matter where you were at the time?"

"I might have been able to see something, an earlier sign..."

"Don't be ridiculous. A cancer that kills in three months is not in the same category with the cancer that lingers for years. Stop feeling guilty."

"How?" She got an urge to wring her hands and lowered them out of sight.

"By rediscovering your backbone; stop being a whipping post for a man who would probably make a splendid subject for any psychologist who deals with deviant behavior. Now, is anything missing from your stuff?"

"No."

"Do you collect stamps?"

"No. Why ask me that?"

"Whoever killed Gomez took out your manuals and reference books, shaking them upside down to see if something might fall out. The ripping part was probably a result of his frustration."

"I don't collect anything that would fit between the pages of a book."

"And definitely no drugs...?"

"Definitely no. Not Mitch, and not me."

"What about the rest of your colleagues? Would anyone of them hide something in your office?"

She shook her head.

"Why not?"

"If anyone in the department does drugs, Errington would know it for sure. The man's a snoop. You saw my office. It's a matchbox with a rickety door that we don't bother locking. The rest of my colleagues have offices, so they don't need to visit mine. Linda Moore, she's Errington's heir apparent, makes a point of reminding me that I don't get visitors in my office because they'd suffocate of claustrophobia."

"What about your students? Don't they come to see you?"

"I hold tutorials in the lab, next to the classroom."

"No one comes to see you?"

She shook her head again and leaned over to pick up her knapsack. She knew exactly where she'd find a tissue but made it into a marathon exploratory session. She had to distract him and at the same time gain control over the emotions swirling inside her. She couldn't look at him because he'd see that she felt sorry for herself.

"This information's not to be shared with anyone, and actually, it's the reason I came. Gomez gained entry through the west delivery door with your old security card."

"What? Old security...how?"

"I kind of hoped you'd be able to answer that question."

"I don't. I mean..." She remembered that her current security card had been re-issued just a few weeks ago.

"What is it?"

"I lost my old security card about a month ago. After I used that excuse not to come in to work two weekends in a row, Errington reminded me to leave my card in the glove compartment on Friday, once I came home."

"Your boss is just a jolly old elf, isn't he? All right, so you left the card in the glove compartment and...?"

"The next weekend, I parked the car and opened the glove compartment looking for it—it wasn't there. I couldn't miss another weekend of work, so I called Errington from my cell phone and he came to open the door. He used the opportunity to lecture me all the way to my office."

"And that's why you didn't call your boss to come down to open the door for you last Saturday, but decided to try your luck on the west door." He nodded his understanding.

"But how did Gomez get inside with the old card? It shouldn't have worked. Bryce Culver, our security chief, would have cancelled it."

"We asked him the same question. It made him nervous."

She smiled. "Bryce sometimes forgets to update his computer records. He's a good security guard, but his computer skills are a little thin. He usually leaves all the computer work to his staff, but must have forgotten to give them instructions."

"Yeah, that's pretty much what he told us. The stolen card that should have been cancelled worked, and Gomez gained entry into the Essex Hall. But this is where it gets interesting."

"How did Gomez know exactly where to go? Essex Hall is an administrative building. Not all the doors are labeled either. My cubbyhole's not exactly a tourist spot."

He stared at her, and for the first time, she noticed a smile tugging at his lips. "Get out of Winthrop College, Ms. Sarasohn, and go claim your rightful place in the world of academics. It took me forty-eight hours to ask that question, and I've been in Homicide for fifteen years."

"Someone must have given him directions...and said to just lean into the door and it would open."

"Yep. And if we manage to establish a connection between Gomez and someone you know, we'd flush out the culprit."

"Sorry." She sighed.

"Keep working on it. In the meantime, I'll have a couple of my guys drive by the college and your house, in the daytime and at night. Did you notice the make of that silver sedan?"

"Maybe a Toyota sedan, larger than a Yaris, that's for sure."

He rose, nodding to her. "Keep in touch. Don't walk alone if you can help it and, if you think you're being followed, go to the nearest public place call me."

"I will," she promised and watched his black leather bomber jacket move along the counter and out the door. Telling Terney her suspicions, real or imagined made her feel better. Especially today, she had to stay in an optimistic frame of mind. She would have to teach her community class tonight without the mineral samples. They not only gave her lessons focus but served as a bridge to her adult students. She picked up a balled tissue and started to shred it, bit by bit.

I can't cry now, she thought. *I didn't cry at my mother's funeral and that's where I should have let it out. Now, it's too late. Things might not have turned out differently, but maybe...*

Chapter 4

THE MOMENT SHE entered meeting room L34, Lauren knew that for once Errington had been right; she should have stayed home. She taught her community center interest class as a tribute to her late mother, who had little free time after running a marina with only two permanent and five part-time staff, but who always seemed to find time for charity. Hannah Sarasohn volunteered ten hours each week at Rockland's food bank and spent two Sundays each month delivering Meals-on-Wheels to convalescing senior citizens all over town.

"I stopped speaking to God after your father died," she'd said to her one day, because Lauren took on the counselor's role and started to reproach her mother for running herself ragged. "Faith is not something that needs to be sent to higher spheres. Faith, like every-thing else, is part of who we are, what we do, and how we treat each other. You were only three years old, so you don't remember, but I sat *shiva* for your father at Rabbi Brolick's house, and suddenly all the voices faded. It felt like the people had left the room. I stared at the Rabbi, saw his mouth moving, but I didn't hear a word of his prayer."

"You went into shock, Mother." Lauren had tried to offer a plausible explanation, but her mother just shook her head.

"No, sweetheart. I think my heart silenced the prayers because it knew that they didn't go anywhere. A week later, I walked into St. Robert's Church on Brown Street and sat through their mass. The same thing happened. I saw people around me praying and singing, but I couldn't hear anything. I went to the Methodist church and the Baptist church, and they all greeted me with silence. That's how I understood that for me, praying is useless. It's our deeds, child, that what we do for others, that speak louder on our behalf than any prayer."

Lauren had little spare time in high school or at the university to do charity work; only after her mother had died did she start to think about volunteering.

Her Mineral Identification class had twenty-two enrolled students. That day, each student must have brought a friend or a couple of family members, because the room felt stifling hot. Those who couldn't find a chair lined up along the walls and in the back of the room.

The moment she entered, the room started to vibrate with buzzing excitement. She knew it would be seconds before the first question flew at her.

"I'm glad to see that interest in mineral identification has picked up," she said, trying to look brave and composed. "But I'm afraid that if those of you who are officially enrolled have brought friends tonight in hopes of learning more about the young man found dead in my office, I'll have to disappoint you. I can't talk about it. Police orders."

A dispirited murmur rippled across the room. People started to move for the door until the room almost emptied.

She looked over the dozen students who remained, and sighed. "Look," she said, "Maybe it's not such a good idea to hold this class tonight. I couldn't even bring any samples..." She lowered her head and started to massage her temples. A few moments later, she looked up to see rows of empty desks.

"Great." She sighed again. She rubbed her eyes and leaned sideways to pick up her bag. The old, cracked leather felt prickly dry. She scrunched it up and started to rise when something occurred to her. Amber had printed out the college class lists for her, but she had one more class list—the one for that night's class. She sat down, opened her beat-up sack—a relic from her Greenpeace days, and took out a bunch of folders. Five minutes later, she found the class list. A quick glance at the twenty-two names showed her that she definitely didn't have anyone with the last name Gomez in her class, and no one with the surname McKinley either. But she knew that already and had said as much to Terney. Neither name rang a bell. Then something caught her eye. Each student's name also had an address in the middle column with a phone number.

"Maria Asuncion Herrera," she read, guiding her finger across to the address. "1367 Roper Drive." Didn't Terney say that the victim's sister lived on Roper Drive...?

She rummaged in her knapsack again until she found her cell phone. She punched out first four numbers of Terney's telephone number, but stopped. What if it was just a coincidence? What if it was nothing at all? She snapped the lid shut and dropped the phone into her bag.

She had parked her car close to the front entrance, right in the wedge of light shining through the front door. The community center parking lot had very few open spots. She glanced at her watch. At seven o'clock, other activities would still be going strong. The center closed at midnight.

For once, Lauren regretted that she didn't get the keyless option. It didn't feel safe to have to bend over to see the lock.

"I'm just stressed out," she mumbled. "It's only my imagination."

However, the moment she sat down in the driver's seat and closed the door, her senses sprang awake. Someone had either hung a pungent air-freshener in her car or spilled lemon-scented cleaner on the dashboard. She turned her head and sniffed the air. The smell was everywhere but when she turned back, the dashboard reeked of it. The nearly overpowering smell forced her to draw air through her nose. She tasted citrus flavor.

She checked the windows, even though nothing seemed to be wrong.

The overhead light winked out. She held her breath and started to count. On the count of three the feeling of being trapped swamped her. She should get out of the car but...that was equally bad as to stay inside. Whoever had been inside her car could be lingering around, watching, waiting...

Her hand shook so badly that she couldn't fit the key into the ignition. She leaned back, trying to steady her breath. She willed herself to turn around and check the back seat.

"Don't be stupid," she said aloud. "This car's so small, a dog barely fits back there." She turned around, but even though she knew the backseat was empty, she felt a hand might reach out from the back and encircle her throat.

Finally, she forced herself to fit the key into the ignition and started the car.

Roper Drive was in West Hartford, just south of St. Joseph's College. The moment she made a right onto the street, she knew that she shouldn't discount her intuition. The two media vans were parked tandem in front of 1365. It was a small, neat white bungalow. According to the logo on the side, the media vans belonged to the WCLO TV station and the local radio station. A camera crew camped outside on the sidewalk, careful to keep off the property, but close by and ready in case the residents of 1365 emerged. So Ellen McKinley, the victim's sister, was Maria Asuncion Herrera's next-door neighbor.

She drove down the street, hating the white color of her car, worrying that someone might spot her vehicle. However, the media crews ignored her once they ascertained that she only slowed down to pass through a narrowed section of street and continued westward.

She should have gone home, but now that the possibility of having the silver sedan parked on her street turned into reality, she didn't want to be alone. She fished out her cell phone and called Mitch, knowing he'd be at his girlfriend's in Wethersfield.

"Come on over," he said. "I'm sure Jenny won't mind you spending the night."

"Mitch," she said half an hour later, when already seated in a padded lawn chair of Jennifer's frugally furnished two-bedroom apartment. "I think I've found the connection to Gomez."

"Well, if you did, I'd advise you not to mention it to Errington, or he'll turn you out so fast your head will spin."

"I'm going to have to tell the police."

He shook his head so forcefully that for a moment his face looked blurred. "No, my friend. No, no, and no. The police may be friendly, but such information will eventually reach Errington's ears. He certainly doesn't need more material to justify why he should fire you."

"Maybe it's time for me to leave Winthrop," she said.

"It's been time for you to leave Winthrop since last Friday. You'd have left with a clean slate. Not now. Errington will make sure that no decent college takes you. Make no mistake about that. Did you know he hates Jews?"

"What?"

"God, Lauren, you've spent five years in that shithole and didn't tweak into anything that's going around that place? Five years ago, then-President Smithers made a pitch for supplemental funding for the college and got gently reprimanded for the lack of minorities in his student body and his teaching staff. Jews, African-Americans, Hispanics and Oriental categories suffered from under-representation. That's what the congressman representing the 1st district had told Smithers. Your application happened to cross Errington's desk right after being raked over the coals for having no ethnics on his staff. He hired you under duress and has hated you ever since. But he couldn't get rid of you while the congresswoman, Beulah Gordon, represented our district. She's African-American. However, two years ago, Clement Palfrey won the seat and the mood changed. Palfrey's a bigot, just the kind of man Errington would worship. For some time after Palfrey got in, gossip and rumors flew that his daddy bought him the seat in the House. Soon after, two journalists supposedly behind such malicious gossip, died in separate car accidents, but only two weeks apart. Now, how's that for fortunate intervention that silences forever."

"How do you know all this?" she asked, shocked that he would be so well informed about issues that certainly no one on college staff would talk about.

"I'm white trash from Louisiana, my friend. I did my undergraduate studies at Louisiana Tech in Lafayette. I pulled in honors and got cocky. I applied to five Ivy League colleges on the East Coast and received polite letters that my academic credentials did not meet the East Coast standards. I ended up doing my Master's at Louisiana State, where I met a bold and beautiful," he glanced at Jennifer and shrugged with a grin, "journalism student who took me under her wing, and proceeded to coach me in minority guerilla tactics of how to get grants and scholarships if you don't have stellar connections."

"You blackmailed Errington into hiring you?" She held her breath.

He hissed, displeased. "No, my friend. I went to see Errington armed with glowing letters of recommendation from no less than two congressmen, one from the House and one from the Senate."

"But if you had those letters, why did you bother coming to Winthrop?"

He grimaced. "You're not supposed to know this, but my grant is three times the size of yours and I have a full scholarship that would knock your socks off."

"I'm happy for you, Mitch. I really am," she said, lowering her head.

"Oh, come on, Lauren. I'm only telling you this to motivate you to get the hell out of Winthrop. You'll never get any support from Errington, especially now since Palfrey's in Congress. As far as defending your dissertation—who knows?—you might not even make it. Errington will see to it that you're humbled. You're no longer a desirable ethnic candidate."

"Political winds change. Why does everything have to depend on politics and political ambitions?"

"Lauren, you were not only a page in Congress, but an intern in the White House. I'm surprised you'd even ask that. Now you have to clean up your reputation before you can leave the shithole."

"I didn't know my reputation had become sullied by having a stranger murdered in my office."

He groaned and motioned for Jennifer to put down the coffees she'd made for everyone and join them.

"Gomez may have been a stranger to you, Lauren, but I don't think it was just a coincidence that he was murdered in your office. I think he came looking specifically for you, knowing you'd be at work Saturday—the day the place is totally deserted."

"I think Maria Herrera and Ellen McKinley are friends. I always thought Maria to be Mexican, but she might well be another Cuban. In that case, the friendship would make sense, especially since they're neighbors," she said, sipping coffee and trying to align her thoughts.

"Very likely," he agreed. "And Gomez must have come to visit his sister with a specific issue in mind. Something that would make her consult with her next-door neighbor, and for some reason, Maria recommended that Gomez go see you."

"But Maria is not a student at Winthrop. She's only in my hobby class, if you will. Most of the time the students just pass around the crystals, admiring them, asking questions whether they can make jewelry from this and that crystal. It's not an academic class," she said.

"Maybe he wasn't interested in crystals," Jennifer said.

"I can't think of anything else that might be of interest to anyone, other than Mitch and myself," Lauren said.

They spent the evening tossing around possibilities, but nothing emerged that would give them a lead or point them in the right direction. Jennifer pulled out a futon and spread it on the floor. Watching her, it occurred to Lauren to tell Mitch that someone had been inside her car at the community center. However, she decided not to complicate an already a difficult situation.

In the morning, she'd have to examine her car inside and out. At least nothing rattled and nothing felt odd when she drove the car to Roper Drive. But one of these days, going over a bump a loosened screw might fall out, or the brakes might lose pressure....

I've seen too many movies. She sighed and closed her eyes.

Chapter 5

O N THURSDAY MORNING, Terney called her at home and asked if anything had been taken from her office.

"Not a thing," she replied glumly, glad that he wasn't able to see her face.

"Are you sure?"

"I haven't exactly pasted together all the scraps of paper, nor did I glue together whatever's broken, but nothing seems to be missing, Lieutenant."

"Is your colleague missing anything?"

"No. Every CD and flash drive we had is accounted for, though half of them are spoiled. Anyway, I can't think of anything that I'd be missing. Did your forensic staff lift any prints?"

He didn't speak for a long time. Finally, he said, "The victim didn't touch anything and the killer didn't leave any prints either."

"I'm sorry, Lieutenant, I really am, but I don't have any useful information," she said, feeling guilty because it wasn't exactly true. However, Mitch's warning had made an impact on her, and for the time being, she wouldn't tell Terney that she'd figured out a possible connection between Gomez and herself.

"Have you seen the silver sedan again?"

"No." She started to say that someone had been in her car, but reconsidered. That morning, she'd checked her car inside and out and found nothing missing, nothing suspicious. But she knew that she didn't imagine the citrus smell. Someone had opened her glove compartment and gone through it, taking great care not to make a mess. She'd also taken her car manual out and sniffed it—and smelled the same citrus aroma.

"Well, keep in touch," he said and hung up.

She knew that the police might eventually find out that Ellen McKinley's next-door neighbor attended her community class, but not for some time. Maria Herrera had no reason to bring up the topic; not with the police if they questioned her, and not with the media. The Cuban community, like most ethnic communities, tended to stick together. They wouldn't be eager to volunteer information that might bring more police into their midst.

She called Mitch, and he told her to come to work.

"Did Errington tell you to ask me?"

"No, but do you care?"

"Maybe I should stay home."

"Lauren, we have to clear out the staff lounge and bring all the boxes back into our office. The police finished their work, and the yellow tape's gone. The chalk outline on our floor has been cleaned off too. I talked to Linda. She said that Errington's going to be tied up in meetings with the Dean and the rest of the faculty for days."

"I'll be over in half an hour," she told him.

Lauren showered and dressed casually in jeans and a sweatshirt. On her way to the campus, she stopped at the only coffee shop in Rocky Hill to pick up tuna sandwiches, coffee, pop, and bottled water.

The media had left the campus but that didn't mean the grounds were deserted. The news of the murder brought out students who seldom attended classes. The tram heading for the Spindler Hall, had students hanging off the sides.

"Good, you brought lunch," Mitch greeted her while she put the bags and coffee on the only table that didn't need repair. Now that the office stood empty, save two small shelves built into the wall, it looked spacious. Shadows and gloom seemed to hang everywhere, but the porthole window still wasn't large enough to let in enough October sunshine to chase the mood away.

"The pop and water's warm," Mitch said, feeling the cans and plastic bottles.

She grimaced. "Go get ice from the fridge. And if the ice cube trays are frozen together, bring them the way they are. I'll get a couple of folding chairs from the lounge."

She finished setting up the chairs. Mitch returned, holding something out to her.

"This yours?" He swung the green canvas bag with some effort.

"No. Where did you find it?"

"In the freezer, jammed way in the back. The ice cube trays stuck to it but I managed to pry them off. Here." He put the trays down on a chair, swung the bag again, and let it drop on the table. It landed with a heavy clunk. "What the hell's in there?" Mitch frowned. "I hope some idiot didn't put a liquor bottle in a bag and hid it in the fridge."

She ran her hands over the cold fabric. "Not a bottle, Mitch, but something solid and heavy. Let's see." She asked him to pull apart the frozen string and make an opening large enough to push her hand inside.

"Careful," Mitch said. "What if it bites?"

She laughed. "It's probably a paper weight...or a doorstop." She grasped the square shape and pulled it out.

"Whoa!" Mitch exclaimed. "What do we have here?"

She stared at an object perhaps six inches long. "Whew!" Her hand dropped down and landed on the table with a painful smack, no longer able to stand the weight of the bar.

She let go of it and instinctively pressed her knuckles against her mouth.

"That's a gold bar, Lauren...."

"No shit. Do you think...?"

"Yep," he said and picked it up with both hands, hefting it. "I'd say about ten, fifteen pounds—I thought these things were bigger, longer."

"Let me see the logo." She reached for the bar, and he put it down on the table. They bent over it, studying its surface.

"That's not any refiner's logo." She traced the outline of what looked like a bird with spread wings and oversized talons resting on a nest of twigs. "No weight or purity stamp either."

"My friend, stamp or no stamp, this looks like pure gold to me," Mitch said.

"It most likely is, but this bar is not a standard size. This gold didn't come out of any refineries we have today."

"How do you know?"

"The international refineries make it convenient for investors to own gold by offering gold bars. These weigh anywhere from token wafers to 400 troy ounces. That's twenty-seven pounds. This is much smaller...very odd."

"How do you know?" he repeated.

She straightened up and braced her back with both hands. "I teach a mineralogy class at the community center, remember? After my father died, my mother lost faith in God's prayer; she also lost faith in our country's currency. Every month, once she paid her marina staff, she converted the rest of the money to gold bars. Mind you, she could only afford wafers, not bars." She motioned at the table. "She refused to keep the gold in a safety deposit box, preferring to keep it in an old steamer trunk at home. Eventually, the police pieced together what happened. During one of her visits to a cancer specialist in Bangor, two of her staff stole all of the gold. The marina went into bankruptcy three days before she died. Once it sold, the creditors took everything. I had enough money left to make it down to Jacksonville."

"I'm sorry," he said quietly.

"Yeah." She slowly breathed out. "We're in trouble, or at least I am."

"Lauren, you didn't steal this. Most likely Gomez stole it from whoever killed him. Your community class student must have told Gomez's sister to come and see you because you know crystals—and gold. He probably wanted to find out its worth, or maybe ask you to help him cash it in. How much is a bar like this worth today?"

She cleared her lungs of stale air with a big sigh. "Mitch, gold prices are usually quoted in U.S. dollars per troy ounce. Let's say we have ten pounds ..." she closed her eyes and did a quick calculation in her head. "That's just short of five kilos and thirty-two ounces per kilo and times five...say, one hundred and fifty Troy ounces, at a conservative estimate of twelve hundred dollars per ounce." She stopped and pressed her hands against her temples.

"Are we looking at two hundred thousand dollars' worth of gold here?" he asked, his voice constricting.

"Yep." Sweat beaded on her forehead and her cheeks grew warm.

"Lauren," he whispered. "No wonder that Gomez guy got spooked if he noticed someone following him. Once he made it here, he saw it was a dead-end, and tried to get out around the corner. That's probably how he found the fridge and decided to stash the bag. He must have come back here, hoping to hide, but the killer found him."

"Yeah, well—see that nest of twigs under the bird's talons?" She ran her fingernail over the lower portion of the bar.

He leaned closer to see and gasped, confirming her suspicions.

"So that's why, my friend, I'm in deep trouble." She continued raking her fingernail over the bird's outstretched wings. "Not a friendly eagle, that's for sure."

Mitch sat down on a chair with a thud. "That's a swastika lying in the nest, not that I'm an expert on such things."

"Yep, Mitch, I'm not exactly an expert either, but this gold bar wasn't minted by any mint that we have today. If it's authentic, it contains looted gold that had been smelted into gold bars and stamped with the Reichsbank logo. But this bar is very different from the ones traded by the Swiss just after the war."

"What do you mean this is different?"

"This Reich eagle has a crown above its head. It looks almost like a Roman laurel wreath. Only an expert in this historical stuff will be able to determine for sure what we have here."

"Lauren, if it's authentic, it must be worth a hell of a lot more than two hundred thousand," he said.

She moaned. "If it's authentic," she pointed at the gleaming bar on the table, "owning this is a crime. And just having it here with us is bad news."

"We didn't steal it," he objected.

"That's not my point. Like you said, Gomez must have stolen it from someone, and that someone will do anything to get this gold back. The last thing the killer wants is to see this in police hands."

"Because of its value." He nodded.

"That, too, but there's more to it. To own this gold is like owning the Mona Lisa. If the logo's authentic, it's one of the bars minted from the treasure that Hitler's henchmen looted from the bank reserves of occupied nations and from Holocaust victims from all over Europe. *If* it's authentic," she repeated, trying not to look at the gold bar.

"Where would you get something like this?" he asked, motioning at the table. "I mean, where would Gomez get it, and where would whoever he stole it from get it?"

"Terney said that Gomez worked in New York, at the Carlyle Hotel as a bellhop. That's a ritzy place; rich people stay there. Gomez probably came across this bar by chance, maybe in a suite, and took it, figuring that in a hotel that size, he'd be safe for a while. I mean, the Carlyle has to have hundreds of employees. I know it sounds harsh, but Gomez is dead so he's no longer a threat. But whoever had this bar in the suite will do anything to get it back and erase all evidence that it was ever stolen. He can't afford to let anyone learn that he has a gold bar that might have come from Hitler's hoards."

"Maybe it's a souvenir. You know—a rich man's trophy."

She moaned. "Mitch, get real! Whether a trophy or a souvenir, it would be in a museum. If this bar became public, every police and government authority would be asking the same question: where did it come from?"

"Maybe a rich collector bought this bar from a museum."

"I doubt a museum would sell something like this bar. A museum would put it on display—complete with its authentication history. And an auction house isn't going to auction off an artifact without making sure its history is legal. I have a feeling that whoever knows this bar exists is either a shady collector or a thief."

"Lauren, that doesn't make sense...the thief part, I mean. If the bar is an unlawful article, where would the thief steal it from?"

"You have a point," she said, biting her lower lip. She stood thinking for a moment. Finally, she asked, "Where would a thief steal something like this except from another thief who would've stolen it from another thief...? The ownership of this gold bar has probably always been unlawful all the way to the original finder."

"Let's see. Maybe there's more in the bag, like a certificate of authenticity." He picked up the bag, turned it upside down, and shook it until something fluttered down and landed on the table.

She picked up the two flattened plastic bags and held them up to the light to better see the ancient-looking brown parchment squares with bluish watermarks. "Well, not exactly a certificate but some kind of parchment with script."

The two squares weren't identical. One looked slightly larger than the other, but they both had the appearance of antiquity. In places, they showed pin-dot crystalline transparency, creating an effect having been poked several times with a needle.

"I have a friend at the Metropolitan Museum of Art in New York," Lauren continued. "We go back to Greenpeace times. We keep in touch, mostly by e-mail. He's in art and restoration. I think he'll be able to tell us what we have here. And if he can't, he has contacts who can." She carefully fitted the plastic-wrapped squares back into the canvas bag.

"I'll come with you—"

"No, Mitch. Both of us gone would only raise suspicions. I'll take the bag with me."

"You don't trust me enough to leave it here until you actually go see your friend in New York?"

"I don't want to come back to my office only to find your chalked outline on the floor." She moaned just thinking about it.

"I think you're being melodramatic, kid."

"Really?" She raised her brows. "What's in this bag," she hefted it, "is dangerous. Whoever wants it back has already killed once for it and still didn't get it back. Do you think a person like that would shy away from another murder?"

"I still would like to come with you to New York. We'll leave separately, meet up some place, and go see your friend at the museum. I have to pick up three reports I ordered last month anyway. The Granger Library usually sends them to Hartford, but I can tell Errington that they discontinued this courtesy service and I have to pick them up."

"Fine. After I contact Hagip I'll let you know."

"Hagip? What kind of name is that?"

"Armenian. Born here, but forever Armenian."

"If that's the case, I can say that I'm born here but forever the son of the Great Gaul," he deadpanned, and for the first time since he returned with the ice cube tray and the bag, she laughed.

Chapter 6

AFTER LEAVING WINTHROP, Lauren hurried home. The moment she put her leather knapsack on the kitchen chair, she felt eyes watching her from every corner, every direction. She stared down her short hallway. The feeling of being watched intensified. She imagined the front door had eyes imbedded in its many layers of shiny black paint.

She grabbed her knapsack. Its weight urged her to fall to her knees. Adjusting her balance, and alternately feeling silly and apprehensive, she walked into the living room, imagining that a camera tracked her every move. Her computer station sat against a wall, wedged between two front windows. She sat down in the chair, careful to lower her knapsack so that it didn't land on the bare parquet floor with a thud. The feeling of someone watching her wouldn't go away, and her thoughts crossed into the fantasy realm. What if the person following her gained entry into her house and planted tiny spy-cameras everywhere? What if he also bugged her house? What if, right now, a sniper sat in his car, out there on the street, his high-powered rifle trained at her window, watching, waiting for the right?

How did Gomez live with the green canvas bag and not lose his nerves? How long ago did Gomez steal the bag? She'd lost her staff security card about a month before. Maria Asuncion must have stolen it from her car in the community center parking lot, probably during a washroom break. How did she get into her car? Maybe she didn't. Maybe she just took the card from Lauren's bag. The community center class was held on Thursday, and she only left the card in the glove compartment once she came home from work on Friday.

No, no. This scenario didn't work. She'd have noticed her card missing on Friday morning because she'd have to use it. Whoever stole her card had to do it on Friday night. But how would the thief know that she would leave her card in her glove compartment? No one knew about this habit...except Errington, because he had imposed the practice upon her.

She leaned into the high-backed chair, holding her breath. That scenario seemed too fantastic to consider. But what if...

What if Gomez had come to see someone else, and once he realized he'd been followed, he tried to get away but ended up in a dead-end corridor? What if it was Errington who told Gomez how to get a security card to gain entry into the Essex Hall? In that case, she'd only be connected to Gomez through theft and nothing else.

In the eighteen months since Errington assigned to her the new office, he'd visited her only once or twice. But hardly a workday passed without receiving an e-mail from him. Even if he couldn't find anything to bitch about, or berate her for, he'd send e-mails asking for her progress on this or that article and whether she'd incorporated *current* material into her lectures.

She shook her head, banishing all such thoughts. Errington was an insufferable asshole and a snoop, but just because he was nasty didn't make him automatically a criminal. He might also be a secret bigot, just as Mitch said, because Winthrop College held the status of a non-denominational, educational institution...that practiced genteel discrimination.

"Enough!" she berated herself and booted up her computer.

Hagip Agopian's message jumped out at her from a short column of e-mails. The back of her neck started to prickle with cold needle-like jabs. She clicked open the message.

"Hey, fellow Stormrider, there's a buzz that there's been a murder at your ivory tower. Call me as soon as you can. And why let your colleague shoot such juicy info across? Are you suddenly too shy to gossip?" He included his phone number underneath his custom-style signature. She recognized his work number at the Metropolitan Museum of Art.

She leaned to one side and stuck her hand into her knapsack, looking for her cell phone. Her fingers brushed against the rough canvas bag, making her shiver. Finally, she found her phone and took it out.

"Is it eight o'clock already?" she murmured. Most likely Hagip wouldn't still be at work, and she didn't have his home phone number. She decided to try her luck anyway.

"Hello, bones and tomes department. Hagip speaking," his characteristically nasally voice filled the line. He had his nose broken, or displaced as he liked to call it, on three different occasions during Greenpeace demonstrations that turned into a skirmish with the police.

"Hagip," she laughed, relieved that she had reached him so easily. "Hi, there, fellow Stormrider. It's Lauren."

"*Vonts es*, Lori, *vonts es*?" He fell into their old routine.

"*Shat lav*, my friend, *shat lav*," she replied even though "very well" wasn't the right response to his informal "How are you?" but "very well" was one of the very few Armenian phrases she knew.

"You must have nerves of steel. What's this shit I hear about a guy being offed at Winthrop and in your office?"

"The victim's body was found in my office all right, but I didn't send you an e-mail about it, Hagip."

He chuckled. "Of course not, you proud and brave soul. Anyone who can put up with that prick, Errington, for five years is not going to run home and cry to mama."

Indeed, during her four years with Greenpeace, Hagip had often played the role of mama to her and offered his shoulder to rest on or cry on, whatever the cause or hardship. He'd joined Greenpeace at thirty-two, and had already been with the organization for two years by the time she came on board. From the moment Hagip raised himself on tiptoes and put a protective hand around her twenty-one year old shoulders, she'd felt a strong kinship with the stocky, baldheaded art appraiser. He held a Master's Degree in Ancient Civilizations from Purdue, a Ph.D. in Fine Arts and History from the Ramsford College of Arts and Technology, a small college in southern California, and was a certified art appraiser. She asked him why someone with his academic qualifications would join Greenpeace. He'd shrugged and said with a fatalistic twang, "I heard I'd find many tall women in the organization. I wanted to find one to look up to." His wife, Isabel, a French-Canadian, stood at least a head taller than Hagip.

"How's the family, Hagip?" she asked. Hagip and Isabel had three children, two born while they still traveled the world with Greenpeace. The third one had arrived after they had settled in New York.

"*Shat lav, shat lav*, Lori, but you didn't call to ask about my family headaches. Your colleague, Mitch, sent me the e-mail. Why wouldn't you sit down and talk to your old friend when trouble visits your office? I'm chagrined, you know." His voice lost some of its chatty, nasal, sing-song quality, and turned serious. "What's wrong, Lori?"

"Nothing's wrong."

"A dead man's found in your office, and you tell me nothing's wrong?"

"I didn't know him."

"What's that supposed to mean? Since when is it a routine occurrence to find dead strangers in your office?"

"I didn't mean it that way," said Lauren. "When did Mitch send you the e-mail?"

"Now. Well, it clicked in on my side about an hour ago. I just wanted to finish going over this newfound Petrus Bertius map of America, supposedly printed by younger Hondius around 1620, before I'd call you. But you beat me to it."

So Mitch must have e-mailed Hagip before she even made it to the parking lot—but from where? His laptop? She hadn't seen him use it since before last Saturday. He must have kept it in his car. But where did Mitch get Hagip's e-mail address? He wasn't the type to go snooping through her computer in her absence. Besides, her computer had been trashed since Saturday. The only places where Hagip's e-mail address could be found were in her computer, her yellow notebook, and in her knapsack. She'd never left the knapsack out of sight with Mitch around.

"You still there, Lori?"

"Yes. I'm wondering...where would Mitch get your e-mail address? Our office is a mess—trashed. My computer's beyond salvation. The only place where Mitch would get your e-mail is from my yellow address book and that's down here, in my knapsack. I talked to him today about coming to see you. "

"Lori, anyone in charge can pull out anything he wants from any computer that's linked to the network. Our director here, Monty, used to perform regular sweeps of staff computers to make sure none of us chose to enjoy our lunch break with a porno site. Mitch might have called the computer services—"

"Why would he do that?" she interrupted. "I already told him that I'd give you a shout and make an appointment."

"Well, if that's the case, come on over."

"Now?"

He laughed. "Not now. Tomorrow, or on the weekend."

"Why are you at work at this hour, anyway?"

"It's a long weekend in Canada, their Thanksgiving. Isabel took the kids to visit her folks in Montreal. I have an empty apartment to enjoy. Come to think of it, you're right. What am I thinking? I have a quiet and empty apartment all to myself. I'll head home the moment I hang up."

"What day can I come down and see you?"

"How about Saturday?"

"I don't want to come to your apartment. I mean—"

"I know what you mean. We have many empty rooms here that no one would think of bugging, simply because they're dungeons. No one in their right mind would think of coming here voluntarily."

She frowned. She hadn't expected him to be so intuitive. Her house might not be bugged, and there might not even be a silver sedan outside on the street, but cell phone conversations weren't protected...not without a scrambler device.

"It's nothing secret or illegal, Hagip. I just wanted to talk to you about something. The police want to know what the link is between me and the dead man, and I can't think of anything. I didn't know him and I have no clue why he came to my office. So, since you're the only one I know who still keeps in touch with the Greenpeace members, past and present, I wanted to see if maybe there's a connection through that organization."

"The e-mail said the man's name is Oswaldo Gomez, a Cuban," Hagip said. "We didn't have that many Cuban expatriates-members, but some folks join the organization under an assumed name. You know, those with great foresight who think their future ambitions might not be served well if connected to Greenpeace."

She blinked, taken aback. "Why would such people join the organization?"

He chuckled. "You know the reasons as well as I do: tall women, glamorous vistas, and tons of booze. Little food, though." He kept chuckling.

"Thanks, Hagip, thanks a lot. Would it be all right if I brought Mitch along?"

"Sure. It'll be good to be able to put a face to the e-mail. Do you like him?"

"Hagip, you should have been a match-maker or a psychologist. Mitch is a friend, that's all. Besides, he's five years younger than I am."

He clicked his tongue. "Younger man, older woman—by now that's a tradition in Hollywood."

"I just want to bring him along because he mentioned he has to pick up some journals at the Granger Library since they no longer forward custom-ordered material to Hartford."

"The more the merrier," Hagip said. "Keep well, my friend, and I'll see you and Mitch on Saturday. Come close to noon so we can enjoy a lunch and we'll chat about the good old days. You do still remember where the Met is?"

"You're a gem in the rough, Hagip. Thanks."

Talking to him should have relaxed her, but once she closed the cell phone, she felt watched from every corner of the room, even from the ceiling. Hagip said "anyone in charge" could pull out anything they wanted from any computer on the network. The only one who scrutinized her computer use in such a way was Errington. Did he send the e-mail, and if so, why?

"You're still not safe, not safe, not safe," voices seemed to whisper all around her.

She rose and stood by the window. After a couple of deep, cleansing breaths, she opened the Venetian blinds and shielded her eyes, peering at the street. It was hard to tell the color of cars parked curbside. She closed the blinds again and sat back down at the computer. Instead of reading the rest of her e-mails, she reached for her cell phone and called Terney.

"I know it's late. I'm sorry to bother you," she started.

He broke in. "I'm a cop, twenty-four seven. It's no bother. What's happening?"

"Nothing much, Lieutenant. The police let us move our belongings back into our office. We've finished going through everything. I even tried taping a few pages together. Nothing's missing. Everything's there. I'm calling about something else." She told him about Hagip and her hope that a connection to Greenpeace might provide a link to Gomez.

"By all means," he agreed. "It's not far-fetched that someone might have given Gomez your name through Greenpeace and he came to see you about some issue."

For a moment, she considered what he'd said. Terney wasn't a fool. He knew that a Carlyle bellhop would have a very slim like-lihood of a connection to Greenpeace.

"It's a long shot, I know," she said, "but I'm so frustrated about not being able to tell you anything useful that I'm willing to con-sider even such a distant possibility."

"A hotel bellhop meets a lot of people. A guest might have even asked him to run an errand or deliver a message to you, even though you might not find many Greenpeace members staying at the Carlyle."

"Some Greenpeace members have gone on to forge stellar ac-ademic, scientific, and even political careers, Lieutenant."

"Very true," he agreed. "Let me know if you find anything useful."

The fact that not once during their conversation did Terney ask about the silver sedan, or raise the issue of her safety, suggested that the Lieutenant, too, didn't trust her home environment—or her cell phone.

Chapter 7

ONCE HAGIP TURNED on the searing white light of his magnifying ring, he seemed to have crossed over into another dimension. The silence in the workroom made it feel like an invisible barrier had been thrown down to separate their two worlds.

Lauren and Mitch found him waiting at the top of the sweeping stone staircase that formed a grand entrance into the palace-like building with its huge columns and tall windows. He insisted on having lunch first, in a Turkish diner just a couple of blocks north at 84th and Fifth Avenue. Somehow, he managed to talk while they walked. His voice wasn't threatened by the never-ending stream of bodies moving along the sidewalk that often forced them to separate. Hagip talked with his hands, flexing his fingers, describing forms and shapes, punching holes in the air to give his words the force that she came to associate with his Armenian heritage. He'd marched in many demonstrations, pushing around policemen who sought to either prevent him from gaining entry or restrain him outright, and the experience served him well on New York's crowded streets.

All through lunch they talked academics, not once mentioning the recent events at Winthrop.

She had initially planned to drive to New York, but Mitch twirled his finger around his temple and said, "You're crazy, my friend." They took the train to New York, and a cab ferried them from Grand Central Station to Fifth Avenue. She didn't ask Mitch whether or how he sent the e-mail to Hagip, feeling that perhaps the mystery might clear up by itself. She said she'd contacted her friend at the museum, and that they had an appointment for Saturday at noon. Mitch nodded and said that she'd made a good choice in Saturday.

Either the world is filled with two-faced people, she thought, *and I've been sleepwalking through life, or Mitch knows nothing about the e-mail.* She didn't want to seriously consider the former possibility, and the latter one sent her rummaging in her knapsack for aspirin.

Mitch noticed that she made an effort to carry the knapsack casually and without obvious strain.

At the train, he offered her a wry grin. "It's not your average purse, Lauren, because it weighs a lot," he said. "I realize that if someone's watching us, it's clever to make them think that knapsack is empty, but don't overdo the swinging bit or you'll dislocate your shoulder."

She managed a feeble smile, holding the knapsack with one hand and feeling the leather strain to the point where she thought it might snap. Once Hagip ushered them into what he called "my spare dungeon," she breathed out a sigh of relief. On the first sublevel, the room's ceilings soared high because some of the still-crated exhibits came in containers ten feet tall.

The workroom turned out to be equipped like the workshop of an ancient apothecary with apocalyptic visions. All the supplies were stocked in volume. The metal shelves and racks practically creaked under all the jars and jugs, vials and cans, bags of powder that came in every color of the rainbow, and boxes of latex gloves. She also saw what looked like a supply of bandages and

sterile patches that would have supplied a Red Cross African relief mission for a year, and a great assortment of brushes, hand-
brooms, and picks in all sizes from a crowbar to a needle set into
a wooden handle.

She motioned at a plastic bin filled with boxes of crayons.
"What do you use these for?" she asked.

"Re-touching minor scratches in leather and wood," Hagip
replied without even glancing at what she indicated.

"What do you steam here?" she asked, pointing at what
looked like a machine a cosmetician might use.

"My face," he deadpanned. "It gets awfully dry in here. Careful
so you don't break that bag," he said, pushing away what looked
like gray dust in a plastic bag. "Fuller's Earth gets awfully messy if
the bag breaks. You'd be sneezing until the end of the month."

"Hagip, we need to know what we have here," she said, and
without further explanation, took out the green canvas bag and
emptied it, dropping the gold bar and the two plastic bags onto
his workbench.

He whistled upon seeing the gold bar and puckered his
mouth as he picked up one plastic-wrapped square. After that,
silence reigned.

It seemed like hours passed, but in reality, it took less than
thirty minutes before Hagip leaned back. He stared into space,
giving the impression he was trying to align his thoughts. Finally,
he opened a drawer and took out pen and paper. He put one
parchment square, still protected by plastic, on the glass plat-
form of a scanner that connected to one of his three laptops. He
clicked something under the workbench. A projection screen lit
up on the wall directly across from him.

"Watch," he said and tapped on the keyboard and moved the
mouse. The magnified projection of the parchment square appeared on the screen.

"The blue watermarks are letters," Lauren said, leaning closer.

"A word," Hagip said tersely. "A single word. *Das*, to be exact."
He scribbled it down, removed the square, and replaced it with

the second one. This time the blue watermarks ran almost from one edge of the square to the other.

"A single word." Hagip's voice sounded crisp, as if filtering through a brand new nose. "It's a mouthful, but a single word nevertheless. *Sibirische*." Once again he scribbled it down.

"It's German," Lauren said. "*Das Sibirische*...what does it mean?"

"The Siberian," he said, tilting his head and staring at a point above the wall screen.

"The Siberian what?" she asked.

"I'm not sure, Lori. I'll have to check it out."

"But you have an idea, a suspicion—?"

"I said I'm not sure," he interrupted brusquely. "I must check it out."

"A Siberian tundra, a Siberian tiger," Mitch offered, but Hagip didn't react.

"Look, Hagip," Lauren pleaded, "tell me what you know."

"Lori," he grabbed her elbow. "If what's in this bag is not linked to you in any way, why didn't you go with this to the police?"

She stared down at his round, fleshly face, noticing wrinkles so deep they looked like scars that haven't been properly treated.

"I told her not to," Mitch said. "Errington would fire her if he could establish a link between her and the victim. Without his reference and recommendation, she'd never be able to finish her thesis—anywhere."

Hagip shook her elbow. "I know you're stuck at Winthrop and not just because of money. Is there a link between you and the victim, Lori?"

"No, nothing more than what I've told you! Maria Asuncion is in my community center interest class. Students there are always asking whether they can make pendants or medallions of this crystal and that gold flake. So she must have suggested to Gomez's sister to come and see me about the value of the gold bar."

"Is this Maria Asuncion a criminal or an ex-con?" he asked.

"No," she grimaced. "She's a thirty-five-year-old housewife who wants to learn how to polish stones into pretty beads. I think she once mentioned rosary beads."

"In that case, Maria Asuncion wouldn't steal her teacher's staff security card. The young man, however, Oswaldo Gomez, was already a thief and probably a very frightened one too. How would he know where you kept your security card?" Hagip demanded.

She moaned softly. "Oh, Hagip, let's not go there."

He turned to Mitch. "Did you know where Lori kept her card?"

"In her knapsack, where she keeps everything else," Mitch said, frowning.

"That's not what Hagip means." She shook her head at him. "The only one who knows my habit of leaving the card in my glove compartment on Fridays is Errington. He's the one who suggested it; although he made it into an order, like everything else."

Hagip cleared his throat. "Well, I think I'm beginning to see your difficulties. You don't even want to consider the possibility that your boss, Errington, set you up."

"He's a prick just like you said, but I don't think he'd do something so...so...."

"Profitable?" Hagip filled in what didn't cross her mind.

"Look," she said, trying to order her thoughts. "Gomez stole this gold bar because he saw a huge opportunity—I mean he could fence it and get cash for a least half of its face value. But he probably wanted to make sure he knew the full value of the gold before he fenced it. He couldn't just walk into a museum and ask for a curator. Hell, he wasn't stupid."

"Of course he was stupid, Lori," Hagip said, his tone gruff. "Gomez was incredibly stupid to steal from people he knew nothing about. He must have learned quickly, though, and the fear set in, but it was too late to return the gold to wherever he found it. Like you said, he probably tried to get rid of it, on the street, through a fence. But someone who has more connections than a tree has branches got to the fence first—with instructions where to point the thief."

"To Winthrop College? To Errington? Come on, Hagip, you're stretching this theory very thin. How can someone like Harold Errington, a university director, be connected to a New York fence?"

"You got it all wrong, Lori. I didn't say your boss is connected to New York lowlife. I said that someone, probably in the employ of whoever had this gold brick in the hotel, told the fence where to send Gomez. That means that the owner of this gold bar is connected to Errington in a way that makes my spine tingle. First Gomez is set up, and next you're set up. The end result is half of what the key players expected. Gomez is dead, but his killer didn't find the canvas bag."

"No, no." She shook her head. "My connection to this is through Maria Asuncion. She's Ellen McKinley's next-door neighbor, and Ellen is Oswaldo's older sister."

"Coincidence." Hagip dismissed her objection with a wave of his hand.

"I'm kind of in agreement with Lauren on this," Mitch spoke up. "Errington is the prototype of a bigoted and self-serving academic, but precisely because he's so selfish he would never get involved in something like...well, like what happened. He's just not the type."

"Not the type, eh?" Hagip snapped his fingers in front of Mitch's nose, threw his hands apart, and quickly brought them together in a crisp clap that reverberated through the workroom like a gun shot. "Well, let me tell you something. Back in '95, while finishing my doctorate degree at Ramsford, I supplemented my grant by doing art appraisals. I worked on commission. One day, two FBI agents came to my office at the college, flashed me their badges, and said to follow them. They took me to a neat pink-and-blue clapboard house, and inside, I shook hands with a ton of FBI agents. A little old lady had lived in that house since she retired in '88 at the age of sixty-eight. She died at ninety-six, peacefully of old age in her bed. She lived frugally, like most old folks with little means other than what our government gives them. The sheriff's people started to go through her belongings—and that's how the FBI came on the scene.

"In a span of more than thirty years, that old lady worked as a housekeeper for at least four of what might be called today the *Fortune* 100 richest families. Each and every one of her employers gave her a glowing recommendation. In the course of her employment, usually several years, each one of her employers reported burglaries at one or more of their residences. And each time, the police and the insurance investigators recovered some of the stolen property—but not all. The sheriff, and the FBI, found in the neat little clapboard house a Degas pastel, a Cezanne, two very vivid pieces by Henri Matisse, a Hals, a Renoir, and a Botticelli for good measure." He raised his brows at Mitch. "A nice old lady, devoted to each of her employers. Upon retirement, her last employer thought he lost a national treasure. There are no types, Mr. Plow. Or there are as many types as human nature cares to create."

Lauren stepped between the two men. "What we want, Hagip, and what I want to know, is can this bar be authentic, and if so, where did it come from?"

"Well now, let's put an ad in the New York Times and see what it'll bring. Or even better, you tell me why the guest at the Carlyle, who owned this, didn't report the theft to the police."

She turned to Mitch. "All right, we're done here. Let's—"

"Stop." Hagip's hand shot out and gripped her elbow again. "I'm sorry. The fault is mine. I apologize. I'm used to staring at all kinds of materials—lambskin scrolls, calfskin bindings, gold-leaf and rice paper, silk and batik, papyrus—but it's not often that I get to study two squares of tattooed vellum—human skin."

Chapter 8

HAGIP REFUSED TO tell them anything more than that the two square patches of human skin had been removed from their owners with expert precision.

"Whether posthumously or still alive, a doctor removed the patch," he said, shaking his head. Lauren saw her friend didn't want to believe that someone who had taken the Hippocratic Oath would participate in such a thing.

"Are these two skin patches from Holocaust victims?" she asked, digging her nails into her palm. The pain helped to offset the shivers coursing through her body, and she needed to remain at least outwardly calm.

"Maybe," he said in a way that suggested he didn't think so, or maybe even that he knew differently but didn't want to say. "Is there any way you can distance yourself from this, Lori?"

"Can't see how," she said tiredly. "Remember what you used to tell me before every demonstration? Stand in your own space and know you are there. I'm not going to run anywhere."

"Back then it was pep-talk, Lori, for a demonstration. But you're not standing in your own space. You're trespassing in someone else's backyard and it's enemy territory. This gold bar," he motioned at it, "is Hitler's gold, but I'm quite sure it didn't come from any known stash that has been recovered by the Allies since the end of the War. That's precisely why the Carlyle guest didn't report its theft."

"What are you saying, Hagip?" Lauren asked.

He ran an open hand over his head and rubbed his eyes. "Hitler built an amazing Tea House on top of Obersalzberg Mountain in Austria. Eagle's Nest is what the historians generally call it. The gold bar you have here bears what I believe Hitler planned to make his personal imperial crest: it's the heraldic crest of Eagle's Nest. A coronation stamp, if you will. The coins issued during the Nazi rule have an eagle with outstretched wings and a glory wreath wedged between the bird's talons. The swastika cross is stamped in the middle of the wreath. The bird of prey here wears a laurel crown, not unlike Emperor Nero, and the swastika cross lies almost like a gift-offering in the nest."

"So you're saying that this bar comes from Hitler's gold that no one knows about...yet?" She wasn't sure whether she understood his implication.

He rose and carefully placed the gold bar in the canvas bag. He took both plastic-covered squares and gently slid them in beside it and said, "There are people today who believe in leprechauns and the pot of gold. They believe in King Solomon's mines and in gold-filled temples of Atlantis lying on the bottom of the Mediterranean. Why shouldn't they believe in the Siberian...?" He stopped.

"The Siberian what?" Mitch asked impatiently.

Hagip ignored him. "Take this." He handed Lauren the canvas bag. "I've scanned the articles. The pictures will be more than sufficient for me to ask around. I'll give you a call if I have something that can be substantiated. In the meantime, where do you plan to keep this?" He glanced at the canvas bag.

"In my knapsack and with me at all times," she said and sighed.

"Lori, my friend, I'd like to see you reach your thirty-first birthday and maybe even finish your thesis." He gave her a quick hug and leaned back. "Well, give me a couple of days. I'll be quick and discreet. And while I'm flushing my channels, it might be a good idea for the two of you to find out, carefully of course, who stayed at the Carlyle Hotel around the time of the theft, say the month of August and September."

He saw them out and once again made a great show of talking with his hands, behaving as if the museum's stone-paved terrace was his stage.

"Thanks, Hagip," She leaned over.

He put his hand around her shoulders and hugged her. He used the moment to whisper into her ear. "If you think you're in danger, go immediately to the police and tell them everything. Show them everything and ask them to lock you up in solitary until they get to the bottom of this."

"Sound advice, Hagip." She laughed and joined Mitch, who'd already started down the stairs.

SHE DROPPED MITCH off at Jenny's apartment in Wethersfield, and by the time she pulled into her street, the dashboard clock showed six o'clock. For once, Elm Grove looked deserted. All her neighbors had either parked their cars in their garages or in the laneways. *Maybe that's why the silver sedan didn't appear*, she thought. *Even in the darkness, it would stand out on an empty street.*

On Sunday mornings, her only day of rest, she usually slept in, but for some reason, she rose just after eight o'clock. After making coffee, she walked over to the living room window, holding a cup and sipping carefully. A blue car sat parked right in front of her house. Two people sat inside. She wasn't sure from their outline whether they were male or female. Terney's cops? He did say he would have his people drive by to make sure she was all right. She turned around, thought about it for a while, and hurried to put on an old sweatshirt and sweatpants. She pulled on a pair of cross-trainers, and with a towel wrapped around her neck, walked outside. She used to jog on a regular basis—ten years ago. Now, she might make it down the street and probably would have to call a cab to give her a ride back. But she couldn't think of any other natural way to go outside and check on the car's occupants.

Joggers usually did a few minutes of warm-up exercises. It gave her an opportunity to look inside the blue Pontiac. She could only afford a brief look but it was enough to tell her that there were two young people inside, a girl and a boy. *Definitely not Terney's cops.* She turned around, preparing to jog away, but heard someone call her name.

"Professor Sarasohn!"

She stopped and looked over her shoulder. The passenger got out of the Pontiac, waving. The voice told her it was a girl. When she came closer, Lauren saw she was young enough to be a Winthrop student. But was she…?

Moving slowly enough to show displeasure, but not reluctance, she walked back to the girl. By the time she was about five feet away, the driver came out of the car, too; a young man, once again with that college student look—casual khakis, white designer sweatshirt, and a touch of exhibitionism in the red and blue checked scarf wound twice around his neck.

"Sorry to bother you," the girl started in a breathless manner. "I'm Megan Smith and this is my lab partner, John Marks. We're psych majors, sophomores, and we're doing a project—" She halted and looked askance at the boy. He spoke up, and Lauren realized that the girl had silently invited the boy to continue.

The boy walked around the rear end of the car, speaking as he approached. "Deviant psychology and motivations underlying violent crimes in various categories—"

"Stop." Lauren raised her hand to silence him. "I'm on a health leave. Until I return to Winthrop, I'm not a teacher. But even if I wanted to help you out with your project, I can't talk about the murder."

"Oh, come on, Ms. Sarasohn," the girl whined. "Please, please, tell us *something*. I mean, how often does a Winthrop psych student get this kind of opportunity? I mean first-hand witness—"

"I'm not a witness, Ms. Smith. I'm just as much of a victim as the young man found dead in my office." She used her uncompromising voice, the voice of a teacher who has the final say by virtue of being the one who assigns the final mark.

"What Megan means is that someone murdered a man who came to see you. What do you think might have been the killer's motivation?" The boy looked at his partner, shrugging and making faces.

"Who said he came to see me? The newspaper only said he was found dead in my office, long before I even arrived on campus. It's actually my boss, Dr. Harold Errington, who found the victim. Why don't you go and interview him for your project, or case study...or whatever." She was careful not to let anything of what she felt inside show on her face. She was a teacher and had to stay in control.

"He's a department director." The boy sounded disgusted. "He won't spare a moment for anyone, never mind a student."

"Well," she smiled at them, "he's the one who found the victim. I only saw my trashed office."

The girl saw her chance and jumped in. "Do you know what the killer was looking for? How badly was it trashed? I mean, was it like totally nuked or...?"

"Sorry." Lauren shook her head, turned around, and started to jog away from them.

"We're going to sit here for a while and spin scenarios," she heard the boy shout after her, but Lauren only waved her hand in the air.

Her jog lasted until she rounded the corner, where she had to slow down to a normal walk before her lungs burst. After a while, walking felt so invigorating that she almost circled the small town and returned from the opposite end of the street. The blue Pontiac still sat in front of her house. She planned to walk by it without even looking at the two students, but the girl opened the passenger window.

"Ms. Sarasohn, can't you even give us a hint of what would be the killer's prime motivation?" she begged.

Lauren stopped, holding the ends of the towel wrapped around her neck, pulling it slightly back and forth.

"Look, kids," she said and moved closer to the open car window. She leaned over so she'd be at the girl's eye level, and caught a whiff of a light citrus smell. They might have polished the dashboard with a lemon cleaner, but such a coincidence would be very strange, given the circumstances. It was the same scent she'd smelled in her car.

"No interviews," she said, fighting an urge to back away and run. "No stalking your teacher, whether she's actually your teacher or not, and no spreading rumors if you can't come up with a bold and sexy motivation that'll earn you a sure A. And that's all I'm going to say other than good luck with your project." She managed a smile before she backed away and headed for her front door.

Chapter 9

AT SEVEN O'CLOCK that night, Linda Moore, Errington's assistant, called her.

"Dr. Errington wants you to take the rest of the month off," she said without any preamble or even a hello.

"I can use three weeks of rest," Lauren said casually, feeling smug because she knew it would confuse Linda, who probably expected an argument.

"Well, yes, I suppose...but he expects you to work on the filtration method paper, you know," Linda recovered quickly. No wonder she was touted as Errington's heir apparent.

"I'll work on my thesis. I'm not in a mood to publish anything until this whole thing blows over, or at least until my nerves settle."

"How can you work on your thesis if you're stressed out?"

"Working on my thesis is relaxing. Trying to write a paper on a filtration process that I don't happen to believe will ever become economically viable, and thus will never be implemented by any sewage processing facility, is a waste of time. At least in my opinion."

"It's your career," Linda said and hung up.

"Kiss my ass," Lauren hissed, even though she heard nothing but a dial tone. "And go kiss Errington's ass too. That's probably his true face anyway." She threw the phone onto the love seat and walked over to look out the window. She didn't see a blue Pontiac but a new car sat in its place. It was Sunday night. She didn't want to call Terney just to ask whether he had an unmarked car sitting in front of her house. She'd feel better if it turned out to be cops, but what if it wasn't?

It was too dark to go for a jog, and the only other way to take a look at the car and its occupants would be to walk out there and confront them again.

She threw on her windbreaker, found a pack of her electronic cigarettes, flipped one out, and headed for the door. Stopping by her car, she put on a show of searching her pockets for a lighter, using the time to look around. Her neighbors' houses on either side had dark windows. That wasn't good. She saw a white car parked in the laneway, at the Cleaver house, three doors down. Well, a manageable distance to run if she had to flee somewhere, screaming for help. She flipped out a lighter from her jacket pocket, and lit it, shielding her electronic cigarette. She needed to explain its glow. She walked leisurely down the laneway.

As she reached the sidewalk, the dark sedan's passenger door opened. She froze, watching a man get out.

"Ms. Sarasohn." He waved at her, obviously wanting to disarm her suspicion with the friendly gesture and the use of her name. "I'm Tom King, Hartford Gazette."

"Look, guys, I'm not giving any interviews to journalists. Police orders." She turned to go back inside the house.

"We're not here about the murder," he said.

"Really?" She turned back.

The guy looked about her age, dressed in a dark, bulky jacket and jeans. The driver, a woman, got out of the car.

"We'd like to interview you about your thesis," she said, joining her colleague on the sidewalk.

"My thesis?" Lauren pursed her mouth. She hadn't expected that.

"I know what you must think," the woman said and flipped out something from the pocket of her black leather coat. Lauren found herself admiring the rippling folds of the three-quarter-length coat because she'd tried on a coat almost exactly like the woman's back in August, at an upscale boutique. How much did journalists earn, she wondered, and should she embark upon a new career?

"My press credentials."

Lauren quickly focused on the badge the woman held out for her.

"Fine, fine, you're the press. So why is the Hartford Gazette suddenly interested in my thesis?"

"It might look like a huge coincidence to you," King said. "I mean, with what happened at the campus, in your office, but we first tried to contact you two weeks ago."

"I didn't get any messages on my phone from the press," she said, flicking the ash off the cigarette.

"We wanted to come to interview you at work, so we contacted your department director, Dr. Errington," the woman said.

"And your name is...?" The woman had flashed her press credentials so quickly that Lauren missed her name.

"Hannah Cohen. Your boss suggested that we make it into a joint interview, you know, the director and his student."

Well, that sounded plausible. Errington would suggest exactly such a thing. Still, something about the two journalists bothered her. Their arrival *was* a huge coincidence. But if they had been trying to contact her before the murder, it might be true that they really wanted to interview her about her thesis.

"We'd have preferred to schedule the interview," King said, "but now it's almost impossible for anyone with press credentials to appear on campus. We also tried to reach you on Friday, but security wouldn't let us into the building. May we come in?"

He slipped the suggestion in smoothly, like only a journalist knows how. She had to admit that it was rather cold standing outside.

"Why is the press suddenly interested in my thesis?"

"It's not sudden at all," Hannah Cohen said. "Last August, we did an interview in Preston with George Wynslow, the general manager of the American Ref-Fuel. We focused on the benefits that communities derive from such a resource recovery facility. Mr. Wynslow mentioned that Winford College's Environmental Management Department has a graduate student doing her doctorate thesis on what he hopes will become a new revolutionary waste management facility."

Well, that was true enough. "So, you talked to Wynslow?" she asked, struggling with the urge to tell them to get the hell out of there and leave her alone, but she knew that if Errington was behind this interview that kind of behavior would only see her on health leave permanently.

"Yes, he mentioned that you came to see him in August, about some details that still troubled you," King picked up.

She stifled a sigh. He should have let his partner do all the talking. In his eagerness to convince her they held genuine interest in her thesis, he'd gone overboard. She'd told Errington that on her drive back from Maine, she took a detour to Preston and met with Wynslow. Except Wynslow had been out until the afternoon, and although waiting a few hours for the general manager would have been what any conscientious graduate student would have done, she'd waited fifteen minutes in the reception area, and left when the receptionist went to the washroom.

She never talked to George that day and doubted that the receptionist even told him that someone from Winthrop had been there to see him. But Errington got the conscientious version. And since Wynslow was a busy man, he most likely didn't call the director either. Errington had a habit of soliciting funding whenever private industry members called.

"Well, Mr. King, Ms Cohen," she nodded at them in the same order, "since my boss expressed an interest to be a part of this interview, you'll have to call him and schedule a regular appointment for it. He'll most likely insist that it should be held in his conference room, and I think that's a much more appropriate place for an interview about an environmental issue than my house. Good night," she said evenly and walked back to her house, slowing down to give them an opportunity to call after her, to try and persuade her to at least give them some preliminary material that they would use to formulate their interview questions.

The fact they didn't told her a lot more than their press credentials did.

The memory of Hagip's whisper, as she'd bent down for his hug, seeped out of the shadows. *"If you think you're in danger, go immediately to the police and tell them everything, show them everything, and ask them to lock you up in solitary until they solve the case."* And while she found his advice always beneficial, for once she couldn't take it. It was just as Mitch told her. Errington didn't need any more material against her to fire her. And since Errington was not just her boss, but her thesis supervisor...no, no. She couldn't take Hagip's advice, no matter how well-meaning.

She tried watching television, but the pictures blurred, and the voices grew distant. After making a pot of chamomile tea and drinking two cups, she still couldn't relax. She thought of calling Mitch, but he'd be out with Jenny.

Grimacing because she didn't want to do it, but knew that if she didn't she'd never get to sleep, she called Terney.

"I'm sorry—"

He cut her off. "Don't apologize. What's going on?"

"It's ten o'clock at night and you probably won't be able to do it until tomorrow. I'd really appreciate it if you checked for me whether the Hartford Gazette has on staff two journalists who just tried to invite themselves into my house: Tom King and Hannah Cohen. They showed me their press credentials."

"Can you hang on for five minutes? Just stay on the phone, okay?"

"Sure," she said, closing her eyes.

It took him a long time. Finally, his voice filled the line again.

From the way he chose his words, separating them with slight pauses, Lauren knew that she wouldn't hear anything good.

"Thomas King worked for the Gazette for five years, covering sports. Six months ago, an anonymous tip to King's editor suggested that King was part of an organized ring that fixed sporting events, in particular, horse racing and boxing. The newspaper put King on leave of absence without pay, pending investigation. King sued the Gazette for defamation of character and unfair dismissal, though he wasn't dismissed outright. The lawsuit is still going on. For those reasons, if anyone calls the Gazette and asks whether Thomas King works there, the answer will be yes but no further information will be given. Is that something you expected to hear?"

She nodded. Realizing he wasn't there to see her agreement, she said, "Yes, Lieutenant. I thought it had to be a fantastic coincidence that two reporters would want to interview me now about my thesis. What about Hannah Cohen?"

He remained silent for a long time.

"Lieutenant, are you still there?"

"Yes, Lauren." He used her first name, which had to mean that whatever he had to say would be even worse. "This is where it gets very strange, and very, very nasty. Hannah Cohen, twenty-eight years old, worked as an investigative journalist for the Gazette. She worked undercover in a joint sting operation with the police, trying to flush out the supplier of the latest batch of designer drugs that surfaced in the Hartford nightclubs. She had diabetes. Someone inside the organization found out her real identity and substituted colorless, odorless lamp oil for her insulin. She died at St. Jerome's Hospital."

"When?"

Once again, he hesitated before saying, "Last night. At this time, no one but a handful of top executives at the Gazette and a few policemen are privy to this information. Lauren, do you have something these people want?"

She held the handset away from her ear, staring at it. It could be bugged. Did they bug her house too? Or did they have the hi-tech tools that the military and intelligence spies employed, the kind that used satellites to let them listen to whatever she said from the end of the street?

"Lauren?" he said louder.

"Still here, Lieutenant. I'm just so...frustrated because I don't have anything. I don't know anything. Errington took me out for the rest of the month. Who are these people? Why won't they leave me alone?"

"They think you have whatever it is they want."

"I have nothing. What can I possibly have? Errington found the body. Why don't they go and intimidate him?"

"Lauren, listen to me carefully. It's not just a one-killer-after-you game. I think we're dealing with a very large organization that has members from every walk of life. The only people who knew that Hannah Cohen died last night are beyond suspicion. And yet these people, whoever they are, obtained the information and not only that, they used it quickly to their advantage. That kind of resourcefulness and brilliance is deadly. Can you think of anything—no matter how inconsequential it might seem to you—that might be at the root of this?"

"Nothing, Lieutenant. I don't know how many times I have to say it—nothing."

"You and Mitch went to New York yesterday."

"How'd you know that?" A cold needle of surprise jabbed her between the shoulder blades. Was Terney one of those members from every walk of life?

He must have sensed what had just crossed her mind. "No, Lauren. I'm not the bad guy. I'm just a homicide cop who has been saddled with another case. I called Mr. Plow's landlady yesterday. She said he might be at his girlfriend's. So I called Ms. Barnes. She told me that Mitch went with you to New York to pick up his research journals at the library and to visit an old friend at the Metropolitan Museum. Besides, you called me and said you wanted to check out the Greenpeace connection, remember?"

"Yeah, yeah, I did." She relaxed but the pain between her shoulder blades wouldn't subside.

"What did you find out?"

"Hagip's going to touch base with some of our old Greenpeace colleagues, and he'll get back to me in a couple of days."

"When he does, you call me, understood?"

"Yes, Lieutenant, I'll call you. I'm sorry..."

"That's all right. Just hang in there, but if you think of anything at all, you pick up the phone. And if you see a suspicious car parked in front of your house again, you call me and I'll have my guys drive by and do what they're paid to do, understood?" And he hung up.

"Lieutenant...!" She wanted to ask about Gomez and whether there was a recent theft at the place where he worked—the Carlyle Hotel. Asking him would reduce the temptation for her and Mitch to embark on an unsanctioned investigation. Well, if he answered his cell phone on Sunday night, he wouldn't mind picking it up again. She quickly re-dialed the number.

"Hello," a child's voice answered.

"Who's this?" She held her breath.

"It's Jaime. Who are you?"

"What's your full name, sweetie?" Her throat felt so dry, she thought she might gag.

"Jaime Terney. I'm not supposed to be talking to you on this phone, but it keeps playing and I can't hear when Mario goes Boo..."

"James," she heard Terney's voice. "What did I tell you about leaving that phone alone? Give me that. Hello?"

She let out her breath. "Lieutenant, I'm so stressed out that for a moment I thought I'd finally lost it. Sorry to bother you again, but—"

"Ms. Sarasohn? Where are you and what do you mean *again*?"

Chapter 10

TERNEY CAME QUICKLY, but still not fast enough for Lauren's frazzled nerves. She passed the time biting her nails and pacing on her front walk, feeling very exposed, but not wanting to waste the precious minutes it would take for Terney to park and walk to her door to ring the bell. Just as she was about to go inside and find a real cigarette, his car cruised up her street, looking like a big blue lifeboat. She spit out a bloody piece of cuticle and ran to his car while it still rolled along the curb. Terney motioned her inside, and sped off the moment the passenger door closed.

She tried to speak, but he raised his hand to stop her. They drove back to Hartford in tense silence. She gave him a questioning look as he drove into the community center parking lot, but she knew that she sat next to the policeman she'd met outside Essex Hall on that horrible Saturday, and not an imposter. She didn't have to fear he'd kidnap her. Besides, the community center was a busy public place. She had nothing to worry about. She shook her head. She couldn't go on like this, doubting herself and everyone else—friends and strangers alike.

"I take my sons here for swimming lessons," Terney explained, heading for the pool area. A teenaged lifeguard approached and showcased his authority by pointing at their street shoes. Terney flashed his badge and said they needed an empty corner for about half an hour. He assured the lifeguard they'd stay on the outdoor-shoes-non-skid strip.

He nodded at the kid, took her elbow, and led her to the far side of the pool. The pool wasn't crowded, but whatever splashing and shouting she heard would act as good white noise.

"Now you can talk," he said.

"I called you Thursday night, around nine o'clock. You were still at work."

"No." He shook his head. "I worked but not in my office. I sat in my car for hours—on a stakeout. If I remember correctly, I talked to you on Thursday morning. I called you. But tell me, how did *our* evening conversation go?"

She closed her eyes and repeated the entire conversation. "You agreed that I should go see Hagip and explore the possibility of a Greenpeace connection."

"How well do you know this Hagip Agopian?"

"I spent the better part of four years sleeping beside him in a sleeping bag."

"Does that mean I'm not supposed to pursue this line of questioning?" He frowned at her.

His solid presence alone had a relaxing effect on her. She laughed. "I trust Hagip in the way I trusted my mother."

"Fair enough. What made you think you talked with me?"

She leaned back, staring at him as if he had declared the rest of the year a national holiday. "Excuse me? You gave me your office number. I dialed it and your voice answered. What was I supposed to think?"

His mouth twitched. "Right. Well, I definitely wasn't within hand's reach of my desk phone. Last spring I went to Quantico, with a dozen homicide cops for a five-day workshop. It's frightening how easy it is to make a print of voice frequency and feed it into a computer. The listener will never know the difference. That's not something that's become standard police procedure. I think we're dealing with a large organization."

"Strange," she said, grimacing. "That's just what you said in our phone conversation tonight," she said.

"It's frightening to know that no matter what I say, I'm not being original. For all I know, whoever they are they might have followed us and know that we're here. If they're smart, and it sure seems to be the case, they'd figure out that you're onto them. Or at least that something happened tonight that spooked you and you got through to the real Terney. Go on, tell me," he said and settled down to listen.

This time she omitted only the most crucial information—that she and Mitch had found what the victim had managed to hide from his killer.

"This means that I can't even call you anymore," she finished, biting her lip.

"Sure you can," Terney replied, surprising her. "Use the same number, but we'll have to come up with some code phrase to make sure that you're talking to me and not to a voice washed through a computer. Why did you call me the second time, the time you got through to the real Terney, or to be precise, Terney Jr.?"

"Would you be able to find out if a theft occurred at the Carlyle around the time my staff security card was stolen?

"Why?"

He kept staring at her. She cast her gaze downward and said, "If the victim stole something and brought it with him to Winthrop, maybe it's still somewhere in our office."

"But you said you've already searched your office and found nothing."

"We'll search again but it might be easier if we knew what to look for."

"We checked with New York. No one reported a theft at the Carlyle during the months of August or September."

"Did Gomez work only on particular floors?" she asked.

He tapped one foot in an uneven rhythm that became faster and more agitated the longer they spoke. "What do you mean?" he asked and turned up his palms. "He was a bellhop. He worked wherever sent to deliver luggage. The Carlyle doesn't have a bell-hop hierarchy, though they do tend to send the senior bellhops to the three Tower Suites."

"Would you have a name of any particular VIP staying at the Carlyle toward the end of August or early September?"

"Carlyle is always full of VIPs. Why don't you ask me what you really want to ask me?"

"Gomez must have stolen something around the same time my staff security card disappeared. You said he worked there almost seven years. That would make him a senior bellhop. So, he'd be assigned to the Tower Suites more often than not."

"Why don't you ask me what you really want to ask?"

"Who stayed in the Tower Suites around the time Gomez would have carried out the theft?"

"It's still not direct, but fairly close. William Clement Palfrey occupied one of the two Tower Suites that overlook Central Park. The other Tower Suite, plus the third one that's on the 22nd floor was filled with Mr. Palfrey's closest friends and associates. The distinguished crowd occupied the suites from August 31st to September 14th." He finished with a dry throat-clearing.

"William Palfrey." She shook her head. "You mean Clement Palfrey, the congressman?"

"Maybe you shouldn't be in such a hurry to get your PhD. You know what they say about PhDs, don't you?" He stared at her, a smile tugging at his lips. She obliged him by shrugging. It seemed to be what he was waiting for. He continued, "They're the academics that strive to learn more and more about less and less until they finally know everything about nothing."

"I'll pass that onto my boss, Dr. Errington," she managed.

"Careful," he raised his brows at her, "or you'll get yourself dismissed. No, I don't mean our congressman. I mean his father, Mr. William C. Palfrey, of the liquor fame. The owner of mega-distilleries and a ton of other money-making enterprises that bring his combined family worth to about two billion dollars."

"Two billion...? Whoa!" She cleared her lungs with a big whoosh.

Terney clasped his hands together and said, "Let me put it to you this way: Mr. Palfrey plays a round of golf with the French president whenever he's visiting the country. A bottle of his *Ste. Mireille D'Or* goes for about a thousand bucks at a restaurant where even the kind of shoes you wear matter. He contributed a handsome sum of money to our president's electoral campaign, and if his Microsoft Windows develops a cold, who do you think he calls to heal his product?"

"The kid down the street who's majoring in IT Business Solutions at the community college?"

"Guess again." Terney no longer sounded amused. "I'm telling you this because if Gomez did steal something from any one of those three Tower Suites at the Carlyle, anyone even remotely connected to him is in deep shit."

"Let's say he stole something from Palfrey—"

Terney interrupted. "Don't take what I've told you lightly. If Gomez stole something from Palfrey's suite, and no one at the Carlyle reported the theft, it figures that whatever Gomez stole is not something Palfrey wants to make publicly known. The man has resources that would make even the FBI gape in admiration."

Terney's intensity started to scare her. "Lieutenant, I'm not connected to Gomez in any other way but through the fact that someone murdered him in my office. Errington found him. Why don't these people go after my boss? He might know something. He came to see me early Saturday morning, knowing damn well I wouldn't be in until nine o'clock. He's the one who found the body. Don't you think that's worth pursuing further?"

He nodded crisply. "Sure—and I already did, but politics got in the way. Your college president, Morgan, is warming up to Congressman Palfrey, hoping to soften him enough to lobby the college's cause and channel some federal grants to Winthrop."

"I'm not into politics," she said, looking over the swimming pool. The lifeguard stood talking to a bunch of kids.

"You're not much into life, period. You keep in touch with a couple of childhood friends from Rockland, but although you had a roommate at Duke, you don't even bother sending her an occasional postcard."

"Denise works for an oil refinery down in Houston, their resident environmental consultant. We don't have much in common anymore."

"She sold out her idealistic principles, is that it?"

"She's earning a six-figure salary," she replied. "What can I say?"

"Do you seriously equate poverty-level wages with idealism? I thought you'd be smarter than that. Dr. Denise Alpen is where she knows she can make the greatest difference—on the frontlines. But she has that coveted academic title, the doctorate, and you're still struggling with yours."

"I'm not struggling with anything but...not struggling, that's all. What's your point, Lieutenant?"

"My point is that I tried to find friends you might have close by, or at least within driving distance, and do you know what?" He paused. She knew he was waiting for her to reply but she needed hours, not just seconds to find something to say that wouldn't sound lame. He continued, "I'm a damn good homicide detective but I couldn't find anyone else besides your colleague Mitch that might be considered even an acquaintance."

"My work keeps me busy," she mumbled.

"What would it take for you to hand in your resignation and call Aileen Summerville or Carmella Perez, and get back where you should have headed in the first place?"

She laughed, hoping it didn't sound bitter. "I haven't seen Aileen in ten years. And Carmella probably doesn't even remember me anymore."

"They both not only remember you, but want you to call them."

"What are you talking about?"

"I told you I checked you out."

"Yes, but I didn't think you'd...what did you do, call them and ask about me?"

He leaned toward her. "Ms. Sarasohn, I'll give you a week to sleep on it. When you wake up, I want the truth and nothing but."

"I don't—"

"Fine! I said I'd give you a week. Now, we need a code phrase to make sure that it's me answering the phone and not my clones."

Chapter 11

O N MONDAY MORNING, she sent Mitch an e-mail, asking to be filled in on whatever happened in the department during her absence, and, if necessary, on campus too. By noon, he still hadn't replied. She grew nervous and called Linda.

"He's teaching your classes," Linda said waspishly. "And after he's done your share of the work, he has to do his. And he also has a departmental meeting. Dr. Errington is going to brief us on the developments."

"What developments?" she asked but Linda had hung up.

She re-dialed, but the bitch let it ring until it transferred to voice mail.

"Fine," she ground out and sat down at the computer. Five minutes later, she rose to look out the window. She saw a few cars parked on the street, but none in front of her house. She tried to work on her thesis, but the words and their meaning didn't want to penetrate her brain. Finally, she settled down to do her online banking. Panic tightened her chest when she saw that after paying her utilities, she'd have no money left for rent. Once a month, the meager salary Errington paid her was deposited electronically into her checking account, along with a payment for her grant, which he had divided into monthly portions and would only advance to her one month at the time. If she wasn't at work, she wouldn't receive the grant money. Hell, she'd be lucky if he didn't block her sick pay, claiming that she took sick leave voluntarily, and therefore, it wasn't a paid benefit.

Lauren calmed down after checking her credit card statement. She had enough credit left to take a cash advance. But that would be a one-shot fix.

"It's a long way until the end of the month," she said, feeling better. She signed out of her bank account and called Mitch's cell phone. He'd turned it off, and the voice-message played. She only heard the last word: Unavailable.

She glanced at the monitor. "Two o'clock. He's probably finishing his classes." Linda also said Errington had called a departmental meeting. Mitch could be tied up for hours.

She stared out the window again. The street looked peaceful, calm. Nothing had changed since the last time she'd checked.

"Calm before the storm," Hagip used to say just as they readied to start the protest march. Isabel would roll her eyes skyward and say something in French. She'd also lean over and kiss the top of his head.

She smiled at the memories. For four years she had been cold, tired, hungry, and often voiceless from shouting so much, but other than the physical discomforts of a Spartan existence, her spirit soared. She was happy...until one sunny day, John Preston McPhend hopped across the planks that connected their houseboat to a dilapidated wooden ramp at a burned-down marina in Corpus Christi, and pointed his camera at her...

She slapped her hands against her temples and squeezed. The pressure helped to banish the memories.

She made a sandwich, poured a glass of milk, and ate her late lunch.

Hagip said it would take him a few days, but she needed to talk to someone...now. But who?

Terney's reproach started to pinch like a tight shoe. She had carelessly cut too many people from her life. When Michelle, a college friend, got a new job and moved to Arizona, she sent her a postcard with a change of address. Lauren crossed out the old address in her daily planner but never wrote-in Michelle's new one. She always had an excuse why a college roommate or a fellow White House intern should be stricken from her address book. She kept in touch and visited her old high school friend, Becky in Maine, only because for a month she could pretend that she came home. That nothing had changed and her mother had just gone to Bangor to look after business issues. Her high school classmates admired her but she wasn't popular. Steve Dennis, the quarterback, took her out on a date a few times, but they had nothing in common, nothing to talk about. He might have stayed around longer if she'd bothered to write down his phone number. But back in high school, things like reading fashion magazines, watching beauty pageants, and gossiping about sexy movie-vampires seemed silly and trite.

She started to dial Hagip's number, thought about someone listening in, and hung up. But they already know, she told herself. What's the use? She redialed.

No one picked up the phone and it went to his voice mail. She glanced at the kitchen clock; it was just after four o'clock.

Five minutes later, it occurred to her to send Hagip an e-mail. Sometimes people refused to pick up the phone because they didn't want to be distracted from their work at the computer.

She always sent everything registered, because she would at least get a confirmation that the recipient had opened the message. An hour later, neither Mitch nor Hagip still haven't replied to her e-mails. Feeling jittery, Lauren called Hagip again.

Finally, a woman answered.

"I believe Dr. Agopian went home early because his family came back from Canada," the woman, who identified herself as Jean Garnet, said.

She laughed out loud. "Of course. I forgot. He did say that Isabel and the kids went to visit her folks in Montreal."

"Can I take a message?"

She thanked Jean, said it wasn't necessary, and hung up. She felt so relieved that she started to hum a commercial jingle. After that, the television must have put her to sleep, because she woke up to an awful buzzing noise. She turned off the TV and went to bed.

She didn't how long she slept but she woke up suddenly and completely alert. She looked at the alarm clock by her bedside. She gasped. Did she really sleep fourteen hours? She sat up and remembered that she had nowhere to rush to, nothing to do but stay home and resume her attempts to reach the two people she counted amongst her friends. Out of habit, she shuffled into the living room and looked out the window. The street, void of any vehicles, looked quiet.

"Good," she said with a nod and strode to the kitchen to fix breakfast. She opened the fridge and stared at the empty shelves, trying to figure out what happened to the food. Slowly, it dawned on her that she hadn't done her usual Sunday shopping.

Now that she had been placed on *health leave*, she'd have to economize, and that meant conserving gas. Rather than drive ten miles to Hartford, she drove to Luther's Price Chex, the only food store in Rocky Hill. Terney's point from the night before started to make an impression upon her as she walked up and down the narrow aisles. She'd lived in Rocky Hill for five years. Considering its population—756—the small town should have been called a hamlet. In five years, she had bothered to learn only the names of five or six neighbors. She'd say good morning or nod and smile at them, but that was the extent of her socializing. She'd seen her landlord, once, five years ago. He came down from Hartford and showed her the tiny house with its neglected garden and crumbling front stone steps. Other than his name, Frank Cooper, she knew nothing about him. Since she had authorized him to electronically withdraw the monthly rent from her account, she had no reason to see him or call him.

The food market had at least a dozen people shopping, but she didn't know any of them.

All through her childhood she'd suffered from asthma. Her mother told everyone about her affliction too. Once, feeling totally embarrassed, she pulled her mother aside and asked her to stop telling total strangers about her daughter's health problems. Mother had tilted her head to one side, braced her hands on her hips, and said, "Sweetheart, I'm doing it to protect you in case you have an attack and I'm not here. I want everyone to know and recognize your asthma attack so they'll be able to search your knapsack or your pockets for an inhaler and help you."

Walking around the supermarket and seeing nothing but strangers, who didn't even bother to nod a greeting, she thought that if she had an attack of asthma right here, no one would even know her name, never mind help her.

Terney was a shrewd judge of character. He may have started checking up on her to find out if the murder might somehow be connected to someone in her background, but he'd learned something else in the course of the exercise. As a person, Lauren Sarasohn has about as much substance as a ghost. Outside of her department, she was a twenty-digit number on the college staff payroll. Other than Mitch and Errington, hardly anyone knew her at Winthrop, and if she went missing one day, they would be the only people to notice. She'd cut herself off from friends and old associates better than if she'd climbed into a glass jar and closed the lid.

Terney tried to raise her profile by calling Aileen Summerville and Carmella Perez. As a cop, he knew just how vulnerable lone or isolated people were. He wanted to alert many of her old connections in order to give her at least a modicum of protection

"Excuse me, honey." A small, chipper voice broke through her thoughts. She shook her head and focused on the speaker.

"I can't reach the top shelf." A diminutive old lady with a frizzy perm and dressed in a shapeless brown coat, motioned at the stacked boxes of cereal with a gloved hand. "I don't know how many times I've told Bill to have his helpers put the cereal in the middle, but kids these days don't listen. They keep stacking them way up there and..."

"No problem." Lauren smiled and turned her back to the woman. She reached for the cereal box—and felt the knapsack on her back jostle. She spun around.

"My grandson has one of those." The lady motioned at her knapsack. "And he says the teacher insists that he bring all his books to school every day. Some days it's so heavy, the poor boy can hardly lift his head. These kids, they'll have back problems someday, and no one knows that better than I do. You should at least put that heavy bag in the shopping cart and give your back a rest." She nodded her head, smiling.

"I will," Lauren said, taking a step back and trying not to show her rising fear. The old lady may have touched her knapsack out of sympathy, but another possibility tightened Lauren's throat. "Which cereal do you want?" She made sure she stood at an angle to the shelves, and as soon as the woman answered, she quickly took the box, handed it to her, and backed away, pulling her empty shopping cart alongside her.

She slung the knapsack over her shoulder to give the appearance that it was empty, or at least that it wasn't heavy. But the old lady's touch would have told her otherwise.

"Thank you, honey, thank you," the old lady called after her, and Lauren forced herself to smile and wave back.

Hurriedly, she threw her purchases into the shopping cart and headed for the checkout counter.

"Joey, help this young lady with her groceries." The man at the counter waved at a teenaged boy, who hovered nearby.

"That won't be necessary," she leaned forward to see the name badge on the man's blue uniform coat, "Bill. Thanks, but I don't have much to carry."

"No bother, that's what we pride ourselves on: Customer service. Hey, Joey, come get these bags." The man ignored her outstretched hands, and instead, handed the two grocery bags to the teen. "He'll help you with your knapsack, too, if you want."

She'd already paid, so she rushed forward, grabbed the bags from the unwilling teen's hands, yanked hard to make him let go, and said, "I'm in a hurry and I don't need help, but I really appreciate the gesture. Thanks again." She flashed a smile at Bill and the boy, and almost ran out of the store.

Her hands shook so badly that she had to sit in the car for a few moments before driving out of the parking lot. She knew that sitting there in an idling car wasted gas, but for once environmental issues took a backseat.

At home, she put the groceries in the fridge without taking them out of the bags, and un-slung her knapsack. She let it fall, and it landed on the tiled kitchen floor with a thud and a telltale clink of metal. The sound seemed to serve as a bell, signaling rest. She sank to her knees, sat back, and wrapped her arms around her body. Whenever she couldn't solve a math problem or didn't quite know how to start an essay or a project, she'd sit back on her heels, hug herself, and rock back and forth. The motion seemed to help settle her anguish and even bring clarity. This time, it failed to do its work. She rolled to one side, curled up tightly into a fetal position, and cried.

She must have fallen asleep on the floor because she woke up disoriented. There was lighting but she couldn't find its source. It wasn't the usual light given off by the overhead fixture in the kitchen.

"I left the fridge open," she mumbled and struggled to sit up. She pushed the fridge door shut and suddenly darkness enveloped her so tightly that she felt entombed. She opened the fridge again, and reached to turn on the kitchen light before shutting the fridge with a kick.

A hot shower restored a small measure of her composure. However, once she sat down at her computer and saw that neither Mitch nor Hagip had replied to her e-mail, her throat constricted again.

"If you think you're in danger, go to the police, tell them everything, show them..." Hagip's warning made a strong argument for confession time. However, if William Palfrey didn't report the theft because he didn't want publicity, she couldn't tell a public official or even a policeman what resided in the green canvas bag. Once she surrendered the bag to the police, her name would become public domain. Terney would seek to protect her, but...it wouldn't take long for reporters to latch on to her name.

National newspapers were filled with stories of big and small crimes. However, to own the gold bar inside the bag hinted at an even bigger crime than murder, because the ownership of those articles led to the most hideous mass murderer in the history of humanity.

Why would a man like William Palfrey, wealthy, successful, and without any public scandal associated with him, own such things? And more importantly, where did he get them? Was this what success and money did to men? Once they had amassed fabulous wealth and easily afforded anything they wanted in their lifetime, did they grow tired of all the finery their money could buy legally and turn to crime?

She knew nothing more than what Terney had told her about William Clement Palfrey. Perhaps it was time to do some research that wasn't connected to environmental issues. But first, she had to find Mitch.

Chapter 12

ALL THROUGH THE five-minute drive from her house to Winthrop, she forced herself not to think about anything but the traffic. The moment she pulled into the staff parking lot, she knew something was wrong.

A white-and-blue campus security car sat parked in her spot. She shut off her engine and got out of the car. At the same time Bryce Culver stepped out of the cruiser.

"Are you warming up my spot, Bryce?" she asked. Five years ago, he'd asked her to call him by his first name and she'd done it ever since.

"Hi, Miss Lauren—nice to see you—hope you're feeling better. I'm sure glad that things have settled down, but there's this thing that has to be done—orders, you know." He always spoke without giving his sentences or thoughts a pause. It gave an impression that he feared he'd forget what he wanted to say if he hesitated too long. He reminded Lauren of Pete Wittlock, one of her mother's two permanent marina helpers. Pete had been a hard worker and also spoke in a breathless, non-stop manner as if afraid he might lose his train of thought if he slowed down. Her mother eventually deduced that Pete was illiterate and didn't want people to know it.

Bryce Culver also didn't want to admit that his computer skills didn't meet his job-description expectations. An admission to such a deficiency might not have seen him fired, but he would have probably been demoted to campus patrol with a corresponding reduction in pay. That's why she never complained if her staff security card didn't work. Instead, she'd remind him in an absent-minded way that her special features needed updating and to remove the weekend access restrictions.

"What's going on, Bryce?" she asked, seeing his discomfort.

He waved at Essex Hall. "Your security card won't work. I mean it won't work on the front entrance, because Director ordered me to suspend all your special access privileges—and I mean all not just weekdays, but all the others. You know, the special weekend access features—until the end of the month."

"So the entire campus is off limits to me," she said, motioning at her parking spot where his cruiser sat.

"He said you need rest."

Well, if Errington had told human resources that he placed her on health-leave, the rest part would be true.

"What if I want to work on my thesis the library?"

He shook his head. "Director said I should make sure you don't come on campus because you need to rest, it's what happened in your office."

"Yes, thanks Bryce, but I just want to talk to Mitch today. Would you at least tell him to turn on his cell phone, or charge it if it's low, and call me, or e-mail me—just to get in touch with me today, okay?"

"Sure thing, Miss Lauren, and you take care and be careful." He seemed relieved that she didn't put up a fuss.

She got back in her car, circled around, and glanced in the rear view mirror to see whether Bryce would move his cruiser; it still sat in her parking space.

Seconds later, something she hadn't considered occurred to her, and she had to pull over on the shoulder. Her hands on the steering wheel shook and grew clammy, cold.

Once again, Terney hit a bull's-eye. Someone had set her up as surely as Gomez had been set up. Errington had to be involved—somehow. Gomez must have stolen her card. No one else's would have worked on the weekend. While listening to Bryce Culver talk, something in the back of her mind had nagged at her. Her staff security card was the only one of its kind—without the normal weekend restrictions. The one time Mitch had decided to come in on Saturday, he arrived at eleven o'clock, and she came downstairs to the east entrance to let him inside. Culver's staff had programmed his security card with restrictions that allowed him to use it only during the weekdays, and only from eight a.m. to ten p.m. That's how most staff security cards worked—with restricted access privileges.

By letting Errington intimidate her into sacrificing her weekends, she'd unwittingly allowed herself to be set-up. She allowed herself to be victimized because she had no spine.

Now I know. She nodded, checked her mirrors, and pulled back onto the road. Ten minutes later, she stood on the porch of a two-story, steel-blue clapboard house on the outskirts of Hartford, trying to understand what Mitch's landlady was trying to say.

"His girl come and pack up for emergency," the woman kept repeating.

"What emergency, Mrs. Gaetano?"

The landlady shrugged. "She not tell me. She just rush-rush-rush and squish-squish-squish things into bags and poof! She gone."

"What time did Jenny arrive?"

"Last night, late too. Woke me up. She said she lose key or maybe she say Mit'chell not give her key. She say a lot. I don't remember."

She thanked the woman and returned to sit in her car, thinking.

What kind of emergency would Mitch have that he would have to send Jenny to pack up his clothes, and where on earth would this emergency be happening?

She had to find out. She drove to Wethersfield. Jenny didn't answer the buzzer, so she waited until a tenant came in and squeezed in behind her. She took the stairs to the second floor of the six-story apartment building, and ran down the corridor to number 2D.

Ten minutes later, she walked back down to the lobby and knocked on the building manager's door.

"She said she'd be out of town for a couple of weeks...something about a family emergency, I think," the man said. He kept wiping his hands into his blue maintenance coveralls as she spoke.

"But did she tell you where? I mean, whose family? Hers or Mitch's?"

"I didn't see anyone else with her, but her boyfriend might have been waiting in the car."

"Can you please look it up in your records—?"

He slammed the door in her face.

Stunned, she stood there for a few seconds and finally turned around and ran outside. She walked down the street until she found a public phone booth and called Terney. His phone rang until it went into messaging screens. She started to leave a message when a dispatcher came on the line. She asked to be connected to Terney's voice-mail and was surprised to hear his voice.

"Hi, Lieutenant. It's Lauren Sarasohn. I'm in Wethersfield, at Mitch's girlfriend apartment. Both Mitch and Jenny are gone. His landlady said that last night Jenny came to Mitch's flat, packed up for an emergency, and left. She didn't know what kind of emergency, nor where they went. The building manager here doesn't know either and won't show me his records, so I can't even find out where Jenny's from. Mitch is from Louisiana, Lafayette...I think." She moaned, realizing that she didn't even know for sure whether her colleague's hometown was Lafayette or some town nearby, never mind having his family's address.

"We'll check it out," Terney assured her calmly. "I'll let you know the moment we find out where Mitch and Jenny went. And do be careful—go home and rest. This is probably the first paid holiday you've had in years."

"I get the summer off, remember?" She waited after giving the *code* portion of their conversation.

"Do you get paid in the summer?"

"Only tenured have that privilege."

"In that case, get moving and finish your doctorate."

"So I can know everything about nothing."

He chuckled. "I think many of us are already there," he said and hung up.

She replaced the phone in the cradle and looked around. Nothing looked suspicious, so she headed back to her car parked in front of Jenny's apartment building.

She stopped in front of an empty space between a red Explorer and a silver Grand Prix. The large parking spot gaped so obviously that she sucked in her breath and held it, waiting...counting to five before letting it out slowly.

Her white Volkswagen Golf had disappeared.

Chapter 13

S HE SMILED, THINKING that not too many victims of car theft would have that kind of reaction. After she decided to drive to Winthrop, she'd picked up the knapsack, wincing under its weight, thought of something—and carried it out.

Now, her knapsack left in the back seat of her car—was stolen just like her car. Except the knapsack was empty. She didn't expect they'd steal her car, but just in case someone broke into it on campus, she put twenty dollars into her pocket, along with her driver's license, cell phone and her VISA card, and left her wallet, her address book, and the rest of her IDs at home.

The green canvas bag rested in its original hiding place, in the back of her freezer. She didn't think they'd find it if they broke into her house.

She flagged down a taxi, asked the driver whether twenty dollars would take her to Rocky Hill. He nodded, and she got inside.

Once home, she checked the freezer to make sure the canvas bag slept in its cold bed, its contents intact, and called the Hartford Police Department to report the theft of her car. She also called her insurance company. She had coverage for the basic compact rental car and arranged over the phone for the Hertz to bring a compact to her house. The car rental agent promised to have the car in Rocky Hill by late afternoon.

Dealing with the details of the car theft kept her busy, and the troubling issue of Mitch and Jenny's sudden departure faded. The moment she hung up the phone, though, worry about Mitch attacked her again.

People had families, and sudden emergencies cropped up, but it was just too much of a coincidence for Mitch, or even Jenny, to be saddled with one now. She tried calling Linda, but either her colleague wasn't in her office or she purposely let the phone go into voice mail. Out of desperation, she dialed Errington's number. Relief flooded her when she heard it transfer to his voice-mail too.

She left him a message, asking about Mitch and whatever events were scheduled in the department. He might not call her, but at least she let him know that she found out Mitch had disappeared.

Half expecting the Hertz guy, who brought her the car at five o'clock, to somehow broach the issue of a leather knapsack, she smiled because he only asked her to check the car's exterior prior to signing off the rental agreement and hurried back to the curb where his colleague waited for him in a Hertz van.

The Pontiac came much better appointed than her Golf. It even had a CD player; she'd be able to listen to her favorite Roy Orbison oldies. She thought of going for a drive but she never did anything without having a firm goal in mind. Aimless driving around, whether on streets or highways, wasn't something she would do, simply because such luxury wasted gas.

I didn't just cut myself off from all my old friends and associates. I climbed into a straitjacket. I can't do anything if the results won't yield something practical or at least applicable to work. How much gas can I waste in half an hour?

Lauren hurried back into the house, dragged her mother's old steamer trunk from the side of her bed, where it served her as an all-purpose night table, and opened it.

She ended up looking at all the milestones that shaped and defined her life; the photographs of herself with Senator Summerville, at work, in public, and at home with Aileen's children close to her age, and their two terriers. Fighting back bitterness and regret, she stared at a photo of herself in a choir formation with all the other pages, standing next to Congressman Braston from New York. She picked up her milestones one by one—the ribbons awarded for excellence in high school, her diplomas and certificates, an eight-by-ten photo of her standing next to Carmella Perez in a White House corridor, the Secret Service agents visible on the fringes—and let them slip through her fingers to softly land in their repository. Her fingers brushed over a brittle photo. In khaki shorts and a faded blue t-shirt, she looked thin and baked brown by the Texas sun. The sheer memories of its glare reflecting off the water made her squint. It's how John saw her when he skipped across the wooden planks onto the houseboat...

She swept it aside, pushing, almost crumpling the paper filled with her memories. Keeping her search focused, she rummaged through the rest until she found the shiny patent leather purse that Aileen's daughter, Melody, made her buy during a shopping expedition in Georgetown. The Louis Vuitton purse, shaped like an oil-drum, looked silly not just because of its odd shape but its eggplant color. It wasn't something she'd carry on any given day, but now that her knapsack had been stolen, she needed something.

The oil-drum shape, however, looked perfect for storing the green canvas bag that she planned to carry with her at all times.

She took out the purse, slammed the trunk's lid, and sat down on the floor. Opening the bag, she turned it upside down to shake out whatever she might have left inside, but nothing fell out.

How fitting that this luxury item I never wanted to buy in the first place is empty. Just to make sure, she turned it right-side up and felt in all the little pockets inside. The last one yielded Carmella Perez's business card. She grimaced. Even the purse wanted to remind her to start becoming visible again—to be someone people not only remembered, but also wanted to stay in touch with.

By the time she finished, darkness had fallen, and she could have used some light. However, she wanted to make the transfer from the freezer into the Vuitton bag in darkness, because it felt safer that way.

"You're not safe, you're not safe, you're not safe," voices whispered around her in the darkness. *"If you think you're in danger...."* Hagip's nasally whisper rose from the generic phantom noise.

She shook her head, got up, and made her way to the kitchen.

She opened the freezer and started to fit the bag inside the oil-drum purse. Pausing, it occurred to her that she hadn't seen its contents since Hagip examined the gold bar and the parchment squares. It didn't bother her that much to handle the gold. In spite of its obscene crest, it was just metal, after all. However, merely touching the squares of human skin, protected by their plastic cover, sent shivers through her. She put them down on the table. Even Hagip, used to handling all kinds of materials, became uneasy while he'd studied them. The patches didn't look much different from a dried and treated hide, stretched to near transparency, but the fuzzy blue tattooed letters crowded together like ghosts locked in a bottle waiting to be released.

The patches of human skin had to bear more than just two words. The tiny dots that looked like pinholes formed a pattern, and the darker outline with irregular edges seemed to define a shape—but of what? She needed Hagip's tools or at least a high-power magnifying glass.

She sat back, looking around her kitchen for something to use. Nothing suitable stood out to her. Back at her office she had a dozen small loupes for mineral identification. Her community class students also used them to examine the finer crystal specimens.

What can I use? She rose, tugging at her hair from frustration. She wandered into the living room, and the moment she saw her computer, she knew—the scanner. She could scan the squares and enlarge them on-screen.

Ten minutes later, she had three more words to add to the puzzle. The pinholes that at first seemed to be random perforations or damage, spelled out *Chateau Dax* on one patch and *Bonnac-Sur-Lot* on the other. She matched the dark outline with the irregular edges easy enough. It corresponded to the map of France.

She deleted the images, replaced both patches in the bag together with the gold, and put it beside her computer trolley. Quickly, she clicked on the browser and searched the Internet. A few moments later, she had a match for *Chateau Dax.*

Aloud, she read, *"Chateau Dax Ste. Mireille,* the French flagship of the Palfrey-Urbanne Industries, is now a wholly owned subsidiary of Palfrey Distilleries, USA."

Bonnac-Sur-Lot had several websites like any other tourist attraction in France that sought exposure through Internet advertising. She studied three in detail and knew she shouldn't have bothered since the first sufficed to give all the information a tourist into the French region of Auvergne would need. *Bonnac-Sur-Lot* was situated about eighty miles south of Vichy, of the water fame, and for the last thirty years had been a tourist attraction. The old gold mine that operated there in the early nineteen hundreds had been converted into a ride-through adventure-prospector's park. The place boasted a gold museum that contained samples of gold mined at the site, old books, manuscripts, and rare collectors' gold stock certificates. Clicking on the history of the attraction opened up a long write-up with a picture of the cultural benefactor who, in 1968, purchased the old abandoned mine. In 1975, he returned it to the French public in its new reincarnation of an historical attraction. According to William C. Palfrey's statement, he made the gift to commemorate his French-born wife's thirty-fifth birthday.

Palfrey's picture was one of those highly stylized formal portraits that an expert photographer takes hours to get just right.

He wore French colors—khaki slacks, and a navy blue polo shirt with a red sweater draped over his shoulders—and stood on a porch of the rustic museum, leaning against a wooden post. The picture was taken when Palfrey was still in his late thirties. Considering that today he had already celebrated his seventy-fifth birthday, his generosity obviously resonated with the French people. In the picture, his blond hair, parted in the middle and slicked back, gave him the classic preppie look. Lauren couldn't find anything outstanding about him. If she closed down the website, a few minutes later his face would surely have already faded from her memory. She might remember his clothes, but only because of their French color-theme.

"What is this about?" she whispered, staring at his features, which seemed to be fading the harder she tried to imprint them into her memory. "Why are two of your business sites in France coded onto the two squares of human skin?"

She needed to talk to Hagip again, or Mitch. Abandoning the websites, she logged into her e-mail. Neither Mitch nor Hagip had read her messages. It brought back the worry and fear.

Well, Hagip might be busy with his family, but what about Mitch? He would have left her a message, telling her he had an emergency, even if he didn't want to say what kind. She had to call Terney.

She'd left her cell phone in the bedroom, along with her wallet. She decided to use the regular phone. In the kitchen, she noticed the portable handset wasn't in the cradle and that a pulsing number in the message window indicated two new messages.

Mitch and Hagip—finally, she thought, relief flooding her chest. She pushed the "play message" button.

Hagip's voice sounded thicker than usual, as if he'd pinched his nose or held a hand in front of the speaker.

"Alice Blumenthal, New York, the Holocaust Museum. Simon Teffler. Anike Van Buren, Piet Meyer, Gertrude Johansen, Adlerina, Cragg's Lake and finally Glathos Pidimentaros' long shot of

Hippolyte. Murillo didn't put dates on his paintings. You date Murillo by his changes in style. La Florista Durmiente. You're in danger, Lori. Go to the police. Tell them everything. Tell them Glathos didn't have an allergy to bee stings. In Sicily we followed bees and stole their honey. They stung us many times. The honey was worth it. Go to the police at once. Give them everything, the double sorrow, and the gold, and talk..." The message had run long, and a beep cut off whatever else Hagip might have said.

The second message started. Hagip again, however, this time he sounded composed and very clear-voiced, as if he had never had his nose cartilage "displaced."

"Sorry I didn't get a chance to call you. Isabel's family has an emergency. I have to head for Montreal, but I promise that the moment I'm back, I'll phone around my old Greenpeace contacts, take a look at what you asked me, and maybe you can come down to New York again and we'll do lunch. How's that?" This time he hung up the phone on his side.

"All my friends are suddenly dealing with family emergencies," she said, swallowing to moisten her dry throat. One message from Hagip made sense, the other didn't.

In her bedroom, she brought back everything she had taken out of her knapsack, including her yellow address book. Playing the first message again, she jotted down all the names that figured in it.

It wouldn't be smart to drive to New York at night, but she couldn't spend another minute in her house. She wouldn't be able to asleep. *Where can I go with Mitch and Jenny gone, and Rockland a few hundred miles away?* Her throat tightened, and the pity she felt threatened to become overwhelming. Fatigue seeped into her limbs and mind. Suddenly, she couldn't move and nothing mattered. She felt the same way back in '05, when Isabel raised her hand to stop Hagip from rushing forward to comfort her. Instead Isa took her hand and made her walk in silence along the shore for what seemed like hours before she finally told her that her mother had died. First she felt disbelief, then anger that her mother wouldn't confide in the child she had raised alone. And finally pity came like an indecent vulture to sit somewhere on a branch above her head. It remained there, always there, hiding in the shadows, waiting for her to collapse. She felt betrayed by the very person she trusted with her life.

A doctor prescribed medication to help with her depression. Everything worked for a few weeks, but finally stopped when body and mind refused to be lulled into neutrality. She thought that doing physically demanding work like waitressing, often sixteen hours a day on her feet and constantly rushing to serve, would exhaust the depression and force it to flee. The liquor and beer she'd tried to use to self-medicate, shot out of her body in violent bouts of vomiting and diarrhea. The doctor at the clinic suggested that she might be allergic to alcohol.

She stopped drinking, not to gain relief but because it didn't work to silence the voices that whispered obscene things at night. Thoughts and images shifted and turned in her head to spell out another message. She had betrayed her mother, not the other way around. The guilt...

"No!" she said out loud. The tears that wet her cheeks had to be just a residue of the pity and guilt that she couldn't afford to feed any longer. At least not until she found Mitch and Jennifer safe and sound, and she could talk to Hagip and hug Isabel.

But where can I spend the night?

The voices obligingly whispered the answer.

Half an hour later, with a suitcase packed full of her clothes in the trunk of the Pontiac, and her oil-drum Vuitton purse in hand, she stood on a charming yellow-painted porch with a picket railing, ringing the doorbell of number 23 Canary Lane, in south-central Hartford.

"I'm so stressed out and so confused about everything that happened that Saturday, that I just can't stay at home, and you're the only friend who might be kind enough to give me what I need the most tonight—company and a friendly ear," she said in one breath when Linda, dressed in a pale blue silk robe and wearing embroidered silk slippers, opened the door.

Carmella Perez, who'd tutored her in White House diplomacy and quick about-face recoveries sure to turn a disaster into advantage, would have been proud of her. She never liked Linda, but that didn't mean Errington's busybody assistant couldn't be turned into an asset. After all, if knowledge was power, Linda wouldn't pass up an opportunity to listen to her colleague's *eyewitness* account of the Winthrop murder.

Chapter 14

THE MUSEUM OF Jewish Heritage, or the Holocaust Museum, was located in Battery Park, Manhattan. Beyond looking up its proper address before she left home, Lauren hadn't made any plans except to see Alice Blumenthal, one of the persons named on Hagip's list. She walked down the street, heading for the modern gray-white building. She wondered whether she had enough money to spend a night in New York, especially in Manhattan.

I'll figure out what I'm doing later. She walked up the wide, shallow stairs. The bare concrete of the three-story museum looked stark, like all glass-and-stone buildings often do. She saw a crowd of children, obviously a tour that had just arrived. She should have made an appointment. After all, it would be a regular workday for Alice Blumenthal.

I'll explain and apologize. With her mind made up, Lauren walked inside.

The uniformed guard at the reception desk smiled at her when she told him why she came, and called Mrs. Blumenthal.

Five minutes later, the guard waved at someone who had to be approaching. A few seconds later he pointed down with his hand. Lauren spun around.

"I'm Alice Blumenthal. How can I help you, my dear?" A woman who might have been anyone's favorite aunt, tapped her chest just above her left breast, and, upon seeing the absence of a nametag, laughed and said, "Oh, dear, I must have forgotten to pin it on again."

She was barely five feet tall and had to be at least sixty. She was portly, dressed in a baggy beige linen blouse and a long black denim skirt. Lauren glanced down and saw Mrs. Blumenthal wore soft leather shoes; the kind that quickly stretch and become almost shapeless, like slippers.

Perhaps because the woman's name came from Hagip, who was heading on forty-three, Lauren had expected Alice Blumenthal to look like Isabel Agopian—tall, well proportioned, with high cheekbones and blonde hair.

"I see I'm not what you expected," Alice said with a smile. "Have we met before? Perhaps in kindergarten, and I loomed over you—a strict but fair teacher?"

"You're a teacher?"

"I've long retired."

"But you work here?"

"Almost everyone who works here has been a teacher at one time or another. I'm the gallery education coordinator. But how can I help you?"

"I don't know. My name's Lauren Sarasohn..."

"You're Jewish, aren't you?"

She moved her head from side to side, and knew it was an uncertain gesture. "That's not why I'm here," said Lauren. "Not that I don't want to honor the memory of Holocaust victims or.... My friend, Hagip Agopian, mentioned your name," she blurted out. The moment she stepped through the entrance of the three-storey building, the guilt had attacked. Mother not only stopped speaking to God, but turned her back on religion in a way that shielded her daughter from her heritage.

Alice Blumenthal's kindly smile and clear gray-blue eyes, magnified through her glasses into almost cartoon-style peepers, suddenly stilled as if flash-frozen.

"Come." She waved Lauren forward. "I've made coffee."

ALICE BLUMENTHAL HAD met Hagip Agopian in California twenty years ago. Her late husband, Martin, had been a dealer of antiques and fine art. While in California doing semi-annual acquisitions tours, he had contracted Hagip on a dozen occasions to second-guess paintings for which Martin Blumenthal doubted the previous authentication.

"Martin's name might just as well have been Mr. Perfectionist," Alice said. "He had an ear for details. Not eye, mind you, but an ear. He'd hear all those pauses and catches in people's voices that happen when a speaker's not sure, but doesn't want to say so. That's why Martin liked Hagip. The kid was very young to be an expert appraiser but he never tried to talk his way around something he didn't know. If he wasn't sure about it, he'd say so."

Lauren agreed that Hagip retained this admirable quality, and the old lady continued.

The Blumenthals never lost contact with Hagip, even after he went to exercise his lungs, shouting for years in support of his green cause, Alice told her. In 2007, Hagip settled into a proper career at the Metropolitan Museum. Martin Blumenthal had already passed away, but Alice, and her son Ralston, renewed the old friendship and business association. The son took over his father's business in Greenwich Village: The Flemish Art Gallery and Antiques. According to Alice, it looked like an attic filled with things that people either gave away to charities, or burned.

Lauren smiled. An art gallery in Greenwich Village had to be upscale, and therefore, top-notch in order to make a profit and continue doing business for nearly thirty years. She found an opportunity to interrupt without being rude. "Mrs. Blumenthal, I'm not here about art."

"I know," Alice said, and her eyes misted behind the oversized glasses. "I just lost myself in memories. I also wanted to tell you that Hagip knew my late husband very well. In spite of their age difference, they became very good friends and always kept in touch. They both loved folklore, legends, and tales of treasure. I considered it all just play talk, but to them—"

"Mrs. Blumenthal," Lauren interrupted.

The old lady raised her cup of coffee. "I'm getting to it, dear. Some treasure tales are healthy, others...vile and obscene. Last Sunday afternoon, Hagip came to see me at home without calling. Not that I wouldn't have welcomed him, but he always called. Manners, you know."

"What did he want?"

Alice sighed, took off her glasses, and polished them. "He wanted to talk about treasures and dark fairytales. My husband, Martin, was a *hidden child*, a Jewish child raised by a Gentile family during World War II. In 1941, Martin was just six months old. His parents smuggled him to Belgium where the von Flemming family in Mechelen took him and presented him as their own. He never saw his biological parents again." She put on her glasses, raised her head as if she was going to read something high above Lauren's head, and resumed her story. "In 1961, Martin undertook the search for his family and found out that all of them died in the Mauthausen concentration camp. Martin was lucky because he was a blond-haired, blue-eyed child, and even resembled his adoptive parents. In the spring of 1944, the von Flemmings briefly gave refuge to a young German girl, Analise von Beyern, with three toddlers: two girls and a boy. Martin was just four years old but he retained fairly strong memories of the girl and the children. The von Flemmings, however, committed the girl's story to a journal and sent it to a relative in Los Angeles.

"Shortly after Martin turned sixteen, the von Flemmings told him about his roots and that his family name was Blumenthal.

But at the age of twenty, once he tracked down his family's fate to Mauthausen, he became so depressed that in 1962, the von Flemmings sent him to America to heal his soul. We met in Los Angeles," Alice paused and drew in a big breath. She let it out slowly, smiling as her chest deflated. Lauren knew what lay behind that smile—decades of memories that sustained the surviving partner after her husband died.

Alice continued, "We married, and shortly after, the Hollywood Flemmings—the American branch of the family dropped the von—approached Martin. They needed a European agent. Martin and I moved to London. You're a very patient young woman," she observed suddenly.

Startled, Lauren looked up and smiled.

"I'm just unraveling history so you'll be able to understand why this is coming into prominence now," Alice said.

"It has something to do with the journal the Belgian von Flemmings sent to their American cousins, right?" Lauren said, showing she had been an attentive student.

"Yes. Martin's parents told him what they wrote down. He asked the Hollywood Flemmings about the journal. They remembered receiving it but thought it must have been mislaid somewhere with the rest of the antiques and knickknacks. I don't think Martin took the story seriously, but it fit into his lore and legends. Maybe that's why he included it in his discussions with Hagip every time they fell into their fantasy world."

"It's a story about a fabulous treasure," Lauren said.

"No, child." Alice sighed. "It's a dark story about the Siberian Oracle."

"*Das Sibirische—Oracle.*" Lauren now had the third word, which Hagip must have known but for some reason didn't want to tell her.

Alice stared at her for a long time. It looked like she was trying to raise the memory of child-Lauren in the kindergarten classes she had taught.

"So, you're the reason why Hagip became suddenly obsessed

with the old tale. I was surprised he came to see me just to talk about it and asked him why. Since Martin died, there's been no talk of treasures and stolen loot. Where did you hear about the *Siberian Oracle*, child?"

"I didn't hear...I have something that has the first two words, *Das* and *Sibirsche*, tattooed...on a parchment," she confessed hesitantly.

Alice clasped her hands in her lap and spoke without looking at Lauren. "If you have the material on which those two words are tattooed, it wouldn't be parchment."

"No," Lauren said quietly. "Hagip examined the squares. He said they're tattooed human skin."

Alice moaned. "I never believed Martin's boy-talk about treasure maps. I always believed it to be a memory of what he must have seen when he went to Mauthausen that made him talk about such maps being tattooed into human skin."

"Hagip said nothing about treasure maps. He just wrote down the two words that appear as watermarks on the parchment squares."

"No, Hagip wouldn't say such foolish things; especially if he thought there was a strong possibility they were true. I prayed for years that the journal was just a myth. I was glad the Hollywood Flemmings mislaid it. I suppose that deep down I felt that it wasn't all just lore and dark legends," Alice finished in a dry, lifeless voice.

"What's the legend of the *Siberian Oracle*, Mrs. Blumenthal?"

"If I tell you, you'll only think that I'm a senile old woman. Why don't you take a tour of the museum for a couple of hours, and once I'm off work, we'll go see Ralston in Greenwich Village. You can read it for yourself."

"Read what?" She thought the old lady needlessly evasive.

"The story of the *Siberian Oracle*, recounted by the young German girl to the Belgian von Flemmings."

"Where's the story written?"

"In the journal, my child, in the journal. It surfaced about a year after Martin's death. Ralston went to the West Coast to help settle the business there and install new management. The staff doing the inventory found the damn journal. Ralston had it translated into English, but he wisely keeps it in his gallery. Samantha, that's his wife, won't have something like that in the apartment in case one of the children found it and read it. It's a foul thing, my child, just foul. Now, I'll get one of the staff to show you around..."

Chapter 15

A SCHOOL TOUR WOUND through the second floor. That particular floor was dedicated to the *War Against the Jews*. The group of sixth-graders started to disperse to look at exhibits that did not figure in the guide's lecture notes.

"I'll be right back." Ariella, Lauren's guide, smiled at her, nodding at the gallery teacher, who obviously needed help to get the strays back onto the pre-selected path.

"I'll be fine. It's all right. Go." Lauren waved to her and hung back so she wouldn't be taken for part of the school tour. The kids filed through the section. Their voices started to fade as the tour moved on. Lauren turned, looking at the photographs. Since the age had creased them badly, many were plasticized or restored. Without the kids' chattering, the silence suddenly felt ominous as if the Nazi uniforms and the peaked hats had the power to once again fill out with living tissue, and Hitler's execution squads would march out from behind the glass.

Ariella had already walked her through most of the second-floor exhibits and stood beside her in silence, waiting until Lauren finished reading the stories of men and women who lived through the Holocaust. Lauren had glanced at her guide now and then, but Ariella just smiled back and remained silent. Lauren got an impression that her guide wanted her to feel the impact of what she saw and read, rather than listen to a guide's voice, lecturing about atrocities captured in the many photographs, or written on blue-lined pages of notebooks such used by school children. Ariella just remained nearby, a reassuring presence.

By the time the school tour filled the open space with echoing voices, Lauren wanted to sit down somewhere with nothing but stone and glass around her and rest her psyche. She needed to calm down, or by the time Alice Blumenthal finished her day, Lauren would be on the floor, balled into her favorite fetal position, crying.

"Very good work, isn't it?" a man's voice said beside her.

"Pardon?" She turned her head.

He had to be at least six-foot-four, maybe more. He looked like a jock, or at least a rich college kid. Underneath his open green leather jacket he wore a beige polo shirt. A gold chain, visible in the hollow of his throat, sat like a thick worm against his skin. It would be expensive. Like many college kids, he favored a diamond nose stud, and diamond ear-studs. He held his head tilted to one side, studying her back.

He motioned with his free hand to include every exhibit on the floor.

"All of this is damn good work. I just wish they'd tell me who does it for them, and I don't mean just the restoration." He let the leather knapsack, similar to the one she used to have but much newer, slide off his shoulder until it hung from his other hand.

She took a step back, careful to make it appear that she wasn't interested in chatting with a stranger, and said, "What *do* you mean if you don't mean the restoration?"

"Aha!" he exclaimed, so loudly that she hopped backward, startled. "You fell for it too, didn't you? Come on, admit it. It's no shame. You believe that all this is real."

Did he have an agenda? Lauren wasn't sure, so she asked, "And you don't?"

"Aw, come on. Don't tell me you believe in all that stuff about the Holocaust and millions of people shot in the back of the head by Germans, do you?"

"Hitler's Nazis, I believe is the correct terminology. The Gestapo, his elite execution taskforce, if you want the corporate schism for it."

He laughed. "All Jewish propaganda. Use your head—think! Do you actually believe that a German soldier like that," he pointed at one of the photographs where the naked victim knelt above the yawning dirt pit and the Nazi executioner held the pistol pointed at the back of his head, "would spend his work day standing on the edge of that dirty hole and keep shooting Jews in the back of the head, one-million, two-million...get real! The man would drop dead of exhaustion at the end of his first week on the job."

"His first week on the job. I see. So you've uncovered a secret, is that it?"

Once again he threw his head back and laughed, showing healthy teeth, no fillings, no cavities. "Of course. And it's not such a huge secret. Air-brushing."

"Air-brushing?"

"Yes, and forensic restoration. You can produce photographs of this antique quality at any decent police lab. But there are also museums. They have restorations departments today that would knock your socks off. Air-brushing and computer graphics and behold—Holocaust tragedy."

She didn't bother motioning around. "So this is all fake. Everything that's on this floor, all these exhibits, are just...?"

"Props," he filled in glibly. "Tools to help spread the propaganda and raise guilt in the rest."

"The rest of what?"

"The rest of the world, of course."

"So you must have visited other such museums or displays of

Jewish propaganda, all over the world."

"Ah, they got to you, all right. That happens a lot, you know. But I have to say, they're good, they're really good."

"Who is?" she pressed, her throat growing dry. A voice whispered in the back of her mind that meeting the cynical young man wasn't a coincidence.

"The people who run this museum. The Jews who want to get rich by claiming they lost family treasures back in the war."

"How did we get from Holocaust is a fabrication and Jewish propaganda to lost treasures?" she asked. Her throat started to close from fear again.

He shrugged. "A few years ago, the Met shook in its boots because some Jew accused them of owning a Monet that used to be in his family. It was supposedly one of the Nazi-looted artworks taken from his ancestral manor, somewhere in Belgium. Well, the Met spent a ton of money on an investigation, and in the end, it came out that Goering actually bought the painting from a Belgian collector. So it was all legal."

"And that particular incident," said Lauren, "convinced you that the Holocaust is a Jewish fabrication?"

"Air-brushing." Suddenly he leaned over and tapped her nose. "Air-brushing, and let me tell you, I'm an expert on restoration techniques. That's why I come here every time I feel the need to be inspired."

Fortunately, Ariella appeared at the far end of the hall. Lauren nodded at young man. "Well, thank you for a new opinion about the Holocaust. I suppose it's possible that millions of Jewish people never existed, and the survivors, who claim their families had perished in the Holocaust, are just publicity hounds. Excuse me," she said and hurried down the hallway.

SHE LEFT ALICE Blumenthal waiting for her on the main floor and quickly walked up the street to the parking garage. By the time she reached the steel door leading to the parking levels, sweat had begun to trickle down her back. The purse kept slipping down her shoulder, its strap digging in with a painful sting. She shifted her feet for balance, thinking about the college student who had been playing devil's advocate with her and if he wasn't—if he really believed that all the Holocaust evidence in the Museum had been manufactured—he had to be...what?

Should she mention it to Alice? Or did people like the preppie come to the Museum to provoke a reaction from a patron just to get their kicks?

By the time she pulled up in front of the building's entrance, she was still undecided whether or not she should mention anything to Alice. She glanced at the dashboard clock. It was just after six o'clock but already dark. Her windshield had started to mist the moment she pulled out onto the street. Soon, the mist turned into rain, and she thought she saw a few wet snowflakes mixed with the water drops.

"Mrs. Blumenthal, where are you?" she murmured, leaning over to see the glassed portions of the building. By now every person coming out was museum staff. The Museum had long closed down. The guards would have ushered the last of the visitors outside. Did she go to the washroom, or had she been called back inside?

The taxicabs waiting ahead of her started to pull away. One or two cabs took their place, picked up their fares, and left.

She shut off the car and ran up the stairs. The rain splattering on her parka sounded heavy with cold slush. Maybe Mrs. Blumenthal saw the slushy rain and hurried back to get an umbrella.

"Excuse me." She grabbed the elbow of a woman who came outside. "Have you seen a lady dressed in a black jacket? She said she'd wait for me inside."

"The Museum's closed now," the woman said. "There's only staff inside."

"She's staff. Mrs. Blumenthal."

"Oh." The woman leaned back. "Alice usually takes a cab. Did you tell her you'd be coming to pick her up?"

"Yes," she said.

"Well, I guess she must have forgotten. I'm sure she's long gone."

Lauren let the woman go on her way and tried to pull the glass doors open, but they wouldn't yield. She rattled them and banged hard with her fists. Finally, the security guard came over and knocked with his metal clipboard on the glass. He pointed at his watch, mouthing "Closed."

She waved at him until he came to open the side glass panel.

"We're closed, ma'am."

"I know. I'm waiting for Mrs. Blumenthal. Actually, I left her standing just inside, waiting for me. I had to get the car from the parking garage."

"Oh, I think Alice left long ago. I'm sure I saw her leave. She usually takes a cab, you know. Did you tell her you'd come to pick her up?"

"Yes. She couldn't have forgotten or gone anywhere. She knew I went to get the car. We're supposed to go to see her son at his gallery." She didn't bother to filter irritation out of her voice.

"Well, maybe she got tired of waiting or misunderstood, and if one of the women asked her to share a cab, she might have gone. She's probably already at the gallery, waiting for you."

"She understood...."

"Get out of the rain, young lady, or you'll catch your death of cold. I think it's mixed with snow. Call Alice. I'm sure she has a cell phone," the guard said and locked the door.

She ran back to her car. Her hands shook so badly it took her a few moments to unlock the door. At first, she couldn't push the button, but finally managed.

No, Alice didn't misunderstand.

A police car pulled up beside her. The cop motioned for her to lower her window.

"I know," she told him, swallowing hard. "I can't park here. I'm supposed to pick someone up but they must have gone. Would you know the address of the Flemish Art Gallery and Antiques in Greenwich?"

The police officer leaned away from the window. A few seconds later he turned back and said, "It's just behind the Washington Square Park between West 8th and Waverly Street. Go up Macdougal, just after Waverly turn left, and I believe it's a couple of stores down the street"

She thanked him and started the car.

The Flemish Art Gallery and Antiques took up what she judged to be three storefronts. It needed the space to be able to carry its name alone. She left the car parked by the fire hydrant and didn't care. She wasn't even sure whether she locked it. Underneath her parka, her t-shirt and sweatshirt had become soaked with sweat. She knew that not all the sweat could be attributed to the fatigue of trying to run with a fifteen-pound handicap bouncing against her hip. For a moment, her heart skipped a beat just as she gripped the polished brass door handles, but the door yielded. The gallery had late night hours, unlike the museum.

Once inside, she felt her gaze drawn upward. She tried to estimate the height of the room. Ralston Blumenthal must have leased not just three storefronts but a couple of flats above. She lowered her head, and saw that the open space concept was necessary to balance the crowded bottom floor. Every way she looked there was furniture, pictures, gilt-edged masterpieces and bric-a-brac. There would be a pattern to it but she couldn't waste time saturating her senses with the rich inventory in order to determine how it all fitted together.

"May I help you?" a woman said.

Lauren focused on the speaker. The woman either had an opera engagement after the gallery closed, or she must have just come back from sitting for an artist whose creativity got stuck in a black-and-white period. Her floor-length evening dress clung to her body. Its top portion was black, while the two slashes in the middle shone with pure white satin sheen.

"That's an interesting dress," Lauren said, feeling that the owner expected her to make some flattering comment. "Very elegant."

"May I help you?" the woman repeated, her round and perfectly made-up face so tight, Lauren wondered whether she wore a mask or whether indeed her perfect skin was a result of many facials.

"Right. I'm looking for Mr. Ralston Blumenthal. Is he in?"

"And who should I say is calling?"

She flinched upon hearing such starchy formality, but reminded herself that she stood surrounded by millions of dollars worth of merchandise.

"I'm Lauren Sarasohn. Is Mrs. Blumenthal here? I mean Alice Blumenthal, his mother."

"You are from the museum?"

"Yes."

"Very well. Just a moment, please," the hostess said, pivoting rather than turning around left.

Lauren didn't get a chance to browse because not a minute later, a man appeared, moving easily and gracefully between the expensive merchandise, giving an impression that he wasn't just mere owner, but a member of these artistic treasures.

"How do you do?" he said, half-smiled, and offered her a handshake.

"Mr. Ralston Blumenthal?" She shook his hand, perturbed for some reason. Alice didn't describe her son. And barely talked about her husband's physical appearance. Lauren had nothing to use for comparison, but she didn't expect Alice's son to be tall. All through Alice's discussion, Lauren imagined that she and her husband would be a diminutive pair. Young girl-Alice must have been petite. Years had added weight to her, but didn't affect her stature. If anything, she'd have lost an inch or two from her height.

"Are you here on an errand from my mother?" he asked, bowing slightly and keeping his hands politely crossed in front of him. He wore a dove-gray suit, double-breasted and probably very expensive, though it wasn't spectacular; just quietly elegant.

"Well, no... I mean yes, sort of. Is she here?"

"No, I'm afraid not. Is she supposed to meet you here?"

"I'm not sure. I think we talked about it."

"Shall we wait until she arrives, and perhaps in the meantime, you can tell me what it's all about?" He smiled, raising his brows. It opened his eyes wider, and suddenly she realized what had perturbed her about him.

Alice Blumenthal's voice came back in its soft, reminiscing quality. *"Martin was lucky because he was a blond-haired, blue-eyed child and even resembled his adoptive parents."*

Two diminutive people could certainly produce a tall child. But it was very unlikely that a light-haired and gray-eyed mother and a blond-haired and blue-eyed father would produce a brown-eyed child. And the man claiming to be Martin's son, staring at her with an indulgent smile, had dark brown eyes and was mostly bald.

"I must be mistaken after all. I think I'll just go see Alice tomorrow at work," she said, turned around, and quickly walked out. The pain in her shoulder, where the strap had been digging into it all afternoon, helped her to make it to her car without shaking.

She started the car, pulled out without looking for traffic, and drove away. She pulled into the first gas station she saw and filled up the gas tank. The attendant asked for her credit card.

"Do you have maps for sale?" she asked.

"A few," he replied. "Where are you heading?"

"Washington, DC," she said.

"Sure. I'll outline the best route for you on the map. It's just after seven o'clock. If you push it on the highway—though I don't advise it because cops never sleep—you'll make it by eleven o'clock. Mind you, if this weather follows the same route, you probably won't get there until midnight."

"I'll drive safely," she promised, forcing a smile.

Chapter 16

"THERE'S PLENTY OF time for talk tomorrow. You must be exhausted after that long drive and you're chilled." Carmella Perez welcomed her warmly. She made it seem as if the gap of ten years since the last time they had met shrunk to mere hours. She literally greeted her with outstretched arms once she opened the door to find what Lauren felt had to be a near stranger, wearing a wet parka, soggy Nikes, and a death grin.

She'd called the ex-presidential science advisor the previous night from Linda's house. Half-turning to hide her smile, Lauren had known that Linda hovered nearby, eavesdropping on the conversation.

Carmella Perez had barely let her get a word in and invited her to come over.

"Anytime, Lauren, anytime. In fact, why don't you just drop whatever you're doing and come on over now. It's only a few hours to Washington. I want to see you, dear girl. I need to see how you are, what you're doing...and where on earth did you disappear to, and most importantly: Why?"

Since Terney told her he'd been checking up on her, calling on her old bosses and associates, she expected Carmella to remember her—quickly—but not enthusiastically. The Carmella she remembered was a smooth, thoughtful talker. The Carmella she spoke with at Linda's house sounded almost bubbly. Had ten years changed the woman that much?

She's overdoing the cheer. Lauren caught herself. *I'm stressed out and getting downright paranoid. I'm looking for sinister reasons and motivations in everything, everyone.*

Carmella Perez dragged her inside, all the while talking reassuringly. Lauren felt treated like a victim of a mugging who needed abundant comfort.

"Your car keys." Carmella suddenly held out her hand to her.

"What?" Lauren asked, dizzy and disoriented. The huge foyer of the stately Georgian mansion in Idylwood, that even in the darkness looked massive, intimidated her with its pinecone-shaped chandelier, the double sweeping staircase, and the dazzling shine shooting off whatever her gaze touched.

"Kingsley will park your car in the back underneath the guest carport. Ah, here he is." Lauren turned to the man, who appeared so suddenly that she thought he had to have come through the wall. She wouldn't have to raise her head much to meet his eyes—but she wasn't sure she'd want to lock her gaze with him. He carried himself in a way that made her feel he looked down on most people. His closely shorn head made him look bald. He wore the traditional butler's attire—a black formal suit and white shirt—but his bearing struck her definitely military. He carried himself like a bodyguard.

"Kingsley, would you please park Ms Sarasohn's car in the guest parking." Although Carmella's voice flexed into a question, a steely undertone made it a direct order.

"Of course, ma'am." He inclined his head.

"Keys, Lauren, dear." Carmella smiled at her, nodding toward the butler, who stood waiting to receive them.

Lauren fumbled in her parka for the keys, found them, and handed them over.

"Did you bring luggage?" Carmella asked.

"In the trunk."

"Kingsley, would you please?" Carmella said.

"Of course, ma'am." He walked away.

Carmella hardly let her say thank you, insisting that she must look after herself first; her health especially.

"Are you hungry?" she asked.

Lauren shook her head, and said that a hot shower would take care of her chills.

"Juanita!" Carmella's voice sounded so piercing that Lauren flinched.

A portly woman in a black dress with a white lace collar hurried down the staircase.

"She'll show you to your room," Carmella said. "We'll catch up on old times tomorrow. I have a ton of paperwork still to go over. A board meeting tomorrow, you know." She served her a conspiratorial wink, smiled, and walked towards the back of the house.

"This way, miss." The housekeeper indicated the staircase with her eyes.

Lauren followed Juanita to the second floor, which had to be at least twenty or thirty feet above the ground floor. *A lot has changed in ten years.*

Linda had been awed that Lauren, whom she considered squatting on the bottom of the totem pole, connected with a mere push of a dozen numbers to the woman who used to be the president's science advisor. Her eyes grew as large as saucers when Lauren said that her old mentor now served as the Director of Argosy National Laboratory in Arlington. Lauren had wanted to say that Carmella Perez also sat on the Board of Directors of six large companies. However, Linda's eyes threatened to roll back in her head. Lauren didn't want to have to administer CPR if Linda fainted.

Back in Linda's apartment, Lauren was sure that upon meeting her old mentor, she'd see a compact woman, who wore minimal make-up even if she faced the media. Carmella that she knew used to roll up the sleeves of her generous, faded North Carolina State sweatshirt, and dig into the sinkful of dirty dishes. She always scrubbed dishes before loading the dishwasher in her tastefully decorated but definitely cozy Arlington town home.

Thirty-eight-year-old Carmella Perez celebrated her ethnic heritage by wearing colorful Mexican wraps at barbecue parties. And if the hosts had a swimming pool, she'd kick off her sandals and sit on the edge, dangling her feet in the water. She'd push up her glasses to sit on her head, unmindful of her hairstyle. Lauren had even seen her bite her nails while reading a brief or a scientific paper.

Today, Carmella Perez not only reigned as an elegant Washington hostess, but everything around her had to reflect her status, her definition of self-worth. The crystal, the marble, the granite floors, vases filled with a colorful anarchy of silk flowers, and the bronze busts of great men of science, who certainly had not received so much recognition while alive, all served as reminders of the woman's status. Wherever she looked, whatever her gazes landed, Lauren saw wealth that spoke even louder than Carmella did.

Yes, her voice sounded different too. She used to be a closet smoker. Today, she probably wouldn't admit to even having the habit—ever. Now, her voice rang crystal clear and harsh.

Why am I being so critical?

"Did you say something, miss?" Juanita's face swam into focus. Lauren realized she must have been mumbling to herself.

"No, ma'am. I'm just tired, I guess." She managed a smile at the housekeeper. She had to get her thoughts and mumbling under control.

"With the weather being this bad all over the Eastern coast, we weren't expecting you until the morning," Juanita said.

"You expected me...in the morning?" Discomfort churned in her stomach. She phoned Carmella from Linda's house, but she didn't commit herself to a visit to Washington. At least not anytime soon. Her decision to drive four hours stemmed from fear and desperation. As she'd filled the gas tank at the station in

New York, she'd debated whether she should head for Washington or go home. Only the fact that she couldn't face going back to Rocky Hill swung the odds in favor of Washington. That and the fact that she needed someone with clout who would be able to help her search for the rest of the people Hagip named in his phone message.

"Yes, miss. In the morning or maybe even afternoon, if the weather turned more nasty. That's why I made up the green guest room. Now I'm glad I didn't leave it until the morning. I'll bring you more towels." Juanita nodded for Lauren to walk into the room. Turning, the housekeeper headed down the hallway.

SHE TOOK A shower in a glassed-in stall adjoining a sunken marble bathtub. If the guest bathroom looked this luxurious, she wondered what the master suite looked like. Briefly, she considered taking the oil-drum purse with her inside the shower, but even though the plastic cover protected the parchment squares, she didn't want to take a chance of damaging them. Of course, nothing would affect the gold. If anything, carrying the damn thing had dug a hole in her shoulder. She undressed and looked in the mirror. Red welts lined either side of a deep purple groove on her left shoulder. She'd have to change the routine and hang the purse on the other shoulder. Should she sleep with the damn purse too? Would Carmella or Kingsley come inside and tiptoe across the room to take the purse from her limp hand? For some reason, she couldn't see the housekeeper doing this, but she had no problem visualizing the new Carmella or her imposing butler doing it.

I'm going crazy. The fucking gold bar has messed up my mind. Why is everyone after it...after me? And if they want it back so badly, why am I still alive? Surely it wouldn't have taken a great effort to dispose of her? They already had many easy opportunities to do it. Even the rental car...all they had to do was cut the brake fluid line and follow her on the highway. Once she had no brakes, and the car went into the ditch, they would stop to assist and take the green canvas bag. Hell, it wouldn't have been hard to bribe the Hertz guys delivering it.

The answer came to her. *They're not sure I have it.* Immediately, doubt cancelled it. *I don't buy it. They have been more straightforward than this. If they weren't sure, why did they take Mitch?*

That had to be the reason why they hadn't tried to kill her. They knew that Gomez stole the bullion and the two squares of tattooed human skin, most likely left in their original green canvas bag, but they didn't know for certain what happened to the bag. The police emptied her office and found nothing, so they would know that. Hell, they probably had contacts to do their bidding in the White House, if not all over the world. Errington might have even told them the bag wasn't in the Essex Hall. And whoever killed Gomez would have told them that the victim didn't have anything on him. Why didn't Terney tell her that whoever killed Gomez had also searched his body? He'd told her everything else.

They didn't know. They didn't know. They didn't know. They let her live, hoping she'd either lead them to the gold bar or tell one of their planted agents about it. They stole her car and her knapsack, but found nothing. They would have searched her house with the same results too. They wouldn't consider a possibility that the bar might be next to her at all times. They probably didn't believe that a hundred-and-twenty-pound woman would opt for carrying the thirty-pound handicap on her person. Now that she thought about it, she hardly believed it herself—except when she looked at her shoulder in the mirror.

While she took a shower, Juanita must have come in with not just an armload of towels, but a snack tray too. She found it on a small marble-and-walnut-inlaid bedside table.

The tiny wedge party sandwiches looked delicious, but she settled for grapes and cheese. Deep down, she knew she'd chosen not to eat the sandwiches, or even take a sip of the garnet-colored wine in the crystal glass, because these might be laced with things that would make her sleep for days—or not wake up at all. She drank tap water, using her cupped hands, stared at her haggard face in the mirror, shook her head, and shuffled outside.

For a moment, fear kicked like a mule in her stomach. Her eggplant purse wasn't on the bed. She held her breath...and suddenly remembered that she slid it under the pillow. She ran to bed, snatched the pillow, and exhaled. The purse indeed looked like an eggplant against the white background of the bed sheet. She wound the leather shoulder strap around her wrist and across her palm, and sank into the cushions.

Mother, I know you stopped speaking to God, but now I'm speaking to you, praying that you hear me, wherever you are. Help me, help me get out of this alive, and I promise to take charge of my life again. I really will, if only you help me....

Chapter 17

IN THE MORNING, over a breakfast of steamed-milk latte, fresh croissants, and whipped butter served in tiny crystal cups, Carmella Perez decided to brief her on all her current involvements, scientific and entrepreneurial. Now and then glancing at her friend across the table, Lauren kept trying to find the scientist and teacher she remembered. What happened to the brilliant, outspoken woman scientist who never neglected to remind young girls that math and sciences were not fearsome things and to study them because such studies would almost assure them independence—financial and spiritual?

"I've been doing all the talking." Carmella reached forward and patted Lauren's hand. The gesture was out of character with what Lauren remembered, precisely because it patronized. Old Carmella Perez might have bullied and pushed, prodded and ordered, but never patronized.

Her hostess continued, "I'm just so excited to see you after all these years. Tell me what you've been up to, and how's your thesis going?"

The previous night, to stay alert while driving in hard rain all the way to Washington, Lauren had played out various scenarios of how she would tell Carmella what happened at Winthrop and why she needed her help. Now, she wanted to get in the car and drive until she ran out of gas.

"The thesis is moving along, but I came because I need help. By any chance, did you get a call from Lieutenant Terney of the Hartford Police Department inquiring about me?"

"Terney? Terney, no, I don't think so. But my dear, I have so many executive assistants that any one of them probably took the call."

"Would your assistants know about me?" She hadn't meant to trap Carmella that way, but it was too late.

Carmella laughed. "My offices are positively wallpapered with photographs. Everyone who has ever worked for me has asked me about my friends and associates at one time or another. I'm sure my executive assistants would recognize the name and make the connection if this Lieutenant Terney had called to inquire about you."

"I'm flattered that you'd display a photo of me in your office," she said, knowing it sounded lame, but she couldn't show doubt.

"Well, why don't you tell me what's finally made you get out of Connecticut? You've been holed up in that place for ten years."

Lauren hadn't been in Connecticut for ten years, but didn't quibble over details. She told Carmella what had happened at Winthrop, and that her colleague, Mitch, had left so suddenly it almost looked like a disappearance.

"I'm also worried about Hagip Agopian, a good friend from my Greenpeace days." Seeing Carmella fall silent, she continued and laid out her remaining worries.

"I'll have one of my assistants inquire into the disappearance of this Mitchell Plow. And you said that this Agopian fellow might be in Montreal, that his wife called him with a family emergency?"

"I would just like to know he's all right, and Mitch and Jenny too."

"Did you know this Gomez fellow?" asked Carmella.

She shook her head. "He worked as a bellhop at the Carlyle."

"Why would a bellhop from Carlyle come to your office?"

She sighed to make it sound convincing and said, "I've no idea, Carmella. I can't even begin to guess why he came to my office and what for. He might have just ended up there, looking for a hiding place. If he thought someone was following him, he probably just ducked into my office."

"What about your research? Anything missing?"

She looked down in case Carmella had learned to read what flashed in people's eyes. "My research doesn't have that kind of value. It has commercial potential but not the kind you'd steal."

"Research piracy and industrial espionage are not just something made up by the police, you know. I find it hard to believe that Winthrop's Environmental Management Department wouldn't have research worth stealing."

It sounded like something Errington might have said to the police just to raise the profile of his department. "The police made Mitch and me check everything in our office. Nothing's been taken."

"Do you think—?" Carmella raised her hand to show she didn't want interruptions. "Don't get me wrong. I'm just looking at all possibilities, but do you think that this colleague of yours, this Mitch, might have somehow been involved and that's why he disappeared?"

"Mitch wasn't involved anymore than I am," she replied, hiding her irritation.

Carmella rose. "So, you want me to check on the whereabouts of Mitchell Plow and Hagip Agopian, is that it?"

"Yes. I don't mean to pry into their family affairs, but I want to know they're fine...wherever they are."

"I'll see what I can do," her friend promised. "Is there anything else you'd like me to look into?"

There was, but Lauren wasn't sure whether she ought to bring it up. Carmella knew she had come from New York. Why hasn't she asked what business Lauren had there? Did she already know? If so, she might be testing her.

"I went to New York to see Alice Blumenthal, a widow of a prominent art dealer that Hagip used to work with on occasion. Hagip thought that maybe Gomez stole something small enough to roll up and carry away inconspicuously, like a small paint-ing...you know, a masterpiece. The Blumenthals used to live in a Central Park apartment. Before her husband died, Mrs. Blumen-thal socialized with a lot of affluent art collectors, so I asked her whether she'd ask around in her circle to see if someone hadn't lost a masterpiece, and didn't report it yet because of insurance problems and such things. She thought that her son, who runs the gallery, would be more likely to catch such gossip, so we decided to pay him a visit. I went to get my car from the parking garage and went to pick her up—but apparently she already left by taxi.

"I drove to her son's gallery," Lauren finished, worry tingeing her voice, "but she wasn't there. And her *son* didn't seem to be worried about her, but I am."

"But of course." Carmella walked up to her and put her arms around her shoulders. "I will check on Mrs. Blumenthal. Are you sure you're still a doctorate student connected to environment? Doing all this worrying and being so charitable, I mean."

"Carmella, someone murdered a man in my office. Wouldn't you find that, at the very least, worrisome?"

"I see your point, my dear. Now, I absolutely must run since I'll probably be late anyway. I'm always the last one to arrive...."

The sound of Carmella's heels clicking on the stone floor had long ago faded, but Lauren sat in the kitchen, sipping coffee and letting Juanita refill her juice glass. The old Carmella would nev-er have admitted to being late simply because the woman was *never* late for any function. If anything, the other interns used to say that you could set your watch by Carmella's arrivals and de-partures. After all, she had a very demanding schedule to keep while in the White House. Obviously, private industry and the many committees that she now chaired forgave a lot.

"Is there anything you'd like me to do for you, miss?" Juanita asked.

"No, thank you...wait. Yes, there is something. I need my car keys."

"I'll bring them to your room, miss. Are you going to do a bit of sightseeing?"

She nodded, thinking that Carmella Perez should have asked her how she planned to spend her day. Then again, Carmella would probably have her followed because that's what "new" Carmella has become—an enemy wearing the soft coat of friendship.

Chapter 18

HER DAY IN the nation's capital, a city of thousands of sightseeing attractions, started on an ironic note. She couldn't think of anything to do.

Kingsley must have brought her car from the rear carport; she found it waiting for her in front of the house, idling and ready. She un-slung her eggplant purse from her shoulder and put it down on the passenger seat, then sat down. She breathed a sigh of relief. She'd only carried it for five minutes but the weight of the gold bar, digging into her hip, was punishing.

Maybe I'll just drive around until I run out of gas.

And what a waste would that be. But the thought of wasting gas, or anything else, didn't sting with the same sharpness as all of her previous self-reproaches. Waste of resources, or even life, had somehow paled in the last few days. For four years, she had been part of a collective of people who cared enough to affect a change of mankind's future.

What had happened? She imagined hearing Terney's voice, sounding clear like the time he'd asked her that question in Hartford.

Nothing happened, she shook her head, nothing at all, other than my mother died. That's what she told Terney, and though he took her to task on that claim, too, she replied that it was true.

But there was more to it.

She ground her knuckles into her eyes to relieve the sting, jammed the stick into drive, drove down the cobblestone drive, and out onto the street, heading for George Washington University. Her Winthrop staff library card wouldn't earn her check-out privileges here in Washington, but university libraries had quiet rooms where a visiting student could to do on-site research.

"Perhaps genealogy is not the right category to use, considering that these names you have here may belong to individuals who are still living," the librarian assistant said two hours later. Neither the books she had helped Lauren find nor a computer search had brought up anything on the names Hagip mentioned in his phone message.

"We have most major U.S. newspapers, online and in the archives," the woman offered. She must have seen something on Lauren's face, because she shrugged and turned around. The woman prepared to leave, but suddenly turned, tapping her cheek. "You know, in my experience—and I've been here twenty years—people searching for names with little else available in terms of information often discover that the newspaper obituaries proves most helpful."

"Obituaries," Lauren whispered after the woman closed the door of the quiet room. *Would Hagip leave me one name of a living person and the rest...deceased?* She shivered. According to Pete, her mother's most loyal employee, if people shivered and thought of cemeteries, someone had just walked over their future grave. Did thinking of newspaper obituaries count?

She found nothing in the recent obituaries of any of the major U.S. newspapers, so settled down to narrow her time period. She reached 1980 with no results, and the archive access went into a pay-service screen. For information older than twenty-five years old, she'd have to pay for access, but the privilege would be good for three months.

She left the room to find the librarian.

"Would you mind if I used your e-mail address here?" she asked. "I'll pay for the service with my credit card, but in order for them to send me a password that will let me into the old archives, I'll have to provide an e-mail."

"I don't see why that should be a problem," the woman said and wrote down the e-mail address on a scrap of paper. "I just hope you won't be wasting thirty dollars," the librarian said, smiled, and handed her the piece of paper.

A few minutes later, Lauren had a password to access in-depth archives.

In-depth archives inquiry proved to be structured differently. The search would pull up anything that had ever figured in a national newspaper and had been microfiched and loaded into the database. Anike Van Buren wasn't a run-of-the-mill name. She chose to start her search there.

Finally, the much-reduced newspaper page of Los Angeles Times appeared on-screen, its November 13, 1964 headlines still hot with China's Chou En-Lai greeting Russia's Aleksei Kosygin. She leaned close to the screen, guessing at the portion that might contain the name she sought—Anike Van Buren. On the fourth try at zooming in on sections on the page, she found it.

She printed the news article, scrolled forward to page twenty-seven, where the rest of it appeared, and printed that portion too. Finally, she sat down to read.

"A twenty-four-year-old fledgling actress was found strangled in her flat on North Harper Avenue, just off Sunset Boulevard, in West Hollywood. Anike Van Buren earned her living while waiting for fame to find her in an interim role of a waitress at Barney's Beanery, a restaurant that claimed amongst its patrons Clarke Gable, Bette Davis and Marlon Brando. Miss Van Buren, who had hoped to parlay her Doris Day looks into a movie career, was last seen alive by one of her roommates, Aby Lincoln, also a fledgling

actress and waitress at Barney's. Miss Lincoln spoke with Miss Van Buren just after eleven o'clock, once she finished her shift at the restaurant and hailed a taxicab to drive her home. Upon returning to her flat, Miss Lincoln discovered her friend's body at about two o'clock in the morning.

"The police have no motive for the slaying of the statuesque, blonde-haired, blue-eyed Nordic beauty. However, in an exclusive Times interview, Miss Lincoln disclosed that the killer had skinned her roommate's back. The Los Angeles medical examiner refuted Miss Lincoln's claim, adding that the small portion of the victim's upper left shoulder did show abrasions, possibly sustained in the victim's struggle with her killer."

Lauren put down the sheet of paper. Anike's roommate didn't make up a fanciful story. The victim's back had suffered more than just mere abrasions. The killer had removed a postcard-sized patch of tattooed skin. According to Alice Blumenthal—a treasure map.

She searched for the other three names. Simon Teffler's drew a blank. Either there wasn't anything newsworthy about him before 1980, or he'd died long time ago and his death didn't merit a column in any national newspaper. She pulled in twenty references to Gertrude Johansen, dutifully examined all the social issues, commercial announcements, and one instance of an ad in the personals, but she didn't find anything that might fit.

Maybe because the year, 1965, started on a relatively quiet note. Other than headlines raising the profile of General Westmoreland and the Vietnam War, the San Francisco Examiner devoted a relatively large column to the twenty-five-year-old victim of what they suggested might be a ritualistic cult murder.

"The Church of Scientology, the recently established Victories Outreach Ministries by Sonny Arguinzoni, the Hare Krishnas and half a dozen other religious cults that have recently sprung up all over California, are currently under police scrutiny. Twenty-five-year-old Piet Meyer, a member of the Sutter Street Commune in San Francisco's Haight-Ashbury District, was found in his second-

floor art workshop-gallery, with his throat slashed. He was a member of the San Francisco Diggers, a radical left political movement that evolved out of combined Bohemian arts and underground theater communities. His friend, another Diggers member and avant-garde artist, Jacqueline, told the police that Mr. Meyer had told her he worried about being followed by "robed men with shaved heads" and that he feared for his life. Although the police didn't discount her information, Jacqueline, whose legal name is Jane Thorold, held two previous convictions for drug trafficking and one for disorderly conduct. Sources speculate that the victim was killed in an aborted drug deal, since he was also a drug trafficking suspect."

She shook her head and moved her shoulders to exercise the stiffness that set in from hours of sitting bent over the computer. Back in the 60s, who wasn't suspected of drug trafficking in San Francisco's Haight-Ashbury District? It was the time of Flower Children, Janis Joplin, Jimmy Hendrix, and Star Trek.

However, Jacqueline boldly spoke her mind in front of the press. She gave them enough information to produce half a news page of lurid detail about Piet Meyer's killer using his blood to deface his books and magazines and skinning him alive. The police admitted that the small patch of the victim's skin, taken from the upper left shoulder in the back, might be considered skinning. However, they brought in the medical examiner's statement to confirm that most likely the victim had a patch of skin removed when either unconscious from loss of blood, or already dead.

She looked down at her feet. The oil-drum purse sat there like a rock. Shivers attacked her whole body. This time she knew that someone must have been walking over her future grave. The chills that attacked her felt more like a warning, a foreboding—an omen. Having read the two articles, all speculation had been removed. She knew that the two patches of tattooed human skin inside the green canvas bag had been removed from Anike Van Buren and Piet Meyer—their deaths came three months apart.

Also, Anike and Piet were the same age. She felt that particular issue had huge significance.

Her subscription into the archives database service gave her three months of free browsing. However, she might not be able to use a computer any time soon. It was much better to have hard copies of information. She printed out the San Francisco Examiner article, folded both printouts and stored them in the canvas bag. Somehow, it seemed fitting that the obituaries should rest next to what had been taken from the victims.

"Did you find anything useful?" the librarian asked her on her way out.

"I had some success." She smiled and thanked her for the assistance.

The woman inclined her head, obviously considering something, and said reflectively, "You know, since you're a student, you might get the staff in the Smithsonian to help you with your search. Are you heading back to Connecticut, or are you staying for a few days in Washington?"

"I'm staying at least a couple of days," she said.

"Then you definitely should try your luck at the Smithsonian. We have a reciprocal link with them. I'm not sure whether they provide the same type of service to the public, but if you explained your difficulties, they might be able to help you. They have links to historical archives almost everywhere in the U.S. and even all over the world. If you talk to someone at the Castle, in their administrative offices, I'm sure they'd be willing to assist you."

"Thank you very much. I believe I'll drive over to the Smithsonian."

"Don't drive if you can help it. Take a cab. Believe me, it'll be a lot faster," the librarian said.

Chapter 19

S HE TOOK THE woman's advice and left her car in the parking lot. Ten minutes later, the cab let her out on Constitution Avenue. The cab driver asked her whether she had her walking shoes on.

"It takes about a day of touring any one of the buildings to do it a justice, and see all there's to be seen," he said.

She thanked him, and he drove off. The Castle, the Smithsonian's first building, which housed their administrative offices, sat just south of the Washington Monument on Jefferson Drive. In October, the two walkways leading to the building looked severe, and the building in the distance loomed, its solid presence suggesting prison rather than a museum. The Vuitton purse felt heavy, and no amount of shifting and re-positioning the leather strap on her shoulder would alleviate the pain.

I have to sit down and rest, or by the time I'm facing an administrator, I'll be crying. The next two stone-and-wood benches she passed were taken, but the third one, still about fifty feet ahead, was empty. She stopped in front of it, fighting an urge to brace her back and massage the sore spots. If Carmella had her followed, she couldn't afford to show fatigue after a short walk. Her gaze fell on the commemorative brass plaque imbedded in the top wood plank.

"This bench was donated in honor of Dr. Simon Teffler, by his grateful friends and colleagues on the occasion of his retirement. 1960-1995."

She stood there, transfixed by the plaque and its message.

"He's dead too," she whispered and sat down heavily, no longer caring whether anyone watched her. Simon Teffler, the name Hagip left in his message, turned out to belong to another ghost. Lauren slid to one side and stared at the plaque again. It said retirement, not deceased, and the years represented his years of service at the Smithsonian. If Teffler retired in 1995, he had to have been no older than sixty-five, and that meant he might still be alive. He'd be seventy-five but that wasn't so ancient. If he worked until the mandatory retirement age, that meant he had to be relatively healthy. She rose, jogging the rest of the way, the handicap bouncing against her thigh almost forgotten.

She didn't lie, but what she told the administrative assistant wasn't exactly the truth either. As a doctorate student at Winthrop College, she definitely needed help with her thesis. She suggested in an oblique way that she needed assistance with manuscript and art identification, rather than ecological issues.

"Dr. Teffler retired almost ten years ago," the woman said, "and I don't believe he's in Washington any longer. I'll see if he left an address to contact him."

Lauren thanked her and asked to use the washroom before she continued on her quest. There, she read Teffler's address in Vermont, closed her eyes, and repeated it until she had it memorized. She put the slip of paper into the green canvas bag with the rest of her acquisitions and snapped her oil-drum purse shut. The urge to carry the bag in her hand became so strong that she started to walk out, reconsidered, and slung it across her throbbing shoulder.

SHE GLANCED AT her watch. It was just after three o'clock. The museums on the mall remained opened until five-thirty. It might look odd if she didn't walk through at least one of the nearby buildings. The Freer Gallery of Asian Art sat practically next door to the Castle, but it still translated into a vigorous ten-minute walk. There were enough people strolling amongst the exhibits that she never felt alone and relaxed.

Why should I worry about being alone? Alone is good. I should feel threatened if people are around, because anyone might be their agent, an enemy. She ruffled her hair, using the motion to rub the back of her neck that ached from the pain shooting into it from her shoulder, and forced herself to focus on the displays.

The Arts of the Islamic Worlds exhibits consisted mostly of ceramic and glassworks, metalwork, and what looked like ivory, leather, and wood. Some exhibits stood on pedestals; others sat on displays inset within alcoves, but most lay behind glass. She leaned closer to reduce the glare and examine the tiny floral pattern of glass inlaid in a ceramic bowl. Suddenly she felt a presence close by.

"I'm all for respecting history and such stuff, but do they have to put these things on display in our capital?" a female voice sounded.

Slowly, Lauren straightened and turned her head towards the speaker. The girl wore a hunter green preppie blazer with a school crest embroidered on the upper pocket. Her short black, pleated skirt exposed her thighs. The green knee-socks lay scrunched around the tops of her sturdy black shoes. The girl adjusted her knapsack higher on her shoulder and nodded at the display.

"Any way you look at it, it's all terrorist arts and crafts. Iran, Iraq, Syria—it doesn't matter that the stuff was made a thousand years ago; it's still made by the ancestors of the terrorists who crashed a plane into the Pentagon. But hey, it's history, so we show off their arts and crafts."

"If you find it so objectionable, why come here?" Lauren managed. The girl's comments didn't make sense. It occurred to

Lauren that the teen might just be messing with people's minds. What the girl said was incendiary, but considering the source, nothing she said could be taken at face value. Her comments were more of a teenage rant than a serious commentary.

The girl curled her upper lip and gave a scornful hiss. "I come here because I have to do a paper on this shit, that's why." She leaned toward Lauren, pointing at a brass bowl flanked by a pair of candlesticks.

"I'll bet you that bowl was once filled with blood..."

"Sorry, I have to go," Lauren said and almost ran out of the room. She'd caught the unmistakable scent of citrus window cleaner. For all she knew, the girl might have polished her shoes with it, but on two recent occasions that citrus smell had meant danger.

She found her way outside, hailed a taxi, and asked to be taken to the nearest department store.

"That would he Hecht's. They're just up on G Street," the cab driver said.

She bought the first sturdy canvas knapsack she found, paid with her credit card, and rushed back outside. The store had five spots reserved for cabs. She walked up to the first one in line, and, leaning over, asked, "Is there a discount liquor store somewhere around here?"

"Discount liquor?" The cab driver stared at her with suspicion.

She let him see her anguish. "I don't have that much money left and I need to buy something for my friend's anniversary."

He nodded at her. "Get in." Once she sat inside, he turned around and said, "If you want a bit of a price break on liquor, we'll have to cruise uptown a bit, if you know what I mean."

She didn't, but said, "Thank you very much."

She used the twenty-minute ride to settle her thoughts. It had to be done. If she returned to Carmella's house with her oil-drum purse still weighing a ton, she might not be alive in the morning. They watched her wherever she went, whatever she did. If she stored the purse in a locker, either at the bus depot or anywhere else, they'd have it five minutes later. Mailing it to someone might work, but to whom? Besides, the post office would want to know the contents of such a small, heavy parcel. Fed-Ex might deliver it, but parcel delivery trucks stopped often, and their drivers might be distracted or bribed. Besides, Fed-Ex x-rayed an odd parcel here and there.

Only one person in Washington would be safe to receive the obscene gold bar. Someone, who two weeks ago, wouldn't have been considered—not even as her last resort. *In a scant two weeks, much has changed.*

At Park View, Lauren stepped out of the cab. The shabby little strip plaza had only two stores with their lights on. One's shingle said: Dominic's Discount Liquor and Wines.

The idea of what to do with the gold bar came to her thinking of Mitch. It was something he did the previous Christmas, a gesture Jenny had thought romantic.

"Would you be able to deliver a case of fine wines to an office here in Washington?" she asked, trying not to stare too obviously at the man behind the counter. He looked like someone who'd just dropped in to rob the cash register. She couldn't decide whether he'd tried to grow a beard, or just hadn't bothered shaving for a month. He chewed on a toothpick while measuring her worth as a customer. His nametag said: Dominic.

"Yeah, sure, I can deliver." He obviously didn't think she'd make it worth his effort.

"What time do you close?"

He took the toothpick out of his mouth and carefully put it on top of the cash register. "I ain't the delivery boy, if that's your worry. I have a regular guy do it. Hey, Vito," he yelled, stuck two fingers in his mouth, and whistled shrilly.

A kid, who might have been a center for his college basketball team, emerged from the back of the store. "Yeah, Dad, what's up?"

"This lady here," Dominic stabbed a finger in her direction, "wants to deliver a case of wine to an office, like today, okay?"

"No problem, Dad. I just gassed up. Where is it?"

"Do you have a fancy crate, you know, something wooden?" she asked, hoping she wasn't pushing her luck. "I'll pay for it, of course."

"Vito, get that fancy wood crate the distillery guy sent with the new brand."

The kid returned with what looked like a banker's box made of oak and reinforced brass corners. Lauren smiled and nodded.

She picked a dozen bottles of wine, praying she had enough credit left on her VISA to finance this adventure.

"I have a card and something small I want to put in the box," she said hesitantly.

Dominic leaned forward, grinning. "Look, lady. I'm not a snoop. You pay for the wine, the fancy crate, and delivery. For all I care, you can pack it yourself. Vito will strip-tie it with steel bind 'cause you don't want all those nice, heavy bottles falling out." He reached for his toothpick and stuck it back in his mouth. "Might be a nice gesture to give the kid a tip too."

She nodded, took out her wallet, and checked her cash. She had just over one hundred and twenty dollars. "How much for the delivery charge?"

"Where is it going to go?"

"3600 New York Avenue, Northeast Washington."

"What's the office building?"

"The Washington Times."

"That conservative scrap of toilet tissue...?" He almost spit the toothpick on the floor.

"Is that a problem?"

"Nah. Say, about twenty bucks for delivery. But that's if you're really sending a whole case."

"A whole case," she assured him.

He motioned for Vito to put the case down and to follow Lauren to the shelves. She selected her choices, and the young man brought them to the cash register. The twelve bottles of wine came to just over three hundred dollars. Seeing that her VISA accepted the charge, she sighed with relief.

"Here." She gave Vito a twenty-dollar bill. "And thank you for the delivery. And here," she gave Dominic two twenties and a ten. "That's for letting me pack the crate."

Finally, they left her alone. The man, who looked like a bank robber, and his basketball-star kid were perhaps the only trustworthy people around. She took out the printed article for the Los Angeles Times' historical, scribbled down all the names Hagip left in his phone message, hesitated, and finally wrote *The Siberian Oracle,* followed by her name and cell phone number. Lauren also penned: *Can you meet me tomorrow, at noon, at the George Washington Library in the Reference and Research Room?* She put the paper in the green canvas bag, wedged them into the bottom of the crate, covered it with some wood shavings that Vito had left behind, and loaded the crate with the wine bottles totaling eight. She reached for the wooden lid but something about the bottles bothered her. It wasn't the gleaming dark glass and it wasn't the elegant labels with gold corners. It had to be the amount of the bottles. Eight was her favorite number. Should she 'gift' it to the last person who deserved it? She took one more bottle and put it on top then stuffed the other three in her new knapsack, and snapped the wooden lid onto the case.

Vito strapped the steel bands around the crate and lifted it without any problem.

"Got a name for Vito to deliver this to at the newspaper?" Dominic asked.

"John Preston McPhend."

An hour later, a taxi let her out in front of the parking lot where she'd left her car. The knapsack with the three bottles of wine felt so light she almost started swinging it around. Her shoulders still ached, so she asked Dominic for two painkillers to get rid of her *headache.* For the first time in what seemed like eternity, she felt invigorated and even optimistic that the morning would find her alive. It also felt incredibly good to be able to dump the deadly gold bar and two patches of human skin in the lap of her enemy.

Chapter 20

"YOU DIDN'T LEAVE me your cell phone number and I was getting frantic." Once again Carmella greeted Lauren with open arms. This time she stopped short of hugging her and continued with her reproach. "It's not wise to walk around Washington in the dark. We have to establish some system where you can leave me a message and your whereabouts. What if your car had been stolen? What if it had got a flat?"

"I'm fine, Carmella," she assured her. "I'm not the kid you used to send home in a taxi."

"Of course not. I didn't mean it that way. But now we have to hurry." She clapped her hands.

"Why?" She let her Vuitton purse drop on the granite tiles, but lowered her knapsack with more care. Still, the wine bottles gave off a soft clink.

"We have a reception at the French Embassy."

"Oh, Carmella I didn't...."

"Of course you wouldn't have brought anything formal, but I took care of that. Michelle, one of my assistants, is about your size. She loaned me a few things from her party collection. Juanita has put them in your room. Choose what you like, or what fits the best, and off we go. What have you got in that bag?" She glanced at the knapsack.

"I thought we'd have dinner here, so I bought some wine."

"That's very sweet of you. We'll have it tomorrow. Tonight, we're the guests of the French Ambassador.

"Maybe you should go without me," Lauren tried, just to see how determined Carmella would be to take her out of the house...away from her purse.

"I wouldn't hear of it. Of course you must come. Don't worry. It's not a formal sit-down dinner. It's a buffet reception."

A buffet reception at the French Embassy would most likely eclipse the average formal sit-down dinner.

"I'm tired," said Lauren. "I'm not in the mood for diplomatic chit-chat."

"We can fix that in a jiffy. I'll send Kingsley up to give you a vitamin-B shot. You'll feel like a million bucks in no time."

"Oh, no thanks. That won't be necessary. I'll just take a quick shower, and hopefully it'll do the trick."

Juanita quietly appeared. Carmella motioned at the knapsack lying on the floor. "Lauren brought wine for dinner. Store it in the cooler and we'll have it tomorrow." She turned to Lauren. "Do you need Juanita to help you?"

"No, thanks. I'll manage."

Half an hour later, Lauren hurried down the stairs. It didn't surprise her to see Carmella standing on the bottom, giving an impression she'd been waiting there all along.

"You look smashing," Carmella exclaimed. "Turn around," she prompted her with a twirl of her hand.

For the first time since she'd arrived at the home of her old mentor, Lauren agreed with Carmella's sentiments. Her old mentor also sounded genuinely pleased.

Michelle had to be not only close to her height and weight, but also her coloring. The tight-fitting silver dress would have only looked good on a brunette with a light olive complexion. Thin straps, studded with diamond stars, crossed just below the hollow of her neck and crossed again in the back, leaving her shoulders bare. The X effect in front and back raised the otherwise plain dress into an elegant creation. Snappy black high-heel sandals completed the look. She'd spent five minutes in the bathroom, massaging vitamin-E lotion into her shoulders until the red abrasions subsided—but they still stood out. She returned to search Michelle's collection and found a loose, short-cropped jacket that belonged to another silver dress. However the jacket's gauzy fabric shot through with silver thread was generic enough to wear with almost anything. Unfortunately, Carmella might notice the slight mismatch.

"Details, details," Carmella used to say. "Pay attention to details. A scientific analysis must be robust and that means attention to details."

"Thank you, Carmella," Lauren said hurriedly when she saw her hostess tilt her head in a scrutiny. "You think of everything." She raised her hand with the elegant black wallet-sized purse she had found with the ensemble, hoping it would interrupt the analysis of her outfit.

"I chose a small one on purpose," Carmella said. "So you won't be able to hide a pack of cigarettes in i, like you must do in that wine-barrel bag. You still smoke, don't you? I've a good nose, you know. I smelled it on you the moment you walked inside."

She had smoked a couple of cigarettes while driving to Washington, but only to keep awake and alert. And this kind of insensitive lecture was the old Carmella Perez, coming back for a brief visit.

"And a final touch." Carmella approached and quickly dabbed something on either side of her neck.

Lauren breathed in, the citrus scent once again awakening memories steeped in danger.

"Smells like window cleaner," she murmured, not really wanting to speak her mind, but the scent seemed to grow, filling her nose, her eyes, and mouth. She felt as if she'd been immersed in a highly citrus household cleanser.

"Do not air such sentiments at the reception," Carmella said, laughing. "The president of the French cosmetics company that has recently launched this fragrance will be there. And so will a ton of very rich and influential barons of such fine industries as wines and spirits, cosmetics and perfumes, and of course chocolatiers."

"It's very strong," she said, smiling guiltily.

"Bold fragrances are in; anything subtle and wishy-washy is out. However, do remember that while bold is in, diplomacy must still prevail."

Kingsley fell into one of his many roles and drove up in a dark Lincoln Continental. He got out of the car dressed in a chauffeur's uniform—but no hat.

"Did you find out anything about Mitch and Jenny, or Hagip and Alice?" asked Lauren.

Carmella reached over and clasped Lauren's hands in hers, squeezing. "Relax, Lauren, my dear, relax. My secretary networked her way through the maze of local police and sheriff's people today.. Mitch is from around Marksville, the real heart of the Atchafalaya bayou country. Heidi didn't want the local police cruising in boats, invading Mitch's folk's homestead, but I understand he's all right. The Plow family's known down there in local corners and they did have some kind of emergency; either someone's sick or dead. Heidi said it sounded to her like every other family down there is either Plow or related to Plow. Mitch and Jenny made it to Marksville just fine. His kinfolk came to get them in trucks; it was a regular convoy, according to Heidi. I'm sure civilization has reached those parts of Louisiana, but I don't think cell phones work in many places. Mitch will get in touch, I'm sure, but it might take days, even weeks because Cajun folks have all kinds of rituals and celebrations."

Lauren wouldn't have thought Mitch to have Cajun roots, but he did say his ancestors were French. And Mitch had referred to himself as white trash—was that the same as a Cajun clan from the bayou country?

"What about Hagip and Alice Blumenthal?" She knew she should have at least sounded gracious and thanked her, but she felt far from pacified or settled.

"I only talked to Heidi for ten minutes, you know." Carmella laughed. "Tomorrow, I'll pass on to her all the rest of the responsibilities."

"Thanks, Carmella. I'm really grateful...."

She wouldn't let her finish and squeezed her hands harder. "Think nothing of it. What are friends for? I still consider myself your mentor...and friend. I should probably say surrogate mother, though I hate to admit to anything over forty."

Well, that part of old Carmella had survived too. Ten years ago, at thirty-eight, she used to say that she hated to admit to anything over thirty.

"You don't look a day over forty," she said, managing to sound ingenuous.

"I'm glad to see you're remembering all my lectures about diplomacy," Carmella said and let go of her hands, leaned back, and started to brief her on the occasion of the embassy function.

Lauren listened to her hostess, concentrating in particular on foreign-sounding names. Marcel Durocher, Comte de Bragaux, an ultra rich perfumes and cosmetics manufacturer, was touring the U.S.A. in tandem with the introduction of a new line of perfume and cosmetics to the American consumer. Additionally, Bolerian Xavier, of the Perigeaux Bolerian Wineries and Distilleries, had just entered into a profitable partnership with Palfrey Distilleries and would come to the reception to shake hands with William C. Palfrey for the benefit of many key political figures in Washington and the press.

"Between you and me," Carmella leaned over, lowering her voice into confidential whisper, "I think Bolerian has been taken over by Palfrey, but that's not something that will be paraded for the press. A while ago, rumors of a hostile takeover ran rampant. The French government was ready to step in. The issue is, of course, the percent of foreign ownership of what is considered a

French institution. However, and just in the nick of time, Xavier and Palfrey announced this partnership deal. It's Marie-Chantal's brainchild, but you won't see Palfrey's wife taking the credit either."

"Do you know William Palfrey?" Lauren asked, inspecting her nails. She wanted to give an impression she'd asked the question only to pass time.

"I sit beside him on two boards of directors, my dear. It's hard to ignore your seatmate since you have to spend hours in cold conference rooms, listening to key terms and numbers. Sometimes, during particularly dull meetings, we play hangman."

How fitting, indeed. Lauren asked, "Who usually wins?"

Carmella made a face and ran a fingertip down the corner of her mouth. "He does. He has an amazing vocabulary, you know. Of course, I'm not permitted to use any of the scientific terms, or names of chemical compounds."

"How large is this reception?" Lauren changed the subject. Playing hangman during board meetings defined William C. Palfrey for Lauren more than anything else Carmella might have told her about the billionaire.

"Three hundred invitations went out, but I doubt that everyone will be able to make it. I'd say about two hundred will show up and that includes the press." Suddenly, she leaned forward and tapped the driver's shoulder. "Kingsley, get us close to the front entrance. It's bitterly cold outside, and I didn't want to wear my fur wrap out of respect for my protégé here." She sat back and pursed her mouth at Lauren, stifling laughter.

"You never used to own furs, much less wear them," Lauren murmured.

Carmella continued to scrutinize her in a way that was difficult to read. Her lips could have curved in a contemptuous smile or a pitiful sneer and then settled back into their placid state of two red-lipstick lines in an exquisitely made-up face.

"Washington gets very cold, my dear, physically and metaphorically. I made sure I bought my fur coats resale; that way I'm only sharing in the crime."

"But a criminal's partner is equally guilty," Lauren observed, flexing her voice to make it come out like a cheeky comment.

"You should have gone to law," Carmella said dryly. "You would have made a splendid Attorney General."

Chapter 21

THE FRENCH MISSION at 4101 Reservoir Road sat on an eight-acre tract of land in northwest Washington across from the Georgetown University Hospital and consisted of four interconnected buildings.

Kingsley came to the fork in the road and chose to follow the sign that said: *La Maison Francaise*. Carmella spoke too liberally, saying they would be the guests of the French ambassador. This part of the mission qualified more like a public facility. The French House was a convention and entertainment center, where the staff and their American hosts would meet at functions designed to promote French culture and re-affirm good will and continued cooperation.

The reception would fit into the corporate/private category. There would be quite a few embassy staff and highly placed U.S. commerce directors, the CEOs and owners of companies and corporations that sought to do business with their French counterparts, but most likely not the French ambassador and few if any congressmen.

Carmella Perez had a double doctorate in chemistry and micro-biology. Lauren remembered she used to identify her specialty—vaccines and viruses, not necessarily in that order. What was she doing amongst the perfume-lovers and wine-and-cheese crowd?

Once, an Intern asked Dr. Perez what she preferred to make: vaccines or viruses. Carmella had leveled a stern look at him that might have been feigned at the time and said, "First you make the virus for free, and the global governments will pay you any-thing you ask for a vaccine."

Lauren's fellow interns had laughed at their boss's deadpan wit. Lauren had laughed too, but something itched in her throat and the laughter didn't want to come naturally.

"Well, what do you think of the *Maison Francaise*?" Carmella touched her elbow, motioning with her eyes at the huge skylight above wreathed in garlands of tiny lights.

"Very elegant and charming," Lauren said truthfully and turned to examine an assembly of multi-colored tubes, one of the three artworks in the entrance hall. It was called *Totem*, and Lauren reflected that the artist had to have a practical streak for the title described the tubular assortment quite well.

A waiter dressed in white coattails offered them a choice of three wines, each in its own proper glas: a red wine in a long-stemmed bulbous glass, a white wine in a slender tulip glass, and champagne in a tall, almost tubular glass.

Lauren didn't drink. Those few beers she had accepted over the years, mostly from Hagip, had been accepted out of friend-ship and solidarity with her companions.

Carmella decided for her. "Here, let's start the evening in style with champagne. Oh, I can just smell the *pâtés* and herbs." She turned toward the reception area leading into the ballroom. "If you see kalamata olives in aromatic herbs, let me know," she told her. "They're absolutely out of this world with smoked Gruyere and red wine. Will you be all right for five minutes? I need to go check my messages. I've left my cell phone on vibrate and it's about to rip through my purse."

"No problem," Lauren said. "I'm sure I'll find someone willing to discuss pesticide use and World Bank financing of strip-mining ventures in Third World countries."

"Excellent. You've grasped the essence of the French sense of humor," Carmella said and rushed off.

Lauren sauntered through the reception area, looking at the paintings and tapestries, which were far more interesting than the guests. According to the title, the four silver tubes by Demarco supposed to represent the four elements. Perhaps molecular bonds might have been a more fitting title for the artwork since there was little elemental representation in the tubular shapes. The blue acrylic paint applied haphazardly over folded and crumpled canvas was aptly named: *Study*.

She stared at it long enough to conclude that she would have to have Hagip beside her, offering insight and interpretation to properly appreciate the artist's whimsy. She turned away from the art, and taking long, slow sips of the champagne, studied the crowd. A few uniforms dotted the room, probably military attaches that might want to slip a French brand into their superior's wine cooler, but most likely just attending the function because it offered free liquor.

The rest of the guests typified those who would have a closet filled with identical tuxedos and another filled with black coat-tails. All such formal attire would be custom-made to fit the customer perfectly and minimized figure faults. The women, wives, diplomatic attaches or executives, would have apartment-size closets filled with designer creations. Those in a diplomatic function might have an occasional attack of modesty and have their designer re-style an already worn creation into a new dress. The corporate executives might favor a dozen styles and own several identical creations in each one. But once a formal dress had been dry-cleaned twice, it would be donated to charity. The wives would strive never to be seen in the same dress twice.

During the six months Lauren had served as a White House Intern, she had two black dresses to wear to formal functions.

Now, her tiny closet contained only five pairs of casual pants and many loose tops worn indifferently each day to work. Her students seldom lifted their heads to notice what she wore, and Errington wanted to see her humble, which meant correspondingly dressed.

If she had dropped by the metallurgy labs and asked one of the teaching assistants to use the firing kiln to smelt down the gold bar and portion it into wafers to be cashed at regular intervals, her bank account would have been happy and warm for a long time. She'd get a wardrobe....

Get a grip. She shook her head to banish such thoughts.

"The champagne has addled their wits," her mother used to say, watching guests who had come back piss-drunk and ran the boat into the dock.

Lauren moved between the guests, heading for the food area and the table with dishes and cutlery set up on one side. Her French wasn't strong enough to allow her to eavesdrop on the conversations around her, and the Americans who spoke it fluently honored the guests by conversing in their native language, so she heard hardly a word of spoken English. At the hot buffet, chefs stood behind their creations. The delicate aromas tortured her taste buds. But if they asked her preference in French, she'd have to confess her ignorance.

"Cheese and *pâtés*," she murmured and headed for a self-serve table.

"Well, how's this for coincidence? Lauren Sarasohn, my favorite environmental advocate," A voice said. It sounded just as fresh and irreverent as it did eight years ago. He used to be a hustler, and hadn't lost the cheerful pitch that she found so hard to resist...or used to, anyway.

"Just a quick shot, you won't regret it once you see the magic I can do with my camera. It'll all go down in the archives some day, and you'll become an imprint in history. How's that for not just making your mark but leaving it for generations to admire?" He used to talk non-stop, pursuing his subject with a ready-held camera, forever busy, forever running and stealing moments in time that would be flattened between the pages of books or newsprint.

She turned around, using the motion to compose her face into a pleasant mask of surprise.

"Why John McPhend, how's this for coincidence?"

"I'm still the Washington Press," he said, bowing slightly. "*Enchanté, Mademoiselle.* You look absolutely great."

Wish I could return the compliment. At thirty-five, John looked like the seasons had conspired to make it eternal winter all around him. His sandy brown hair shot with gray, looked almost white at his temples, and time had ravaged the man's hairline. The black tux hung loosely on his body, and its dark color gave his skin an almost unhealthy pallor. The voice may have retained its youthful, fresh quality, but nothing else.

"I see I no longer measure up to the brash young man who used to coax you to walk a tightrope," he said and took a sip of his wine.

"How are you?" She avoided the trap.

He shrugged. It was something else that he never used to do because of shoulders always weighed down by his tools—cameras, batteries and knapsacks full of snacks.

"Too many hours spent in rooms where you can't even open windows, and neon light strips without a dimmer switches forever glaring down on you since."

"You've finally settled into the corporate good life."

"I still keep my hand in the earthenware pot, but these days I'm more liable to approve headlines than to write them."

"You should be doing quite well now that the current White House administration is polarized along the beliefs fostered by the Times and its illustrious owner. Tell me something, I've always wondered, is everyone who works at the Times a member of the Unification Church?" she asked, smiling and keeping her voice neutral.

"I'm an editor of the commerce and technology sectors. And the Washington Times is a privately owned newspaper whose owner happens to be a religious leader. I don't get involved in controversial issues anymore than I have to."

"So you've left religion and the environment far behind. How refreshing. I feel safer already." She kept framing her sarcasm in a polite diplomatic smile, not allowing her mouth to twitch with her true feelings. Eight years ago, John had gained admission into the Greenpeace ranks with lies and deceit. Once his series of investigative articles came out, five Greenpeace members became indicted in Texas on charges of piracy, trespassing, and destruction of private property. The last article attempted to twist some of the close-knit individual groups into private teams of militant gays and lesbians. And those who couldn't be so easily stereotyped, like Hagip and Isabel, became hippie throwbacks. He'd spared Lauren. Foresight must have showed him that someone he'd slept with would be capable of fighting back perhaps more meanly and underhandedly than he did.

"The articles didn't represent accurately what I submitted to my editor. My information was fair and correct. But the editorial powers—"

"Oh yes, the editorial might," she interrupted. "Now I understand why you pulled short of suggesting that I was really an Israeli spy, using the Greenpeace umbrella to move freely all over the world and engage in subversive activities. However, a man who calls the Holocaust a Jewish indemnity for killing Christ must have the kind of people on his newspaper staff who are able to see the true vision that's floating before his privileged eyes...."

"All right. I'm sorry," he said, raising his voice.

"Are you, John, are you really? I rather doubt it, because if that was true, you wouldn't still be at the Washington Times."

"I tried to get out after the series published, but the Post wouldn't hire me. I didn't want to leave Washington. Diane didn't want to leave Benson and Hardwick, either. She made partner, so...."

"Oh, yes, how is your wife?"

"Ex-wife, and she's doing well with a law firm down in Houston."

"So, you're thirty-five, have two ex-wives, no children, and are now an editor at the Times. My, you do like to live dangerously, don't you? A second divorce is not something that the great leader, and incidentally the owner of your livelihood, would condone. Hasn't he just celebrated a forty-fifth anniversary with his second wife? One divorce may be glossed over; everyone's entitled to one mistake. But two failures to live up to the principles advocated by Moon's church." She shook her head and let out a theatrical sigh.

Eight years ago, he told her he'd divorced from his first wife, Amelia, a high school sweetheart, but not that he was still married to his second wife, Diane, a lawyer with a high-profile Washington law firm.

"You used to be cranky before rain and afterward, when your sleeping bag got soggy. You used to cringe upon hearing thunder. You used to be bold and brashly advocated your cause, but I've never heard you sound so malicious, so...spiteful," he said.

"You're a newspaper man, John, you should know that words sting far more than any dagger." She no longer bothered to hide her smirk.

"Let's walk out on the terrace."

He changed the subject so suddenly that it confused her. If he came to the reception, he probably hadn't received her crate of wine yet. Where would the crate be now? Was it sitting somewhere in the Times' reception area, or inside his glassed-in office?

Chapter 22

ONCE THEY WALKED outside he said, "I wasn't talking about words, Lauren." He kept his voice so low voice that she had to lean toward him. "I'm talking about wine—and the articles that accompanied it. Here." Suddenly, he thrust his wine glass into her hand, took off his tux jacket, and draped it around her shoulders. The terrace wasn't glassed-in, and the October wind, laden with moisture it picked up over the Potomac, blew cold. The resulting chill sliced right to the bone.

"You got my gift." She also lowered her voice, although no one else had walked out for a breath of fresh air.

"How did you get those...articles, and what is this about, Lauren?" he asked, staring out over the darkness twinkling with lights.

"There's probably a story in it, John, a blockbuster of a story, but I suspect it won't be the kind that might be allowed in the Times. This isn't the place to go into the story. Can I see you to-morrow, somewhere safe?"

"If I had the story, the Post might take me on," he murmured.

Suddenly, she felt a pang of guilt. Maybe she shouldn't have dumped the deadly bag with the gold bar on his doorstep. The thief who stole the bullion bar had been murdered. Carmella might have tried to reassure her that Mitch and Jenny were down in bayou country, cut off from the rest of the world by its unspoiled charm and totally in keeping with Mitch's white trash roots, but she didn't believe her. Hagip might be in Montreal, but what if he wasn't? Also, what about Alice Blumenthal and the man who'd impersonated her son, Ralston?

"I shouldn't have sent you that case of wine, John," she said quietly, drawing his jacket around her shoulders.

"Probably not," he admitted laconically, "but you've done it, so it's no use to backpedal now. I'm in."

She flinched upon hearing his statement. Memories resonated within her. He used to say that, pretending he didn't care, whenever she'd ask him if he wanted to join the rally or come along and take pictures of the group's activities. After all, he joined them—a much-needed photographer, the media liaison who'd be willing to not just sit in the office and collect news, but be a part of it, out there on the frontlines in the field.

He remembered too. "I know." He turned his head, gazing into the darkness. "I don't volunteer for anything these days."

"It's safer that way," she said.

"Safer and I have more control over what I'm doing, but it's all just fool's gold."

She looked in the direction where the city lights burned so strong they cast a halo for miles around. The illumination gave the impression that the sky had a huge flashlight shining into it. *The Fool's Gold People's Summit,* sought to spotlight irresponsible and damaging gold mining all over the world. It had been the last Greenpeace function she attended with him by her side. They'd just come back from Venezuela, documenting how the Pemon lands and rivers steadily grew ruined by people panning for gold with high-pressure hoses. The process destroyed much of plant and fish life. The situation had its mirror image in Nevada where most gold in the country was mined, and where the process consumed more water than all the people in the state. The water table in Nevada had fallen a thousand feet in the vicinity of the largest open pit gold mines in the northeastern parts. The cyanide contamination around the mines had reached dangerous limits.

It was years ago but she still remembered how she lectured him about the detrimental effects of mining gold, saying, *"And the use of the mercury in the Philippines has resulted in the worst ever outbreak of the Minamata Disease. Do you think that jewelry, which is what more than eighty-five percent of gold mined today will be used for, is worth hundreds of thousands of human lives and livelihoods?"*

She also remembered his reply as if he just spoke the words moments ago.

"So what you're saying is that all that glitters is not gold," he had deadpanned, taking the camera for a moment and staring at her without the lens.

"Where would be a good place to meet tomorrow?" she asked sharply to break the flow of memories. The silence had also grown uncomfortable.

"Lunch, at the Gypsy Rose," he finally said after a long moment.

"What kind of restaurant is it?"

"Environmentally responsible, if that's what you mean. Pasta and seafood, but they don't torture the shrimp all that much and they don't even serve lobsters. Just regular, approved fish, seaweed salads, no turtle soups, and of course the pasta's made of wheat—trashed but I think that's acceptable, no?"

"I still like your wit, but not much else," she said turning around and using the motion to take off his jacket. She handed it to him. "Thanks. I appreciate the gesture. Now, let's go inside and be diplomatic and politically correct."

"I thought I did just that...?" She heard him murmur behind her.

CARMELLA CAUGHT UP with her near the washroom.

"Who was that?" She motioned at the crowd that already swallowed John.

Lauren was tempted to say that it was the man she used to like and trust but now she intended to use him to stay alive and find her friends. However, truth framed with sarcasm was not a form of diplomacy.

"John McPhend of the Washington Times," she replied, curling her upper lip.

"Not a friend, I gather."

"He used to be. Or at least I thought so. He gained admission into the Greenpeace ranks by lying about who he was. He stayed with us eighteen months. No sooner had he left, the Times came out with a series of articles that sought to sully the Greenpeace work and reputation."

"Did he apologize now?"

She shrugged. "He wants to explain, make it up to me, and take me to lunch tomorrow."

"You'll go, of course."

"What's there to explain? He's still with the Times, and I'm still the environmentalist."

"Lauren, haven't I taught you anything? If you let him apologize, he may become useful at some point down the road if you have a cause to showcase in a way that you'll be in control."

"I don't have any more causes, Carmella," she said morosely. "I just want to see my friends again, and make sure they're all right. And I want the Hartford police to solve the damn case so I can return to work and pay my rent."

"Not finish your doctorate?"

Lauren uttered a displeased sound. "Well, of course I want to finish that too."

"Good." Carmella nodded. "Because the moment you do, I want you to come work for me. Or at least work in the same sector for someone I'd like to introduce you to. Come." She grabbed her arm and almost dragged her along.

"Bill, I'd like you to meet Lauren Sarasohn, my protégé and friend. I took Lauren under my wing ten years ago back in the White House. She served as an intern." Carmella made a smooth introduction, not embellishing anything, but Lauren felt it ran needlessly long. She just had to introduce her by her name and let the rest come out in the course of the conversation—that's if William Palfrey showed interest or cared.

"How do you do, Ms. Sarasohn?" Palfrey shook her hand, leaned back, and raised his wine glass. "What do you think of this champagne?"

"It's very good, sir, but I'm not a wine connoisseur," she said. "I hardly ever drink."

"I like honesty." He smiled and inclined his head. "Half the people in here came because of free liquor and food. So, if you aren't a drinker, you must be here for the company."

William Palfrey was a big man, not corpulent but square and solid, like a chunk of stone. His presence alone intimidated, and even though his voice sounded genial and he kept smiling, she felt threatened. She grew up on cartoons where size always carried a threat to the other, tiny characters. She preferred rooting for the little guy, the underdog. Hulking men, whether cartoons or real life, would always be the enemy.

"Carmella invited me to come along. I haven't been to one of these functions in years," she said.

He raised his wine glass to Carmella in a dry toast and said, "She tells me that your doctoral thesis is in pollution control."

She didn't want to start an argument there, or embarrass her old mentor because of misdirection or slight misrepresentation, so she said, "Pollution control is the outcome of what a resource recovery facility that my thesis deals with would accomplish. My proposed facility is somewhat similar to the American Ref-Fuel Company in Connecticut, but quite a few key-treatment processes would be different."

"I own two gold mines in Nevada, and others in the Philippines and South America. But it's the Nevada operations that I'd

like to overhaul in terms of implementing pollution control processes. My engineers are already working on designing a
catchments process that would effectively stop any seepage of
dangerous chemicals into the water systems. I'm also working on
drastic modifications to the existing mining methods there that
rely heavily on water to at least decrease the present water con-
sumption. I'd like you to come work for me in Nevada, be part of
a team of environmental specialists." He took a sip of champagne, peering at her above the rim of the glass.

She saw it coming. The same kind of offer that Denise, her old
roommate at Duke, must have received—a resident environmental consultant on site, where the actual crimes against Nature
and humanity are being committed. Who'd resist the gleam of
such a golden carrot?

"That's a very tempting offer, Mr. Palfrey, but I still have some
time to go on my thesis. I'm not happy with some of the new
processes I'm introducing."

"Maybe you should leave Winthrop and finish your doctorate
at a more...advanced academic institution that would be able to
offer you not only its research facilities, but the guidance and
expertise that you deserve," he said.

Carmella must have told him Lauren was doing her doctorate
at Winthrop, but Palfrey made it sound like a household name.
And yet he'd only recently heard it. After all, Winthrop College
wasn't in the top ten ivy-league academic institutions. Even lo-
cals who'd lived around Hartford all of their lives might have
difficulty giving directions to the campus.

Palfrey must have seen something on her face. He said, "My
son, Clement Palfrey, is the Congressman for the First District
that includes Hartford. He mentioned something about working
with the Winthrop College administration to get a portion of the
federal grant that's going to be released soon."

"I'm sure that my boss, Dr. Errington, would be happy to
know that Congressman Palfrey keeps involved to a degree
where he discusses it with his father," she said, forcing cheer into

her voice. She wondered if Palfrey would show knowledge of other things that have recently raised the college's name from obscurity.

"Yes, Carmella told me about what happened recently on campus, in your office, I believe. I will definitely keep my eyes on you, Ms. Sarasohn. And I look forward to our next meeting. Now, if you'll excuse me...."

"You mustn't be so humble." Carmella nudged her arm after Palfrey left to join a new group. "You have to learn to make a sales pitch when an opportunity presents itself."

"I found him...overwhelming," she said. It was mostly true.

"Yes, I know. You've been out of this kind of networking action for ten years. Now, have you eaten?"

Chapter 23

THE GYPSY ROSE restaurant was on 20th Street just north of K Street. John waited for her outside the restaurant.

"Let's go." He grabbed her arm and tried to turn her around, but she resisted.

"Let's go where, John? Isn't this the restaurant?"

"Yes, but if you're starving you'll just have to tighten your belt. We'll grab a bite later. He's here."

"Who's here?" She didn't like to be dragged, and he wasn't making sense.

"One of the names you wrote down on the piece of paper you've enclosed with the wine, Simon Teffler."

"Where?" She freed her arm and looked around.

"I mean here in Washington. He's giving three lectures at the university. The first one's today but it should be over," he glanced at his watch, "soon. So let's hurry up and catch him before he goes back to his hotel."

"Simon Teffler is here? What would he be doing lecturing at the university? He's long retired."

"Look, I'm not trying to kidnap you. Trust me, the old guy's here. By pure stroke of luck I suggested Gypsy Rose. The Foggy Bottom campus is just a stone's throw away."

"Very lucky," she agreed dryly.

He stopped, moved his shoulders up and down and then let them sag rather than just drop. The forward hunched stance looked like a sign of capitulation if not outright surrender. She certainly didn't remember seeing him like this before. His face looked even more tired and gaunt than it did the previous night at the reception.

"I haven't slept a wink all night," he stated, "and no, I wasn't thinking about you. I worked on what you commissioned me to do. And once I finished that, I worked some more, catching up on backyard news, namely in Connecticut at Winthrop College. Has anyone been following you?"

She threw her arms wide. "Hell, John, the whole world for all I know and at this moment for all I care. I'm starving."

He cracked a smile. "I forgot about that. You used to be very cranky when starving, which happened to be most of the time. I'd have thought you'd have grown used to it by now. But if we want to catch Teffler and not have to spend hours on the roads with ridiculously low speed limits to get to him in Vermont, we'd better get going. Let's go. It's only a ten-minute walk."

The clerk in the administration office told them that Dr. Teffler held his lecture in Stuart Hall just a block down on G Street.

The woman glanced at the office wall clock. "The lecture would have finished just about now, but Dr. Teffler stays around for fifteen minutes to answer students' questions. If you run you just might catch him there."

"You're out of shape," Lauren said, waiting for him to catch up to her on the steps of Stuart Hall. Suddenly she remembered something and grabbed his bulky green parka sleeve. "Where did you leave the wine crate?"

"In my office," he said urging her to get moving.

"Is that safe?"

"No one would dare to take a bottle of wine from their editor's office. Actually, I think my staff fears me."

"I meant...."

He interrupted, "I know what you meant. Don't worry, the bag is safe."

"Where is it?"

"Next to my very rapidly beating heart," he said and tapped his chest. She noticed that though the down-filled parka bulged, his hand didn't sink into it.

"How did it feel to run with a thirty-pound handicap?" she asked, holding the door open for him.

"It's the only reason why you beat me," he grumbled, and they hurried down the corridor to lecture room 212.

Teffler sat on the edge of the desk, chatting with half a dozen students. He looked his seventy-five years with his frizzy halo of white hair. He was dressed in a casual brown-checked shirt and corduroy slacks. He held his jacket in the crook of his arm.

They waited politely just inside the lecture hall until one by one, all the students left. Teffler must have noticed them the moment they appeared in the open doorway, but he didn't react to their presence.

"Dr. Teffler." Lauren took the initiative. "I'm Lauren Sarasohn, a student and a teacher, but not here in Washington. A good friend of mine, Hagip Agopian, left me your name for reference. I wonder if you'd have a few moments to talk...maybe not here, if the classroom's going to be used."

"Why not here, Ms Sarasohn?" Teffler asked without looking at her. He grew busy collecting his lecture notes and overheads from the desk, packing them with exaggerated deliberation into his briefcase.

She looked around. The classroom could seat about hundred and fifty students. Teffler would have used the mike—standard equipment in theater-style lecture rooms. Without it, his words wouldn't carry farther than perhaps the first row.

"All right," she said, looking at John and received a puzzled shrug. "We can talk here, but I'd have preferred somewhere more private."

"A police station, perhaps?" Teffler stopped loading his brief-case and jerked his head up, staring at her with definite hostility.

John stepped forward. "If we wanted to disrupt your lecture we'd have come sooner, not when it's over. We're not from any government commission and we're not here to make a sales pitch for anything. We simply need information."

Teffler stared at them for a long time and finally said, "The police that came to question me yesterday in my hotel room needed information, too, but I couldn't give it to them. I had nothing to give them."

"What are you talking about, sir?" she asked.

"You said you're a good friend of Hagip Agopian?" He waited for her nod and continued, "In that case you must know that he's dead."

"Dead?" she repeated. The room started to swim out of focus. "What do you mean dead? He can't be dead. He's in Montreal." The room blurred until she couldn't distinguish anything; not the blackboard, or the lectern, nor faces that melted down to brown uniformity.

Her sight cleared slowly. It felt as if a hand mopped her eyes from inside. She moved and the backrest portion of a desk pushed against her back. She realized that John had probably caught her and dragged to a desk in the front row. Teffler stood nearby, staring at her, pensively fingering his chin.

"You didn't know?" Teffler asked.

"Take another sip," John pressed a glass to her mouth, forcing her to take a drink of water.

She pushed his hand away. "I'm all right. Dr. Teffler, what happened to Hagip? How did he...?" The word stuck in her throat.

"From what the police told me, the weather killed him. His car spun out of control on a highway, rolled over a few times, and ended up in the ditch. The police identified the culprit as black ice. The funeral was held yesterday in Montreal. His wife's staying there with the children at her parents. Didn't anyone call you, Ms. Sarasohn?"

"I've been on the road," she said, blinking back tears and wiping her cheeks. "New York and Washington. I saw him on Saturday. When did the accident happen?"

"Monday night, I believe. I understand his wife called him about a family emergency."

"Is that what the police told you?"

"More or less. They weren't quite sure. The accident occurred near Plattsburg. The Plattsburg Police contacted his family in Montreal and reported to the New York Police."

"How would the Washington Police know?" John asked.

"The Plattsburg Police found a note in Hagip's pocket with my name, address, and phone number. The New York Police called my home, in Vermont. My housekeeper told them I left for Washington. The New York cops must have contacted their Washington counterparts to come check with me, but I haven't seen Hagip in two...three years now. We kept in contact though, phone and e-mail. So why did you go see Hagip on Saturday, Miss Sarasohn, and more importantly, why would he give you my name and address for reference?"

"Hagip examined some articles for me. He offered to check out their authenticity and history," she said, taking the tissue John handed her and dabbing at the tears that wouldn't dry up.

Teffler put on his jacket and took his coat from the back of a chair.

"Come, a walk in the fresh air will do you good." He motioned at them and headed out the door.

Once outside, Teffler lost his taste for a walk and motioned at the first empty bench that sat in a small parkette set well back from the street. He put down his well-aged briefcase. He must have noticed her staring at it because he patted the briefcase fondly and said, "It's a gift from my late wife, on our third wedding anniversary. She loved traditions. First anniversary you give paper, second is cotton, and third is leather. She never made it to our forty-fifth anniversary, the one where the tradition calls for sapphire. She died just a few weeks short of it, five years ago."

"I'm sorry," Lauren said.

"Thank you." Teffler patted her knee in a fatherly way and added, "Sunday morning, I went to check my e-mail. I found one from Hagip. I thought nothing of it; nothing urgent or dangerous, that is. That's why I didn't rush to open it. I finally got to it by late afternoon and discovered it had a bit-map attached to it. I printed out the picture and deleted the e-mail—permanently." He leaned forward and clasped his hands together. He lowered his head, speaking to the ground. "That's a very dangerous picture Hagip sent me. A gold bar and two squares of what appears to be parchment with blue watermarks."

"Dr. Teffler," John said. "What you just described sits in a leather pouch that's hanging from my neck, making me about thirty pounds heavier than I should be."

For a moment, it looked like Teffler might rise and leave.

"What is it all about, Dr. Teffler?" Lauren put a hand on his coat sleeve. "Hagip knew the moment I showed him the articles. I knew he knew, but for reasons of his own, he didn't want to tell me yet. He said he had to check it out."

"Hagip would have known and he probably didn't tell you to protect you...for a while. The history behind the *Siberian Oracle* is grim, like anything that has to do with Hitler and his insane schemes. I first came across it almost forty years ago. I had yet to finish my second doctorate, so I apprenticed in library and archives. One of the curators bought a lot from an estate sale at an auction in Zurich. The lot contained quite a few rare first editions, mostly French and German books, old photographs, journals and manuscripts. The contents came from a once-wealthy aristocratic French family.

"Some of the journals and correspondence suggested that the de Augais-Perigord family were Nazi sympathizers. But that's open to interpretation and mostly depends on the translator. It's possible the Augais-Perigords, not having much choice or choosing to live instead of being slaughtered by the Nazis, surrendered their chateau to Hitler's doctors. The journal is really a medical log, documenting experiments conducted at the chateau, mostly in genetics."

Chapter 24

AT FIRST TEFFLER spoke haltingly, groping for words which was strange considering he still gave lectures. Lauren reached for the old man's hand, prepared to apologize if he took offence, but Teffler welcomed her touch. He squeezed her hand, nodded and the words of a difficult tale started to flow.

Throughout the history of humanity, healers have always been considered saviors; they were people who sought to protect life, or at the very least, ease the pain and suffering of their patients. The doctors of the Third Reich could only be called inhuman monsters.

Hitler's ultimate goal was to have the Aryan Race rule the world. The blond-haired, blue-eyed *ubermensch* would be the only race in the Nazi empire once all the undesirable imperfect factions—Blacks, Hispanics, Jews, Gypsies, and homosexuals— became exterminated.

From 1939 to 1944, the Perigord Chateau housed one of the more ambitious of Hitler's programs: *Die Goldenen Kinder*, literally meaning The Golden Children. The translators subsequently found two more references in the journal to such custom-made offspring of high-ranking SS officers and *pure* German women, many still teenagers. They called them *Kinder des Lichtes*, or the Children of the Light, and *Die Kinder des Adlers*, the Eagle's Children.

The journal entries started in January 1942, upon the arrival of the writer at Chateau Perigord, who appeared to be a lab technician and not a doctor; some entries contained criticism of his superiors and derogatory remarks about their *leuteschinder* or slave-driver work ethic. The author liked to eavesdrop on *fortschritt-sitzungen*, on progress meetings of his superiors. He found a trap door that allowed him to move through the crawl space between floors and he'd listen through the holes he'd made around the light fixtures in the ceiling and walls. He was after all a Nazi technician in a chateau that had been converted to Hitler's breeding-farm laboratories.

On six occasions, large truck convoys arrived at the chateau, presumably delivering medical supplies, but the writer learned otherwise. The trucks contained looted treasures, art, coinage and gold bullion that Hitler's henchmen stole from wealthy families all over Europe.

The technician, a part of a team under two doctors, Rolf Halsig and Claus Menner, had assisted them on a rather peculiar medical procedure performed on three of the children whose mothers had been removed from the chateau once they had carried out their supreme duty for the Reich and weaned their children. The three children, two girls and a boy, nearly identical in appearance—blond-haired, blue-eyed, and in every way perfect specimens of the Aryan Race—were *geschmückt* or decorated each with a single word of the phrase *Das Sibirische Orakel*. The phrase, according to the journal's author, was Hitler's brainchild. However, the next journal entry detailed what the technician once again overheard during his snooping expeditions. Hitler was superstitious, and had his officers periodically bring in fortunetellers to either confirm or refute what his personal astrologers must have forecast. An old gypsy, calling herself *The Siberian Oracle*, told him that he should hide his stolen treasure in the living icons that would walk ahead of him—heralds of his glory. If a soldier wished to draw a map showing his enemy's positions, he should sketch it on the back of the man marching ahead of him. That way it would always be in sight.

The technician assisted his bosses in etching maps made to look like skin imperfections, or large birthmarks, onto the backs of three eighteen month old toddlers. He concluded that the maps marked the three sites where Hitler had hidden his looted treasures and gold. Each child was also tattooed with a single word from the code-phrase, since, according to the technician, the gypsy who called herself *The Siberian Oracle* didn't live long after giving Hitler her deep-eyed advice.

At the time, twenty-seven Golden Children lived at the chateau. They ranged in age from infants to four year olds, cared for by nine caretakers, or *Adlerinas*. Each one had responsibility for three children about the same age. The technician decided to befriend Analise, the marked children's *Adlerina*.

Twenty-year-old Analise worried about her charges and her own fate. She wasn't recruited into the breeding program. However, young and pure German women grew scarce, and she felt she would soon be persuaded to join the ranks of mothers of the Golden Children. The technician promised to help her and the children escape.

Analise told him she had a much older sister working for an American banker who had visited Berlin in 1928. She was supposed to return home after five years, but remained in America. Her parents had died a long time ago, and Analise never told anyone that she had a sibling. The technician wrote down the sister's name, Wilhelmine von Bayern, and made notes on the margin to remind himself that the sister might have married, and therefore have a different name, not necessarily a German one, either.

The last journal entry, dated February 1944, read more like an exercise where the technician sketched out possibilities for getting

Analise and her three charges out of the chateau, perhaps to Switzerland, perhaps to Belgium. Since his journal surfaced in 1963, found by a team of clean-up crews hired by the estate lawyers representing the surviving members of the Augais-Perigord family, it's doubtful that he ever left the chateau, since he would not have left it without a journal that contained incriminating evidence of Hitler's breeding program and his looting."

Teffler stopped talking as if he'd been reading from a teleprompter and the text had finished.

"Two days ago in New York, I saw Alice Blumenthal," Lauren said, glancing at Teffler to make sure he had finished the tale. When he blinked and nodded, she continued, "She said that the von Flemmings from Melechen took in her late husband, Martin as a child and also gave a brief refuge to a young woman. In the spring of 1944, Analise von Bayern took care of three toddlers, two girls and a boy. "

"How is Alice?" Teffler straightened so suddenly it startled her. John, too, leaned back to give the old man more space on the bench.

"How is Alice?" he repeated, staring at her with almost the same hostility he showed after she first spoke to him in the lecture hall.

"I don't know," she whispered, clasping her hands and feeling pain in the joints. "I left her in the museum lobby, waiting for me. There were people around, guards.... I went to get the car from the underground garage. I pulled up and waited, but she never came outside. Mind you, the guard said Alice must have felt ill and took a cab...or shared it with a colleague."

"Did Hagip send you to see her?" Teffler's tone didn't soften.

"Hagip left me a phone message. Yours and Alice's names and other names figured into it. I never spoke with him again after I left him on Saturday."

"Did you ever think, Miss Sarasohn, that perhaps you should have surrendered that bag to the police and let the authorities deal with it?"

"Yes," she said quietly. "I spoke with Lieutenant Terney several times and he kept asking me over an over whether I found something missing from my office...and did I know the murder victim...."

He said, "So why didn't you take it to the police?"

"Once I finally got through to the real Lieutenant Terney, who had not participated in any of those calls from the police, I realized that if I surrendered the bag, I'd be dead within twenty-four hours. At the time, I spoke with the impostor, only Mitch and I—he's my colleague; we share an office— knew what was inside the bag. We went to see Hagip and showed him the articles in the bag. But the next day, Mitch and Jenny, his girlfriend, disappeared, and though I'm once again being offered plausible explanations for Mitch's continued silence, I don't believe he's safe...or still alive..." She couldn't finish. A hard knot lodged in her throat, and tears flooded her eyes.

"That would make sense," Teffler said, his hostility fading. "Telling old folktales and stories about treasures is one thing. But actually having a piece of evidence in your possession...yes, that would make sense. They don't want anyone to see what's inside that bag, much less have it in someone's possession. And you're probably right, as harsh as it may sound, your colleague Mitch is dead just like Hagip. He shouldn't have sent me that picture. It's what killed him. You're only alive because they're not sure where you're hiding the articles."

"The articles are hanging around my neck," John spoke up.

Teffler chuckled dryly. "I hope you've put your financial affairs in order and made a will. Do you know who you're dealing with here?"

"I can guess. The party who obviously found the location that's etched on those maps—maps of sites where Hitler hid his looted gold and art treasures," John said. She leaned across Teffler's lap to stare at him.

"I did a bit more research than I told you." John nodded at her. "Glathos Pidimentaros was the photographer I replaced upon joining the Greenpeace."

"I don't remember hearing the name. Hagip never mentioned him. Besides, we ran without a photographer for years before you joined," she said.

"Glathos brought Hagip into the fold, so to speak, back in '92. You didn't join until '95," he said.

"I knew Glathos Pidimentaros," Teffler said. "Or at least I met him on a few occasions through Hagip. He struck me as a brash young man, and if you believed any of his usually inflated tales of his youthful exploits, he was a pearl diver, a tour guide, a diving instructor, and I think at some point he claimed to be a mermaid hunter. His less fanciful employment, however, was to take scenic shots and make them into naval postcards or seaside prints. And whenever an occasion presented itself, he turned into a celebrity hunter—a paparazzi. He specialized in taking shots of the boat-crowd celebrities. He didn't settle just for stalking ports and annoying harbor authorities. *Enterprise* might as well have been his middle name. On several occasions he hired a motorboat to take him crack-close to a yacht anchored way out of the traffic and he'd snap the rich and beautiful, sunbathing or enjoying lunch, or even having sex.

"In '94, while pursuing a Greenpeace cause on assignment to document harbor pollution around Preveza, he snapped a few quick pictures of a French-flag yacht, *Hipollyte Vivant*. Hagip sent Glathos to see me at the Smithsonian. He couldn't come due to some rally commitment or something. Glathos had already washed the pictures through the computer, using what graphics packages existed in those times. He enlarged it and toned down the background, but even without such brushing you clearly saw the two men standing on deck, admiring a painting displayed on an easel. Glathos had identified both men and said Hagip wanted me to confirm his suspicions about the painting. One of the men in the picture was a Middle Eastern oil sheik, well known for his art collecting passion. The other man was William Clement Palfrey, our own homegrown billionaire. The painting by Murillo, was lost during World War II. Its last owner, a French

Jewish aristocrat, Marcel Amarens, Comte du Roschilde, and his entire family, save the youngest sister, died in Auschwitz.

"The sister, Celine Bolieux, escaped the Nazis by posing as a nun amongst one of the Ursuline cloisters. Subsequently, she made it to New York. When the Roberts Commission, a unit established to investigate Hitler's art looting all over Europe, made available to the French Government all information they had on German art looting in France, the list of stolen assets included *La Florista Durmiente*, the Murillo once owned by the Amarens family. Celine Bolieux smuggled much of her family's official documents, certificates of ownership, and banking information. You may ask what's an American billionaire doing, selling a Nazi-stolen-but-never-recovered Murillo painting to an oil sheik in 1994?"

"A painting that might have rested for years right next to the gold bar with Hitler's personal crest that is now digging into my ribs," John said.

Teffler nodded, momentarily closing his eyes.

"Hagip's phone message said that Glathos died of a bee sting," Lauren murmured.

Eyes still closed, Teffler replied, "Yes, three days after he came to see me. How's that for coincidence? And I apologize, Ms. Sarasohn, for my earlier rudeness. Ten years ago I just wanted to enjoy my retirement,and spend time with my ailing wife. I lied. I told Hagip that it wasn't a Murillo. I said he made a mistake since Murillo seldom if ever dated his paintings. A Murillo is dated by his changes in style. I said the style came very close to Murillo and that it was a great forgery. Hagip never questioned my professional opinion. I don't think he quite accepted it, especially after Glathos died, but he never once questioned my decision. I betrayed him, betrayed my own heritage, my professional integrity, and for what? Ten years in Vermont, grieving my wife, lecturing through e-mails and taking long nature walks." He opened his eyes and wiped them with his coat sleeve.

"There wasn't anything you could have done, Dr. Teffler." Lauren leaned closer but didn't dare try to comfort him.

He abruptly raised his voice. "I had not just the authority but directorial power—I *was* the authority in the Smithsonian. I routinely attended receptions in the White House. I had friends in congress who owed me a ton of favors. Hell, I should have called for an inquiry before a congressional panel...." His breath ran out and he started to cough. He pushed her hand away when she tried to help. "Glathos left me his negatives. I had evidence that would have been more than enough to raise serious doubts about William Palfrey's source of wealth."

"What do you mean source of wealth?" John moved closer to Teffler, making a calming motion with his hand. "I'm not following you. You had a chance to point a finger at Palfrey owning a stolen masterpiece that would have forced him to disclose how he acquired it—"

Teffler silenced him with a raised hand. "Who are you, other than Miss Sarasohn's friend or associate?"

"I'm an old friend, but I'm not her associate. I'm an editor with the Washington Times. She came to me for help. I've been doing research on the names she asked me to cross-reference."

"Someone ought to make a bid for the Times and buy it from Reverend Moon," Teffler murmured. "If you think that the Times is the newspaper that would run a damaging story about William Palfrey, you must be sleeping in your office, not running the headlines."

"That's not why I'm involved in this, Dr. Teffler," he said. "But what did you mean about Palfrey's source of wealth?"

"You've been researching for Miss Sarasohn. Well, research some more. Go back to about 1962 and trace the meteoric rise of Billy Palfrey, the kid from Pittsburgh who never finished high school and whose fifth-grade teacher, Sister Rosalie, used to call him 'the little hoodlum.' Twenty-seven-year-old Billy Palfrey cleaned meat-grinding machines in his father's butcher shop and that's after being fired from a job at a leather factory for his laziness. One day, like a miracle, he hears the higher calling and works his way as a deck hand on a freighter to southern France.

He heads for a small border town called Tarnos, where the voice of his personal fortuneteller advises him to tour the vineyards and learn the art of fine wine making—which he does in a scant two years. A year later, he's made his first million, and after that, it's just like an avalanche in the Alps, it all just keeps coming and coming." Teffler rose, smoothed his coat, and looked around.

"I'm staying at the Washington Suites in Georgetown. That's just for reference. I don't think you should come to see me again, or seek contact. I'm an old man. For ten years, I lived with not just my eyes but also my heart padlocked. I lied when I should have stood up and marched for a worthy cause. I used to berate Hagip for wasting his talent and his education, shouting into deaf ears, and marching for an unattainable cause. At least he stood up for what he believed in." And without looking at them or even saying good-bye, Teffler picked up his briefcase, turned, and walked down the pathway toward the street. He hailed a cab, got in, and the cab drove away.

Lauren shivered, once again reminded that someone just walked over her future grave. Except she felt that this time she'd shivered on someone else's behalf.

Chapter 25

"I F YOU'RE STAYING at Carmella Perez's little cottage in Idylwood, it might be a good idea for me to put it in the paper in bold letters—a public announcement," John said after Teffler's taxi disappeared down the street. "Let the world know where you are so you'll wake up in the morning, alive."

"She took me out in public last night," she said. "I think I'm safe; at least for the time being."

"She took you out for one and only one purpose—to let William Palfrey size you up. I saw her dragging you along for an introduction. I understand now why you sent me that crate of wine; that was pretty clever too. Did you carry this," he pressed his hand against his chest and moaned, "on you all the time ever since you and Mitch found it?"

"I have gouges on my shoulders from where the leather strap of my purse dug in."

"I'm going to look as if someone tried to strangle me with a wire." He rubbed his neck. "What now, Lauren? Teffler didn't just tell us the story of the Oracle. He confessed, unburdened himself of what must have been preying on his conscience all these years. He's the only one in a position to point a finger at Palfrey—whether ten years ago or now. Since he didn't do it, he must have known all along that he'd not live to testify in front of any congressional committee. So, I'm afraid we're in no man's land. The way the story stands today, I can't think of a newspaper that would dare to suggest that the roots of Palfrey's wealth are not the stuff of the good old American dream. He's not just the father of a congressman; he's our leader's most generous campaign contributor. I'm afraid we need more than just an editor who's willing to stick his neck into a noose."

"Those two patches of human skin in the bag most likely came from two of the golden children, Anike and Piet." Lauren paused, thinking. Finally, she said, "Analise obviously made it to America with her three little charges and joined her sister, Wilhelmine von Bayern, who probably married so she wouldn't be von Bayern. We still have the third name, Gertrude Johansen, and a place, Cragg's Lake."

He shook his head and moaned.

"What?" she asked.

"Your instincts have always served you well," he said. "That's something else I remember. You suggested that we go some place indoors or stay in the lecture hall. You should have insisted. Teffler probably felt claustrophobic just remembering the story, since he lived with guilt for ten years...but it's too late to worry about it. We're being watched. These days, they cannot just read your lips, but your thoughts...or it seems like that sometimes."

"Are you saying that by insisting we go outside Teffler may have signed his death warrant?" she asked, looking around.

"He may have signed ours, Lauren. That's what worries me. Teffler seemed resigned to whatever fate would find him. It's October, and although we're having a cold spell all over the Eastern Seaboard, I don't think there'd be black ice yet on Interstate 87 around Plattsburg. And why would the Plattsburg Police deem it necessary to track down the person whose name figured on a piece of paper in Hagip's pocket? Once the police would have ascertained it wasn't direct family, they'd have left all notification of friends and associates to the victim's kin. Palfrey has snitches in what sounds like any police department he damn well chooses. If he needs something, he just flicks his finger, and activates it to do his bidding."

"I'm going back to Carmella's, and in the morning, I'm driving home," she said. "Walk me back to my car. You can leave the bag with me. You shouldn't be a part of this. I sent you that crate because..." After a moment, she shook her head. "It doesn't matter. I shouldn't have done it."

"You sent it to me to punish me because you finally had the means of revenge. I knew it the moment I read your note," he said, not sounding bitter or even accusing, just flat.

"Maybe, but now that I think about it, I sent it to you because I considered you my last resort. I couldn't come back to Carmella's with it. She worked hard to get me out of the house last night so her associates would be free to go through my belongings without worrying about interruptions. I didn't know she'd use an embassy reception to get me out of there, but I knew that if I came back with the bag still inside my purse, I'd probably be found in a day or two, back in my house, in my bed with maybe a bottle of sleeping pills by my bedside."

"I never lied to you, you know," he said, rising and pulling her along.

"You probably did, but I can't think of a specific example so I won't argue with you."

"I'm not asking you to trust me. I'm just asking you to spend the night at my place."

"Carmella would never...."

"Carmella Perez has three failed marriages behind her, two of which ended in divorce because she slept around with anyone who'd further her political and corporate ambitions. She'll understand a weakness that would see you back in bed with the man who betrayed you. Believe me, I know."

Chapter 26

THE HISTORIC THREE-STORY Carriage House brownstone in the Lincoln Park area had to cost more than she'd earn in this lifetime. Ten years ago, if you didn't have at least half a million in disposable income, the real estate agents wouldn't bother showing you houses in this neighborhood. Today, they'd probably even ask a millionaire for a financial statement before they gave him a tour of any property between Florida and Maryland Avenues.

She wondered just how much John earned in his position of a senior editor with the Times.

The house didn't have a garage but the laneway was wide enough to let two cars pass. He drove his Land Rover to the end of the laneway, got out, and waved to her to pull in, motioning to park beside his SUV.

"The bottom floor's my workspace, office, laundry, storage and washroom," he said, walking in through the side door. "The kitchen is the next level up. You'll find the dishes in the cupboards, glasses above the center-island, and drinks in the fridge. I'll just check my messages and will join you in a jiffy."

They had returned to the Gypsy Rose but ordered a take-out of: soups, pasta, seafood salads, garlic bread, and Italian puff-pastry for dessert.

"I'm sure that even without your crate of wine, I have enough beverages at home," he said.

She opened the Sub-Zero fridge, and stared for a moment, confused by what looked like a caterers' convention. *Either he's expecting a nuclear holocaust soon or he's invited his entire staff over for dinner—for the next couple of weeks.*

The last time she saw a granite countertop it gleamed expensively in Aileen Summerville's kitchen in Georgetown. But even the Maine Senator didn't have a marble-trimmed gas fireplace—in the eat-in portion of the kitchen. She put the three take-out bags on the center-island, cringing at the clink, and hoped it wasn't something breakable in the bag, and took a quick look around the floor. The dining room had a thick oriental rug over its gleaming hardwood floor. Another marble-trimmed fireplace stood in the living room. The requisite crystal chandelier, offset to one side of the skylight that in daylight would let the sun shine down on the spiral staircase with wrought iron railing, looked imposing. The walls that must have once defined the rooms had been mostly removed or reduced to half-walls. What wall space remained had either an alabaster tulip fixtures or paintings and lithographs.

"No diplomas, no awards, no citations, no framed photographs with the Times brass," she murmured, returning to the kitchen. Just good taste and the finest that money can buy—but no pride, no showcasing of accomplishments that define milestones in a man's work and life.

"Nice place," she commented, sitting down at the round kitchen table with a beveled glass top. He opened a bottle of Cavalier Blanc and poured for both of them.

"Diane chose it," he said indifferently. "And immediately she hired an architect and a wrecking crew and gutted it. What you see here is a result of excellent renovation. The expensive kind," he glanced at her and smirked. "I bought out her share as part of our divorce settlement. We parted...amicably."

"Really?" She loaded her plate with pasta and seafood salad and put a slice of still-warm garlic bread beside it.

"It just happened one day. I was having an affair, and she was between affairs, so we decided to part company. That way we'd be able to concentrate on making better choices—for our affair partners."

"A very civilized approach to ending a marriage," she remarked dryly.

"For two years our marriage worked. But slowly, we both became unhappy and let our unhappiness grow, preferring to mask it with affairs."

"Did you assign numbers to your affairs?" she asked, prodding the pasta with a fork.

"What you mean is that you want to find out where you stood in the lineup of my affairs?"

"Number one," she said, shrugging.

He chuckled. "There's nothing wrong with your self-esteem."

"There's nothing wrong with my math or my memory. Eight years ago, you told me that you just separated from your wife of two years. Except you meant it metaphorically, and I took it literally."

"I lied to you. So there's your example that you couldn't think of earlier. But that's the only thing I lied about. No one asked me whether I worked as a reporter with the Times. I'm a good cameraman and a great photographer. I always have been."

"If that's the case, where are your awards, prizes, and recognitions?" She motioned with her head at the living space beyond. "I walked around and although you certainly have very good taste in art, there's nothing on your walls that would honor or even recognize your excellence as a photographer or an accomplished editor."

He took a sip of wine, stared at some point in space above her head, and said, "I haven't been proud of what I'm doing for a very long time."

"The Times is a conservative newspaper that gives every bit of news a conservative slant," she said. "That's just the part of its missions and values. All businesses and corporations have those."

"Do you believe in your thesis?"

"I believe in the responsible treatment of our environment," she said, stirring the pasta around the plate.

"That's not what I asked, Lauren. Do you believe in your thesis? What you're doing?"

She put the fork down and lowered her hands into her lap. "No...yes...it's something else," she said quietly. "I still believe my processes are viable and that the resource recovery facility is a good thing to have anywhere, not just in Connecticut, but I don't believe...in myself anymore. I don't have anything to contribute."

"Wouldn't it be great to be a part of a team of environmental advocates who are even more ardent about the cause than you used to be?"

"What?" She raised her head, staring at him with suspicion.

He laughed and flipped a calamari ring in the air with his fork. "You had a friend at Duke, your roommate, Denise something-or-other. You felt she sold out to the corporate interests by accepting a job down in Texas as a corporate environmental consultant. You became so incensed every time you talked about her. Ten years later, Denise is probably pulling in a quarter-million salary, and you're still hiding under the bleachers, holding your knapsack with your brilliant project inside and fear showing it to anyone. Not because you don't believe in it, but because you don't believe in yourself. That's what being alone for five years, hiding in some backwoods Connecticut college will do to your self-esteem. Your mother's death was a tragedy, but you didn't even want to share your grief with anyone. You just mothballed yourself in Winthrop out of the life's stream. Why didn't you answer my phone calls, letters? I even sent a letter to the law firm handling your mother's bankruptcy. They phoned and told me you wouldn't accept the letter."

"I didn't have just my grief to deal with, but the backlash of your articles and all the bankruptcy fallout issues." She ran her hand through her hair. It was better than what she wanted to do—hit him squarely on his chin.

"Hagip never reproached you for anything, and Isabel wanted to put a stick of dynamite in my car on your behalf far more than punish me for my articles. Once all the dust settled after the inquiries and indictments, you came out of it an innocent victim. I even got the editor to include an apology to you in my last installment of the series," he finished.

"I didn't want an apology, John. I wanted the truth. I would have been able to handle it, you know—the truth about who you were, why you joined us, and that you were still *married*."

"Our marriage looked like campfire ashes by the time I joined you in Corpus Christi. I came back to Washington, and we both knew it was over. We only stayed together another year to sort out the financial details and to finish the renovations on this house since initially we both planned to put it up for sale and divide the proceeds. I thought I still had a shot at getting a decent job with another newspaper, not just the Post, but maybe in New York or even back in Charleston."

She put down her fork and leaned back in her chair. "I should have just driven home tonight and picked my stuff at Carmella's."

"Come on, Lauren, you knew the past would come back; whether bits and pieces or all of it, you knew we'd have this kind of conversation. Actually, it's long overdue. You're here because you have a chance to do something that will make a difference. You already had so many chances in life to make a difference, but you turned your back on all of them. You went to hide in Winthrop and chose to be a footstool for that idiot, Errington, who most likely set you up."

She looked up, alarmed. "How would you know that?"

He laughed. "You're forgetting that I started my career as an investigative journalist and I retained my analytical skills. A Cuban bellhop sees an opportunity and steals something he thinks is going to get him at least fifty to a hundred grand on the street. But something panics him and he heads for Winthrop College— a very strange choice to make, I'd say. Early in the morning, your boss goes to look for you in your office, knowing damn well you won't be in yet—on a Saturday, I might add—and finds the body. I'm surprised the Hartford police didn't pull him in for questioning or didn't charge him outright. I read the papers, you know." He grinned at her.

"Congressman Palfrey represents our district, and our college president, Burke, is lobbying him to channel some of the money from the federal education grants to Winthrop. Errington's on the committee too."

"It's true what they say, you know," he said, flipping another calamari ring onto the fork. "Everybody has a price. You just have to find what it is or how much."

"Do you, John?" she asked

"Probably." He grimaced. "But I doubt anyone will ever offer me happiness."

She took a sip of wine, arched her brows at him to show appreciation and started to eat her pasta. Long ago, in another lifetime, once the annual Lobster Festival left only a buttery taste in her mouth, mother and Pete would spend a couple of weeks closing down the marina. They had to make sure all the boats, Mother's rentals and those the owners kept at the marina year round and paid for storage, were safely berthed and covered for winter.

Afterward, Mother would send Pete and one of the part-timers upstate to buy berries by the bushel and spend the next few weeks making homemade jams and preserves. Lindstrom's Delicatessen in Rockland would put them up for sale and charge a modest agent's fee. Mother would volunteer three or four days a week at the food bank or deliver meals to old folks, but come Christmastime, she would always take two weeks off, and all three of them would go to visit Pete's uncle and aunt at Sebago Lake. She suspected Mother adopted this regimen to lessen the stigma of her being one of the few students who didn't celebrate Christmas. And since Mother no longer spoke to God, they didn't celebrate Chanukah either.

Pete's kinfolk had raised him ever since his parents had died. They were a nice old couple that never asked them why they had chosen to join relative strangers at Christmas or how come they didn't come with them for midnight mass on Christmas Eve. Once the high Christian holidays passed, the three of them would set out for their "quiet adventure." That's what her mother called their ice fishing on Sebago Lake. With Mount Washington overlooking the lake from its majestic vista, and the cold still-ness of the frozen lake, they didn't feel the pressure to talk other than an occasional pointer or warning about this or that pressure ridge that might be an area of weak ice. Mighty Sebago Lake could be very deceptive according to Pete. It didn't like showing its weaknesses—or its strengths. He said the lake liked to fool those who ventured out in wintertime to do ice fishing and pre-sent its weak spots for strong and vice versa. But it couldn't fool Pete.

He'd make sure the spot they had chosen for the day was a true strong spot and only when he made sure he'd put down the set of ice picks he carried on the lanyard around his neck. They wore survival suits because Pete refused to be lulled into security by the lake. Sometimes they would pitch an icehouse but more often they would just sit on the wood stools, their lines vertical in the drilled hole, and breathe in the incredibly crystal-fresh air, waiting for fish to nibble the bait. That's where she spun her dreams, staring at the majestic snow-frilled mountain in the dis-tance that made such an excellent point for environmental safety and preservation.

In Iceland, Lauren took John ice fishing at the Reynisvatn Lake, a small lake just outside Reykjavik. She'd brought Isabel's portable propane stove, and they pan-fried trout sprinkled with what he said were almonds. She stuck a hand in his parka pocket and groaned, seeing she'd brought out a handful of cornflakes.

Afterward, driving back in a Jeep that a local Greenpeace member loaned them, he said that if he ever got around to writing his biography, she should remind him to include the adventure and mark the day: Happiness Day.

"In college," he told her, laughing. "My roommate told me that meditation would show me a route to happiness. Wish I'd have known about ice fishing back then. It sure beats sitting with your eyes closed, trying to remain upright and not keel over." He chuckled harder. "The moment I closed my eyes, the rest of me wanted to go to sleep. Ice fishing gets you in touch with your spirituality...physically." He'd patted his stomach. "What a great lunch."

"It's just after nine o'clock," John said. The sound bounced around, coming back amplified. She jumped in her chair. His voice in her memories was a lot softer...kinder, friendlier.

"Sorry, didn't mean to startle you." He nodded at the kitchen wall clock. "If you're tired, there are three bedrooms upstairs. Pick any one you like. I usually sleep in the office downstairs, on the couch; most of the time I'm too tired to climb all the way to the third floor. There's a washroom on this floor and two more upstairs; once again, your choice. Anything in the closets that's clean and fits you is yours to wear."

"What are you going to do?" she asked.

"More research."

"I'm supposed to sleep while you're doing research?"

"You used to sleep on my shoulder while I changed a film in the camera," he deadpanned.

"Only when I had an empty stomach. I'm fed now. I'm good for a few hours."

Chapter 27

THE GEOGRAPHIC NAMES Information System didn't have a listing for Cragg's Lake or any other Cragg for that matter. Widening the search globally brought in a Cragg in Ireland as a town or city, but not a lake.

"Maybe it's not a lake," she said. "Maybe we're taking it literally and it's simply a name...of something."

"But what?" He leaned back into the ergonomic chair and stretched. They had been searching and cross-referencing databases for hours with no luck.

"I've known Hagip to be thorough, detail-oriented, and analytical. He left me the phone message with names in order in which he wanted me to follow; the so-called path of discovery, I'd say. Alice Blumenthal would have shown me the journal where I'd have read about the Oracle and what it referred to. Simon Teffler's name figured next, and Teffler provided additional details about the golden children, Anike, Gertrude, and Piet. We can safely assume that their caretaker, Analise, is Adlerina and since in Hagip's message Cragg's Lake followed

Alderina it has to be...." She stopped, unable to offer even a wild guess.

"How about a place where this Adlerina/Analise can be found?" he offered.

She stared at him with admiration.

"Is my worth rising?" He pursed his mouth, his eyes narrowing. "You're definitely looking at me more charitably than you did at that embassy reception. Did I really look that shopworn?"

"It must be three o'clock in the morning. Don't you have to go to work? I'm going to bed." She rose, pushed back her chair, and walked around him. She hadn't expected him to move that quickly.

"I'm the editor. No one expects me to be in before lunch." He blocked her way to the stairs. "Lori..." His hands around her felt the same way she remembered. Back then he used to do it for warmth or to get her out of harm's way whenever the crowd around them surged. However, regardless why he did it, she'd always reward him with a kiss.

This time he kissed her. She didn't resist. He leaned back, staring at her with slitted eyes. "You never used to yield this readily. Are you worried that your last resort will quit on you if you don't?" He caught his lower lip with his teeth.

He was just the right height for her to put her head on his shoulder. She maintained it was his greatest asset. It used to make him laugh. Maybe time had come to find another reason to make him laugh.

"You know I'm a terrible liar and I wouldn't want to have to lie to Carmella about my purpose for choosing to spend the night with you."

"Choosing...?"

"Yep," she said and raised herself on tiptoes to bring his head down where she wanted it.

Chapter 28

S HE DIDN'T EXPECT Carmella to be home at ten o'clock in the morning. After all, she made such an issue of being fiend-ishly busy, skipping from one board meeting to another. Once again Carmella opened the door for Lauren and smiled. This time, however she didn't rush to embrace her.

"Don't tell me. I don't need to know where you spent the night, but it must have been a great lunch," Carmella said.

"We had a lot to talk about. You were right. He had much to apol-ogize for," Lauren said, walking inside. "You're not working today?"

"I'm always working," Carmella put a hand around her shoul-ders, "but I'm between meetings and forgot a portfolio at home. Kingsley's having the car serviced at the dealership, and Juanita doesn't drive. So I had to cab home and am very glad you made it before I left again. How well did you know this Alice Blumen-thal?"

Lauren stopped abruptly and turned to face Carmella. "New York was the first time I met the lady. But she was very sweet and very sorry she couldn't be of any help."

"Well, I have news that will explain why she didn't wait for you to pick her up. She must have felt unwell and took a cab home. She called her son to come over. That's why you didn't find him at his gallery shop. He's the one who found her dead of a heart attack. Of course, he called 911, but by the time the police and paramedics made it to Brooklyn, they just transported her body to the hospital."

Lauren made a fist and pressed it against her thigh. The pain of her fingernails digging into her palm helped her stay calm and show only polite concern.

"I'm so sorry," she said, shaking her head to alleviate her tightening throat. "I just hope it wasn't my visit that stressed her...."

"Of course not, my dear. What a silly thing to say," Carmella hugged her, then stepped back. "She was an old woman and a heart attack—well, you know how there's nothing anyone can do about a heart attack. Healthy young people, like you, can even collapse in the middle of the street dead before they hit the ground."

"Yes, I suppose," she turned away so Carmella wouldn't see her face. Her hostess would never resort to threats. But Lauren knew that's precisely what the diplomatic reminder was about. Carmella made her point, elegantly as ever. She understood now why her mentor had waited for her at home between meetings. Carmella had one evening and a whole night to have the staff search her belongings and still found nothing.

"Oh, and your boss called...."

"Dr. Errington?" Lauren spun around. "How would he know where I am?"

"I think one of your colleagues, Linda something-or-other, suggested that you might be making rounds of your old contacts and gave him my name."

"He put me on health leave until the end of the month. Actually, he more or less barred me from the campus. What did he want?"

"He's worried about you, my dear. He wants to make sure his student and teacher is all right."

"Why didn't he go to the police if he worries about me?" Lauren smirked.

Carmella laughed. "My dear, I think Dr. Errington is pretty much fed up with all the police he had to suffer on his campus."

"Department," Lauren said.

"What?"

"Only the environmental department is his, not the whole campus, although I'm sure he'd like to hear what you've said. John's going to track down some of the Greenpeace members, you know, mutual associates we once had. He thinks Gomez might have overheard some information at the Carlyle and figured he'd try to check out its significance with the experts before he embarked upon blackmail." She had made it up on the spur of the moment.

"Blackmail?" Carmella shook her head, sighing. "What kind of information can a bellhop at Carlyle overhear, for heaven's sake?"

"Environmentally sensitive," Lauren wagged her finger at her hostess. "I'm surprised that it wouldn't occur to you; vaccines and viruses used to be your specialty. Carlyle guests are the movers and shakers of industry, banking, financing, and politics. What if Gomez overheard a business discussion about a pharmaceutical complex that's an umbrella for manufacturing chemical weapons? There are two in Connecticut, and if I remember correctly, one of them spent millions installing sophisticated catchments systems to contain dangerous chemicals seeping into the water. If someone had damaging information about a bona-fide enterprise used as something else, a chemical manufacture that calls for dangerous processes with deadly by-products discharged into the environment that would certainly be worth a lot of money to the blackmailer."

"But he'd have to check it out first with the experts." Carmella tapped her finger against her cheek. "And his sister lives in Hartford, so she might have suggested that he go to see someone at the college in the environmental department."

"Precisely," Lauren said, wondering how Carmella learned Gomez had a sister living in Hartford. Surely she didn't read the news with a magnifying glass, and if the newspapers would have printed that detail, it would have been only a by-the-way mention.

"So it probably has no connection to Greenpeace," Carmella said.

"I told John to keep that option open, but I'm now leaning more towards this information-blackmail theory. I just came to clean up and change clothes. I'm meeting John later this afternoon to see what he managed to find." She headed for the magnificent staircase.

"Have you thought about Bill Palfrey's offer?" Carmella's voice floated after her.

She turned around. "Very tempting," she said.

"But...?"

"I have at least another year to finish my doctorate."

"You can finish it here in Washington. It would certainly reduce the distance between you and Mr. McPhend."

"Dr. Errington will never let me go. He's been my thesis advisor for five years. He needs to show his student finished her doctorate under him."

"I'll talk to him. I'm sure he'll change his mind," Carmella said and waved good-bye.

"VERY CLEVER," JOHN said after she told him about her inspiration that suggested Gomez had a reason to come and see the environmental experts.

"I don't think Carmella bought it, but at least I gave her a plausible explanation why I had to see you again."

"You mean she didn't wink at you," said John, "and say she didn't want to hear any explanation?"

"She did all of that...except maybe wink. Why didn't you want me to come upstairs? Afraid your staff might start rumors?" She told the security guard at the reception desk that she wanted to see Mr. McPhend. He'd picked up a phone, and when he put it down, he'd said that her party would come down to see her.

"We're leaving, and I didn't want to waste time," John said, guiding her to the door.

"Where are we going?"

"Cragg's Lake."

"I thought there wasn't any such place, lake, or town."

"It's not a lake or town."

"What is it, for God's sake?"

He answered once they sat in his Land Rover. "I had a brain storm too. Last night, we agreed that Cragg's Lake might be a place where you'd find this Analise/Adlerina. Well, if this Analise were a twenty-year old girl back in 1941, she'd be eighty-four years old today; that's if she's still alive. And where would you look for an eighty-four-year-old lady?"

"A retirement village" She stared at him, smiling.

"Well, I must have searched every retirement village and complex between two oceans that frame our country and didn't come up with even a related term or feature called Cragg's Lake."

"So, where?"

"I did cemeteries too, you know," he said, staring at her, mouth pursed in a speculative pucker.

"She's dead?"

"If she is, she can't be buried at any cemetery that features Cragg's Lake in its name."

"Tell me now or I'll never sleep with you again."

"You said that last night...or actually this morning because I wouldn't let you take the green canvas bag and it's still here with me." He motioned with his head at the back seat.

"Where or what is Cragg's Lake?"

"So young, so impatient...."

She swatted him with the rolled up newspaper he'd brought along.

"Come on, Lauren, think! Where would you go to visit an eighty-four-year-old lady?"

"In a nursing home?"

"Close, very close. What kind of nursing home would you use if you wanted to hide an eighty-four-year-old relative—and could afford it?"

"A private nursing home? A sanatorium?"

"Well done. That's what Cragg's Lake is: a very private, very discreet and very unknown private sanatorium in upstate New York."

"How far upstate?"

"Not too far from Lake Placid. I suspect that a lot of wealthy people have family members they want to hide or at least make invisible but they want to be able to visit them out of decency, too, I suppose. Cragg's Lake's proximity to Lake Placid is ideal for that purpose. The relatives can take a vacation in a well-known vacation spot and discreetly slip away to visit an infirm relative so they can live the rest of the year with warm and happy conscience."

"So what you're saying is that it's a place where you hide Uncle Phil, the one who left you his millions, but who can be quite an embarrassing feature at the dinner table if he's mentally and physically infirm or has Alzheimer's."

THE EIGHT-HOUR DRIVE saw them passing the sign announcing Lake Placid city limits just after ten o'clock at night. Ten minutes later, John pulled underneath the canopy in front of the Holiday Inn's entrance. He took out his wallet and handed Lauren his gold VISA card.

"Go check us in. We're a couple with the same last name. Say your partner is parking the car and will bring in the luggage, what little we've brought."

"I can afford a room, you know," she said, ignoring the credit card.

"If I didn't know, I would have asked. Come on, Lauren, don't you remember the drill? One couple checks in and lets the other three couples in through the back door. We've shared lot of those adventures in eighteen months."

"That's because between all of us, we'd only come up with enough money for a single room."

"Would you like me to buy the hotel for you? I'm sure that gold bar in the back seat would make a decent down payment?"

She snatched the credit card from his hand and got out.

Chapter 29

CRAGG'S LAKE SANATORIUM was not a Lake Placid landmark but the Holiday Inn staff knew it existed and gave them directions—about ten miles north on a local road, Randal's Route, and another mile along a private road, at the Cragg's Lake sign cutoff.

Last night, after they collected their passkeys, they ate a late dinner at the hotel's restaurant.

"You realize that we're facing two huge problems, John," Lauren said, picking through her salad.

"Of course." He nodded, sprinkling Parmesan over his pasta dish. "How to get in the place and how to find a resident named Analise who might not be registered under that name. Don't worry. The Force will be with us."

"I only wish you were a Jedi Knight. I wouldn't have to worry about anything. I'd feel safe no matter what."

"I see you're not a true Star Wars fan," he remarked and twirled his fork in the pasta. "Almost all the bad guys used to be Jedi Knights."

"Seriously, John, how are we going to get inside that place and how do we find Analise?"

"Eat." He motioned at her barely touched food. "You'll need your energy."

"For what?"

He raised his brows at her and grinned.

The next morning, he threw down the *key* to gaining them entry into the Cragg's Lake Sanatorium. She stared at him, wondering if he lost his mind.

"What's that?" She pointed at the bed where he threw down his *key*.

"It's a wig; can't you tell?"

"I can see it's a wig. What's it for?"

"To transform you into a Nordic beauty, or at least a girl from South Dakota where I hear there are a lot of cute blondes."

"Why do I have to wear a blonde wig? No one's going to know us. What's the difference?"

"Yesterday, after I met with such huge success, I made two calls: one to my good friend, Leslie, the senior partner in a very respectable Washington law firm, and the other to the Cragg's Lake Sanatorium. We're not only expected, we have an appointment. We're legal representatives of a certain wealthy Maryland family that's looking for a suitable place for their elderly family member. We're coming to check the place out."

"Fine. I understand, and that was very clever, but why do I have to wear a blonde wig?"

He grinned at her. "I always thought you'd look good as a blonde but never dared to suggest you color your beautiful, black hair. A few gray strands give you that distinguished look of a seasoned academic."

"You're just indulging a whim, a male fantasy, is that it?"

"Guilty."

She didn't argue anymore but she didn't remember him having fetishes or fantasies. However, they spent only eighteen months together. It probably wasn't long enough for her to have learned about such appetites.

Later, once they turned onto the private road, she noticed cameras and floodlights mounted on trees lining the road. The technology anchored to the trees in an otherwise beautiful un-spoiled green forest with faint sprinkle of early snow on the pines looked odd—and disconcerting. The iron gate between the two large concrete posts was definitely another security feature.

"A castle surrounded by a stone wall. We might get in but will they let us out?" he remarked after they drove up to the gate. She saw the stone wall stretch on either side until it disappeared into the woods.

The building looked more like a colonial mansion with tall pillars upfront and green wooden shutters pinned back on either side of the windows. In the summertime, the expanse of grass surrounding the place would be manicured. The large mound off to one side with a clump of pine trees providing shade looked a perfect place for staff to take their patients.

"It certainly is a good place to hide someone if you want them out of the mainstream," she said and motioned for him to get out and announce them at the gatehouse.

Dr. Belzer, who greeted them, had pleasant blue eyes greatly magnified by his glasses.

"How do you do? I'm so pleased to meet you, Mr. McPhend, Miss Sarasohn." He shook their hands. Lauren wondered why John would make an appointment under their real names since he insisted she wear the silly blonde wig. Was it really just his fetish, his fantasy...?

They spent half an hour with Dr. Belzer, the chief administra-tor of the facility and he handed them over to a young woman wearing a short white lab coat over her neat light gray suit.

Lauren glanced at the woman's nametag. "You must be Ar-menian," she said, pointing at the name: RN. Nella Cherkidjian.

Ten minutes later, John nudged her elbow and whispered, "Good work."

Hagip impressed upon Lauren that all Armenians knew each other, no matter what the country, no matter what the planet.

"If you meet an Armenian, just mention my name," he used to tell her, "and you'll find out what I'm talking about."

She couldn't bring herself to mention Hagip's name and used the name of his cousin, Vahe Amadjian, instead. She'd met Vahe on a couple of occasions when still with Greenpeace. He lived in Montreal with his wife and two children and owned a restaurant. Isabel used to work at his restaurant in the summer as a high school student.

Nurse Cherkidjian knew Vahe, and Lauren felt instant kinship transferred through this seemingly slim link.

The sanatorium had thirty residents. Nella smiled and corrected John after he called them patients. She said that while many of the residents required constant care and a few might be bedridden or in wheelchairs, the majority were simply a little bit worn down by old age but their health was quite robust.

They gave Nurse Cherkidjian an impression that their client's relative was old but in fairly good health. The second story of the sanatorium had apartments for the staff who didn't commute from Lake Placid, and the first floor was reserved for the residents. An addition in the back provided a medical wing with treatment rooms, a therapy whirlpool, a small exercise room, and lounges for residents able to move, whether by the help of a walker or a wheelchair. It's where they gathered to play card games, watched TV, or read and make crafts. Everything was double-width to accommodate wheelchair access, and doors had push-plates for automatic opening. Soft elevator music floated down from the ceiling wherever the nurse took them. Occasionally, a particularly wistful melody made Lauren tighten her mouth. The whole place looked like an expensive spa or a country club. The care was probably better than what the residents would have been given at home. What about the ninety-nine percent of the old folks who couldn't afford such excellent care or any care at all?

"Would it be possible to perhaps talk to some of the residents?" John asked their guide. "Of course, if that's stressful...."

"No, not at all. I'm sure whoever is in the lounge today won't mind chatting with visitors," the nurse assured him.

The lounge was furnished and decorated more like a luxury hotel than a common room in a nursing home. The floors were covered in a Berber-style wall-to-wall carpeting; the kind that would give the residents sure footing but also softness to minimize stress on fragile feet. The high-sitting couches were upholstered in light colored tapestry fabrics. Wooden arm rails with strips of non-slip fabric protruded from the sides to assist the resident in sitting or rising.

Lauren knew what John pursued. Two men playing cribbage suspended their game to chat with them and had nothing but praise for the nursing home.

"My only complaint is that Nellie here won't be my date for the Saturday night dance." One of the men winked at the nurse, who raised her hand and poignantly wiggled her engagement ring.

"Now, Mr. Snowie, you know I'd like nothing better than to take you up on that offer to teach me to dance the Charleston but my fiancé wouldn't like that," she said, also winking at the senior citizen.

Out of fifteen residents in the lounge only four were women. Lauren turned around, intending to approach them where they sat at a hobby table and suddenly heard a high-pitched voice.

"*Wo sind Sie, Trudie so lang gewesen? So, überkommen Sie, überkommen Sie darüber, so kann ich einen guten Blick auf Sie haben.*" The old lady sitting in the cornflower-blue chair motioned for her to come on over. The other three women wore glasses. Their white hair was permed and cut short in a style of her mother's generation. The old lady beckoning to her had braided hair. The effect gave an impression she wore a white crown.

Lauren approached and saw the woman's eyes almost matched the blazing-blue of the chair's tapestry fabric.

"That's Addie," the nurse touched Lauren's shoulder. "She speaks English well enough but if something triggers a memory, she reverts to her native German. Come." She motioned with her hand to precede her, speaking on approach. "This is Lauren, Addie. She came to see our place so she can tell her grandmother back home how nice it is here and maybe she will want to come too. Addie...?"

"Hello," Lauren started to lean over, reconsidered, and sat down on the edge of the couch across from the old lady and offered her a hand.

She flinched as the old lady grabbed, hungry for human touch.

"*Trudie, mein Kind, sind Sie so dünn. Essen Sie genug?*" She kept stroking Lauren's hand with her fingers, passing over the wrist and shaking her head, all the while making displeased sounds. Lauren glanced at the nurse who leaned forward and gently turned the old lady's face toward her.

"Addie, Trudie would like you to speak English. You speak English, don't you?"

"*Ach, ya*. I speak English all the time. *Ihre Hände sind so dünn.* So thin." She rubbed her fingers over Lauren's wrist. "You must eat, my child, eat. *Würste und Kartoffeln.* I taught you to cook sausages and potatoes. Did your boy, Greer, propose yet?"

"Soon," Lauren managed once again glancing at the nurse who nodded encouragingly.

"*Bald? Bald ist nicht gut genug.* Soon not good. You will be an old maid."

"I'll ask him tonight," Lauren said, smiling.

"*Bitten Sie einen Mann zu planen?* Trudie, a good proper girl does not ask a man to marry her. Greer should have asked you long time ago. He gave you a ring, ya?" The old lady's fingers skipped over her ring finger. "No ring. Trudie, Trudie, *das ist nicht gut, überhaupt nicht gut.* I thought you came to show me the ring." Her mouth pulled down at the corners with sorrow.

"No, no, I'm so forgetful. He gave me a ring, a beautiful ring but I rushed so much to get here that I forgot it at home," Lauren said hurriedly, carefully patting the old hand that in spite of its bony look, didn't feel fragile. Indeed, the old lady had to be in her eighties, even nineties. Her skin was heavily scored with wrinkles particularly around the mouth but her high-cheek bones gave her a patrician look of someone who had been a great beauty in her youth.

"Greer is a good boy." The old lady let go of her hand and sagged back into the chair with a sigh. "*Er hat ein sehr gutes Herz.* A very good heart. I know the first time I see him he is a very good doctor. *Herr Wyndham ist ein sehr guter Arzt.*"

"Addie," the nurse stroked the old lady's arm, "Trudie has to go. And it's time for your nap. I'll just see Trudie—" she looked around and found John hovering nearby, " and her friend out and I'll come back to take you to your room."

"Who is your friend?" Suddenly, the old lady grew agitated, pulling her pink-and-blue shawl closer to her chin, tucking it to protect herself.

"He's her chauffeur," the nurse hurriedly supplied to calm the old lady.

"I never learn to drive," the woman said and sighed.

Lauren said good-bye but the old lady didn't seem to be a part of the scene anymore. She kept fingering her shawl and making inarticulate sounds as if the conversation had moved inside to her head.

"Her health is remarkable," the nurse said, leading them outside. "But her mind isn't strong anymore"

"Who is she?" John asked.

"I'm afraid I can't divulge that information, Mr. McPhend. Such rules are for our residents' protection. I'm sure you understand."

He nodded, apologizing. The nurse saw them through the door. They had left the Land Rover parked close to the bottom of the stairs. Lauren climbed inside the car and turned her head slightly to see if the nurse still watched, but saw no one hovering behind the glass.

"I think we've met Analise von Bayern," John said as they began their trip back to Lake Placid.

"We've met an old lady whose mind is faltering far more than her eyesight. That's what you expected, or at least hoped for, and that's why I'm wearing a blond wig," she said, staring ahead.

"Oh, come on, Lauren, I played a hunch, that's all."

"You could have told me why you wanted me to wear the wig. You could have trusted me to understand your reasons."

"Would you have agreed to wear it had I told you?"

She moved her head from side to side, undecided, and knew he saw it.

"That's precisely why I didn't tell you, Lauren. You have ethics."

She snapped her head around to stare at him. "You've spent a better part of last night convincing me that you're not unethical."

"We needed to find out and we had one chance to do it, in case you haven't noticed."

"Well, now we know that Analise von Bayern is a resident in Cragg's Lake Sanatorium but that's it."

"No, Lauren. We know a hell of a lot more. We saw just how happy Analise was to see Trudie. She would have been equally happy to see Doctor Greer Wyndham."

"Wyndham?"

"Trudie is diminutive for Gertrude, and Doctor Greer Wyndham is dead. I did his obituary shortly before I joined with you at Greenpeace. He was my first serious investigative assignment."

"Well, if this Doctor Greer Wyndham is dead, we still have nothing."

"Oh, we have a hell of a lot because Gussie Wyndham, his wife, is very much alive and very vocal around midnight. That's the time her talk show airs on the East Coast. Look in your side-view mirror."

"Gussie Wyndham? The talk show host?" The name didn't sound familiar.

"Look in your side-view mirror. How far are they?"

"They? What am I looking for?"

"A dark Lincoln. It's been following us."

"Try to shake him."

He laughed. "What for? We haven't done anything wrong."

"What about that?" She jerked a thumb at the back seat where he once again put the canvas bag.

"Who would ever suspect we're traveling with a bar of Hitler's gold in the back seat?"

"And two patches of human skin," she said dryly. "Don't forget the rest of the bag's contents."

Chapter 30

J OHN DROPPED HER off next to her Grand Am in the parking lot of the Times building.

"Do you want me to follow you to Idylwood just to make sure someone won't try to run you off the road?" he asked.

"If Carmella had us followed to Lake Placid and had orders to get rid of me, then upstate New York would have been an ideal place to do it without anything threatening her in Washington. She can't afford for me to die in a traffic accident in Washington. It's not just her turf; it's where she's made her reputation. I'll be all right," she assured him. and he said he'd put in some time, doing research on Gussie Wyndham.

"Like Hamlet said: we'll be ready to stage the play." He winked at her and stole a kiss.

"Hamlet wanted to flush out his father's murderers." She grimaced. "Gussie Wyndham is a TV celebrity, not a criminal. If anything, she's a potential victim, like her two siblings, though technically speaking they weren't her brother and sister. We want Gussie Wyndham on our side. She's probably the only one who'd be able to point a finger at Palfrey and be taken seriously. John, that canvas bag...I'm not sure you should be the one to carry the burden, so to speak. I don't want to hear about you on the evening news dead of a heart attack in your office."

"I'm much too young to die of a heart attack." He laughed. "For me, they'd have to be more imaginative. Not to worry. I won't let the bag out of my sight and I'll live to give you a call to-night," he promised.

She drove off thinking that Carmella had obliquely warned her of young people dropping dead of a heart attack on the street, never mind discovering them dead in their offices. And if the victim was an editor, it would be chalked up to job-related stress.

She pulled into the driveway just as the big, dark Lincoln Continental pulled up behind her, its headlights in the rear view mirror almost blinding her.

"Hello, Kingsley," she nodded at the chauffeur as he got out of the car. She noticed the vehicle was super-clean and shiny. He probably took it through the car wash close-by before coming home. It had rained all the way from Lake Placid to Washington, and John's SUV was covered with snowy-slush.

"Hello, ma'am." He tipped two fingers to his forehead. He wore a dark hunting parka and a black toque. It gave him the disconcerting look of a mercenary. His black boots were just as shiny as the car. "Have you already had dinner or should I tell Juanita to prepare something for you?"

She wanted to say that she just came to get her things. His presence alone made her uncomfortable, but she had to stay at least until John confirmed that Gussie Wyndham was Gertrude Johansen and they managed to see the talk show hostess.

"I am rather hungry," she said, managing a tight smile.

He inclined his head, and without saying anything else, he headed for the house.

Carmella wasn't home. Juanita told her that her hostess had another reception and wouldn't be home until very late.

"Can I take my dinner upstairs to my room?" Lauren indicated the tray with the veal dish, salad, and a fruit cup

"Of course, ma'am." Juanita started to pick up the tray, but Lauren reacted faster.

"It's not necessary; really, it's not. I can carry it upstairs."

"As you wish, ma'am." The housekeeper nodded and returned to her duties, at the counter.

Just after nine o'clock, John called her cell phone.

"Good news," he said cheerfully. "We're going on another trip tomorrow to Greenwich—that's Connecticut."

"Actually, I'll be heading home to Connecticut tomorrow, so we'll take my car. You can come up, visit me afterward, and take a flight home. How's that?"

"You've been my guest so now you feel you have to return the hospitality?"

"I'd like you to meet my boss, Dr. Errington, to create the right impression that I'm not without friends—or connections."

"I'm going to be a trophy, is that it?"

"Safety-net, John, safety-net." She laughed. "What's in Greenwich, Connecticut?"

"Gussie Wyndham's Pallisades Estate. We have a formal and confirmed appointment. I understand it's a great honor since she grants very few in any given year."

"Make sure you bring along the bag."

"Ah yes, the albatross around my neck. I wouldn't dream of leaving home without it."

She felt much better after talking to him and took a shower. Afterward, she settled in bed to watch TV. An hour later, sleep still wouldn't come. She rose and started to pace around the room. After a while, even though the room was the size of her entire house, she felt confined, claustrophobic. She put on her jeans and sweatshirt and walked out in her socks. The long corridor had several doors, presumably other bedrooms. She didn't want to snoop, but take a little look around and admire a beautiful residence.

She knocked on the door, waited a while, and entered pre-pared to gush with apologies if necessary but the bedroom proved empty. Every which way she looked, she saw yellow. Not brash lemon-yellow but soothing hues of the yellow-and-cream color spectrum. Her feet sank into the plush broadloom. The wreath of daisies in the center had to be a custom design. She wondered whether Carmella had psycho-catalogued her guests and assigned them to a particular color room according to their personalities. Did she choose the *Green Room* for Lauren be-cause green stood for environment and optimism, or did it stand for money?

She shook her head, banishing the memory of meeting Wil-liam Palfrey at the French Embassy reception. Carmella would certainly put his job offer into the optimistic category. She al-most missed seeing a door that had been wallpapered over; only the brass handle gave it away. Once again, she knocked. No one answered. She turned the handle.

"Ah yes, the Blue Room." Lauren sighed. She had entered into a Ralph Lauren country-chic, thunder-blue decor. Carmella probably assigned this bedroom to her male houseguests, or would that be considered sexist stereotyping?

She toured what back in Rocky Hill would have been several houses of her neighbors. Time to end the unofficial tour and re-turn to her bedroom. She turned around, looking for the exit in what once again looked like wallpapered uniformity. There, off to the side, sat what Aileen Summerville used to have in her bed-room: a daybed. White ceramic knobs adorned the brass rail. The fancy throw cushions should have been framed and hanging on the wall. They looked too delicate for use. However, she sucked in her breath at a rather strange article lying on the bedspread. She approached, wanting to avert her eyes and at the same time drawn by some perverse force to keep looking and make sure.

"No, no...." A whimper escaped her. Carefully, she touched the briefcase that once had to be light brown or taupe but age had scored with a web-work of cracks such that it now appeared almost black.

A few days ago, Teffler had put this briefcase down and sat on the bench. He'd taken it with him and left in a cab, having unburdened himself of the tale of the Siberian Oracle.

What was Simon Teffler's briefcase doing in Carmella Perez guest room?

ON THE WAY to Greenwich, Lauren told John about finding Teffler's briefcase in her hostess' bedroom. He replied that it made Gussie Wyndham that much more important. Very possibly she was the only person alive who knew the tale behind the Siberian Oracle—other than William C. Palfrey.

"And us," she said, flexing her voice so he'd not miss the significance.

He smiled at her. "You and me...what a pair we are—again. Don't worry, your knight in shining armor will protect you."

"And who will protect my knight?"

"The Force," he said in a mock-deep voice, and they laughed.

Three hours later, they took the Greenwich exit and ten more miles brought them to a private road. Gussie Wyndham's Palisades, a contemporary fortress, sat on the seacoast just north of Greenwich. It was as magnificent as it was forbidding.

"I'd like to see someone without a confirmed appointment to approach this place," John said after they parked the Grand Am in a guest parking lot, well outside of the actual estate grounds.

It took five minutes to reach the first sentry station. The gatehouse stood at the padlocked entry onto the private road. After the guard opened the gate, they spent another five minutes driving to the second sentry post that opened another gate to the guest parking lot.

The third and hopefully the last gate still awaited them in the distance.

"What is she afraid of?" Lauren murmured, pulling her scarf up to shield her face from the cold coastal wind.

"Mobs of her adoring fans," John said. "Or the media rush."

"She *is* the media, John."

"Not exactly. She uses the media to shock and delight her audiences. Have you seen her show?"

"Once or twice. I don't watch much TV."

"Last year, she interviewed an inmate on Death Row in South Carolina's Lieber Correctional Facility. On her show a month later, she had a leader of the citizens' coalition for the return of the lynching as the preferred method of dispensing justice in America. She had Malvern Pynchon, the author of *Pedophilia is Natural* on her show one month, and the next month, the parents of a child-victim of a convicted pedophile," John said.

"It seems like she offers her viewers both sides of the argument."

He made a soft hissing sound. "Balancing some issues seems fair, but others...I'm not so sure about. I heard she got a ton of hate mail after her show with Pynchon aired. Maybe that's why she lives in a fortress."

The two uniformed guards at the third gatehouse let them wait for fifteen minutes before one finally cracked open the window and said they could enter.

"The small gate on the side," the guard said not bothering to even stick his hand out and point out the direction.

"The big gate must be rusted," John remarked.

"Don't antagonize them." She poked him in the back. "They're just following orders; after all, it's their job to maintain security."

It took them another ten minutes to walk up to the five-tiered stone entrance. A portico-type of canopy supported massive stone pillars.

"Want to make a bet that if I ring a bell I'll be electrocuted or at least get a nasty shock?" John said, holding his hand inches away from an ornate brass plate with an inset button.

"Well, if that happens, I'm sure our hostess has enough staff on hand to drag your paralyzed body inside," She chuckled.

The door opened before he had a chance to ring the bell.

"Well, have you changed your mind or are you still inhaling

this fresh seacoast air," a woman's voice sounded crisply. It was tinged with a provocative tone of one who's used to arguments.

"Mrs. Wyndham. How do you do?" John dropped his hand and stepped aside, glancing at Lauren. "This is Lauren Sarasohn, and I'm John McPhend—"

The woman silenced him with a hand wave. "I may be a senior citizen but there's nothing wrong with my memory. The two of you are the only ones I'm expecting since you're the only two people cleared to get this far. And if you want something to boast about, be proud of the fact that you're only my third set of properly cleared visitors here this year. Get in, get in!" She motioned for them to come inside "It's damn cold out there. I bet my guards wouldn't even stick their noses outside."

Lauren moved ahead of John. She expected to be overwhelmed even more than when she first set a foot in Carmella's estate.

"Thank you for seeing us," John said behind her.

A hand tapped her back. "Well, how do you like my fortress? Impressive outside but cozy inside, huh?" Gussie Wyndham's voice churned with laughter.

The white marble double spiral staircase swept upward in graceful half-moons. It only needed Fred Astaire and Ginger Rogers to dance down the stairs to complete the Hollywood illusion. The store where Gussie Wyndham's decorators bought the crystal chandeliers must have closed for a few months to restock after her order had been filled. And any museum would have been proud to own the collection of art that hung on the walls.

"I see my foyer has struck you speechless," Gussie Wyndham said, nudging Lauren in the back again. "So let's retire into my library. I'm sure the office environment will revive you."

The library was larger and much better appointed than the manuscripts and rare books section at Winthrop College Library.

"Sit down." Their hostess indicated a puffy-looking dark green leather couch. She sat across in its match, leaned back and put up her feet on the brass-and-glass coffee table. She dressed like a rich woman who didn't care what anyone thought of her appearance, a departure from her polished and buffed look on her show. She wore a loose faded orange cotton sweatshirt over comfortably baggy coffee-colored sweatpants and Aladdin slippers. Her six-foot statuesque figure served as a bottomless well of jokes for her "Rubbing Shoulders with the Audience" feature. She changed her hair color according to her show's ratings. High ratings meant vibrant colors of orange, red, and sunset-fire; low ratings would correspond with dark colors. That no one remembered the last time Gussie Wyndham went brunette testified to her show's staying power in the rating polls.

"Dr. Belzer phoned me," Gussie Wyndham said, staring at them. Lauren got an impression that the great talk show hostess was deciding where she should draw targets: on their hearts or their heads. "Lord knows, I pay him enough for such excellent service and security. I haven't yet decided whether your conversation with my aunt at Cragg's Lake was merely meddling and intrusion or whether you've endangered her life."

"I'm sorry, Mrs. Wyndham, we didn't mean to...." Lauren started.

Gussie silenced her with a loud handclap. "I don't need apologies, Ms Sarasohn. If I wanted an apology, I'd have slapped you with a lawsuit. You gained admission into the facility under false pretenses." She nodded in a way that included John. "Cragg's Lake is a private sanatorium and I mean entirely private since I own it. I can have both of you charged with illegal entry and trespassing with intent to cause harm and put you away until you're ready for retirement in a state-run facility."

"Fine," John said, leaning forward, his voice hardening. "You can charge us, but before I disappear behind bars, I would make sure that the next headline in the Washington Times reads: Is Gussie Wyndham Gertrude Johansen, one of Hitler's custom-made children? The story of the *Siberian Oracle* would appear splashed all over the front page. All would be presented as a conjecture, of course. American public loves to read dark history disguised as fiction."

"Blackmail, Mr. McPhend?" Gussie laughed. "What a unique tactic for a mere newspaper editor. Print whatever you like in that conservative rag of yours. I don't give a shit. I'm Gussie Wyndham, the beloved talk show host of American audiences who know only too well that I have a ton of enemies. I'm the queen of controversy. I've been accused of being a Ku-Klux-Klan member after I had one of their leaders, suitably disguised, on my show. I've been accused of being a bleeding heart liberal after I had anti-war activists on my show. Hell, Mr. McPhend, I've been accused of just about everything you can think of. Do you think accusing me of being a neo-fascist is going to rattle me?"

"I didn't say neo-fascist," he said, lowering his voice. "I said you were one of the children custom-made, so to speak, according to Hitler's guidelines for the pure Aryan race. You're a product of breeding program conducted in his secret experimental laboratory, in the Perigord Chateau, in France. In 1944, the caretaker assigned to you, Analise von Bayern, smuggled you and two other children out of France and made it to Belgium where the von Flemming family took her in. Analise had an older sister in America: Willhelmine von Bayern. She brought Analise over here with the three toddlers, Anike van Buren, Piet Meyers, and you, Gertrude Johansen. I'd bet anything that you didn't become Gussie Wyndham until much later in life—a stage name, perhaps?"

"A stage name?" Once again she clapped her hands together. The crisp, naked sound reverberated around the huge library. "Do you think I'd have so little imagination to come up with nothing better than Gussie Wyndham? It happens to be the name that figures on my birth certificate, Mr. McPhend. Augusta Marie Green, born in Goldmine Junction, California back in 1940 after all the gold ran out. Wyndham is my married name. Didn't do your homework did you, Mr. Editor,?" She stared at them with a smirk.

"John," Lauren turned to him. "Give me your knapsack."

"What are you doing?" He resisted, but she tugged at it.

"Give it to me!" She yanked it from his hands. She opened it, took out the green canvas bag and with little ceremony dumped its contents on the glass table. The glass top crackled as the thirty-pound bar landed on it but it didn't shatter. The plasticized patches of human skin flitted down like butterflies and settled on either side of the bullion.

"A young Cuban bellhop at the Carlyle stole this from one of the suites and for some reason came to Winthrop College where I teach. He was killed in my office, nothing was stolen from it. The police found nothing on the victim. A couple of days later, my colleague, Mitch, went to the fridge in an alcove on our floor to get ice. He found this bag. Now, Mitch and his girlfriend are missing. Another friend, who examined these patches and the gold bar, is dead. After I spoke to a woman in New York, she died hours later—supposedly of a heart attack. I went to Greenwich to her son's art gallery. Someone impersonating him greeted me. I drove to Washington to see Carmella Perez. She used to be my mentor. I don't know who she is now. I suspect she's working for whoever wants these articles back."

Lauren gestured at the table. "Hagip Agopian, my friend from the museum, left me a phone message with a string of names. The same names that John has already told you about; Simon Teffler, Glathos Pidimentaros, Adlerina-Analise, and Cragg's Lake. We found Dr. Teffler giving a guest lecture at the George Washington University. He told us the story of the Siberian Oracle. Those two patches," she pointed at them, "are human skin, tattooed with the words *Das Sibirische*. The pin dots spell out *Chateau Dax*, and *Bonnac-Sur-Lot*. Why would the names of William Palfrey's flagship French industries figure on two patches of human skin that came from Anike van Buren, killed in 1964 and Piet Meyer, killed three months later?" Her intense recital drained her of energy. She waited for her hostess' reaction.

"I don't know," Gussie Wyndham said laconically. She looked bored. "But you go ahead and tell me. I'm curious whether this preposterous tale has an ending."

Confused, Lauren stared at her, and for the first time since they left Cragg's Lake, felt unsure whether they had followed the right trail. What if they assumed wrongly that Trudie meant the talk show hostess just because her late husband's name was Greer Wyndham? What if it was just coincidence and Augusta Marie Wyndham was not Gertrude Johansen?

"I'll make this simple, Mrs. Wyndham," John stood up, pointing at the patches on the table. "These pieces of human skin had been stripped from the backs of your...foster siblings. Would you mind showing us your bare back?" He smirked and added, "You can call your security here to make sure we won't stab it."

"Ha!" Gussie exclaimed and also rose to her feet. "If that's what it'll take to get rid of you, I have no problem doing a strip-tease for you. Actually, at my age, it's kind of nifty to take off my clothes...." She pulled off her baggy orange top and turned around.

"Oh, John!" Lauren bit her lower lip.

Gussie Wyndham's back was padded with flesh that kept accumulating with years of good living. And though there were folds in the flesh, it looked unmarred by any remnants of a scar or even birthmarks. It looked simply pristine clear.

Chapter 31

"WHAT NOW, JOHN?" she asked. They headed for Hartford an hour away.

He shook his head, turned, and grinned at her. "It might look like we hit a dead-end but don't despair. I'll think of something yet."

"No, John. It was stupid of me to think I could bring someone like Palfrey to justice, stupid to think that I would do better than the police if I kept the evidence. That canvas bag will spend the night at my house, along with you, but tomorrow morning we're going to Hartford to see Lieutenant Terney. It's what I should have done in the first place."

"I can still flush my channels; see who else might be able to help us—"

"No, I want you to stay alive," she said with conviction. "You said yourself that your newspaper would never print the story that would show Palfrey in an unfavorable light, never mind label him a criminal. Hagip is dead. Mitch and Jenny...well, I'll probably learn to pray if I ever hear from them again. Alice Blumenthal is dead, and if her son Ralston had the journal the von Flemmings sent him, it's probably gone too. Palfrey's just too powerful; maybe even for the police to do anything, although I think Terney will believe. I'll just tell him the whole story."

He stayed silent for some time. Finally, he said, "Lauren, if you go to the police you might be signing your death warrant."

"I know that, John, but it's what Hagip kept telling me to do. I should have listened. He would still be alive and so would Alice and Dr. Teffler."

"You don't know that Teffler's dead."

"I hope not, but seeing his beat-up briefcase in Carmella's house...it wouldn't take much to kill an old man, especially for someone like Kingsley. He's ex-military for sure. Carmella hired him to be her bodyguard and also do her dirty work getting rid of an old man who might still be a threat to her board member, Mr. William C. Palfrey. Carmella told me that she sits next to Palfrey at a board meeting. If he gets bored, they play hangman. He always wins. In the morning, the gold bar and the patches of human skin go to the Hartford police."

"And you?"

"I'll tell Terney the whole story and go back to my office at Winford and wait for Errington to deliver the bad news about Mitch and Jenny. He's another one that Palfrey bought—his lackey."

"Where is your drug store?" he asked.

"What?" The change of subject confused her.

"A pharmacy, you know, where you get your prescriptions filled. I want to pull in somewhere that's innocuous."

"Why?"

"I think we're being followed—again."

"Actually, there's a campus drugstore...."

He groaned. "Somewhere en route to your house so whoever's following us won't get suspicious. I don't want to take a detour to your campus."

"Stop at Myrtle's Coffee Shop. That's my regular spot."

"You have coffee at home, don't you?" He grimaced at her. "I want somewhere where I can spend a few minutes inside while you stay in the car and watch for a dark Lincoln."

"Oh, I see. Well, how 'bout Ellesmere Drugs in Wethersfield? It should be coming up. Make a right at the next intersection and then another right. It's in the strip plaza. Get some Advil or Tylenol."

He looked at her, wiggling his brows. "I wasn't going to browse through headache medicine. I prefer to browse through another...uh...more pleasurable section."

"How can you think of sex at the time like this?" she pretended to be outraged.

"Who said anything about sex? I meant rubbing alcohol."

She stayed in the car while he went inside the store. The dark automobile that drove leisurely through the plaza and parked at the very far end might have been a Lincoln, but unless she got out and went to check....

It started to rain again. Winter kept bullishly pushing its way in. Snow mixed with the water splattering on the windshield. Lauren stared at the slush accumulating behind the windshield wipers. Fatigue seeped into her mind. Everything she had done in the past two weeks, she'd been doing in vain. Even connecting with John again felt artificial. He seemed to remember a lot more of their eighteen months together than she did. Had he spent eight years thinking about her while she strove to forget him? After all that, was it possible that they could have a future together?

She rubbed her eyes and, feeling chilly, she turned around to get her parka from the back seat. The green canvas bag lay there looking deceptively ordinary like a pouch one might use to store shoes in. She twisted to pick it up with both hands and brought the bag with her, setting it down in her lap.

Absent-mindedly, she picked on the strings, twirling and pulling without opening the bag. The windows became steamed with cold condensation. John was taking too long. Should she get out?

"Let's see what you look like," she murmured and pulled the strings apart. She sunk her hand inside and felt the cold metal.

Lightly, she traced the engraved logo with her finger, shook her head, and pulled the shape out the gold bag. The moment the bar peeked out of it, her nostrils twitched. The tangy citrus smell—where did it come from? She let go of the bar, brought her hands to her nose, and recoiled. They reeked of Windex. Someone must have polished the gold bar with it, except she now knew it wasn't household cleanser. It was the new French perfume, the same one Carmella had dabbed on her the night of the embassy reception. She cleared her throat because it started to close. She could be allergic to the scent, but someone who wore it had handled the gold bar. Should she ask John? How would she ask him without sounding like an idiot?

"No, no, can't ask him nothing," she murmured and hurriedly stuffed the gold bar back in its bag. She heaved it over and let it fall down on the back seat. Not caring about smearing the glass, she rubbed her hands against the passenger widow and wiped them into the seat's upholstery.

By the time John returned, she had put on her parka and if he asked why she shivered she had an excuse—without the car running, it turned chilly.

"Advil and Tylenol," he said, shaking the plastic bag at her. He put it down at his feet. "Sorry it took me so long. There were a couple of customers ahead of me at the cashier. Whoever's following us didn't come in. Did you see anyone?"

"No." She hugged herself, stifling shivers. "Let's go. It's only ten minutes from here to Rocky Hill."

"I'm sorry. I should have left the car running to keep you warm."

Normally, after it rained, Elm Grove Street looked fresher, cleaner, even at night. The rows of nearly identical white-clapboard houses looked like they had put on clean nightshirts before bedtime. Tonight, the street looked desolate. The old elm trees that in the summer provided much welcome shade had lost their leaves.

"Fifth house on your right," she said. All the houses had well-lit numbers except hers. Five years ago, her landlord promised to install an overhead light. She knew not to hold her breath.

"Very Connecticut," he said, pulling into the laneway.

"It's all I can afford," she mumbled, getting out and heading for the crumbling stone steps. She would get her luggage out of the trunk tomorrow morning.

It took her five tries to fit the key into the lock. By the time she opened the door, she vowed she would call her landlord and insist he put up an outside light beside the front door.

The house smelled stale but she found it preferable to that other throat-scratching fashion smell.

"Did you turn off the heat?" John asked as he walked up behind her.

Oh God! Did the utility company turn off the gas? But she wasn't behind on her utility bills—yet.

"I probably just didn't turn up the thermostat," she said and reached to turn on the light. She sensed him behind her. His hand reached around, brushed by her cheek. Her throat constricted.

"John, come on. Let me at least...." A sickening stench entered her nostrils. Her hands flew to her face, clawing at something pressed over it.

LAUREN WOKE UP feeling dizzy and nauseous. She tried to move and met with resistance. Her lids drooped heavily, and she had to will them to open. She felt dizzy and disoriented. She drew in big breath, but it caused her throat to spasm with the rush of cold air. She started to cough and retch.

"What's happening...John?" Her throat felt raw. She tried to move her hands and discovered that they were tied behind her back. Slowly, her sight cleared. She sat on a chair behind her kitchen table. John sat across from her and for some reason, he had stacked two Advil bottles, one Tylenol bottle and two of what looked like prescriptions filled with tiny blue pills in front of him.

"It's a pity that you didn't take Palfrey's job offer, Lauren," he said and started to flick the lids off the plastic bottles. He'd found her glass pitcher and must have made hot lemonade. The cloudy liquid steamed upward in curly tendrils; its sour flavor-like odor assaulted her nose.

"What?" Her vision blurred. His voice grew hollow. He sounded as if he talked through a tin can.

"Just a little chloroform, Lauren. It'll clear soon enough. But I'm afraid you'll have to go to sleep forever."

"Are you insane?" she managed, fragments of what he meant starting to penetrate her numbed senses.

"On the contrary. I'm very sane. An insane man would have done what you did at that embassy reception—laughed at Palfrey's offer. You said it was tempting, but no thanks. Basically, saying it's *tempting* means ridicule."

"Untie me right now!" She strained her arms, but he'd used something very strong to tie her. She couldn't even move to gain relief from the pressure. The pain between her shoulder blades grew unbearable.

"Soon. In about half an hour or whatever it takes to fall asleep forever."

"You sold out, you son-of-a-bitch. Palfrey bought you, didn't he?" she whispered, the depth of his betrayal still not making its full impact. She couldn't believe it of him.

"I told you. Everyone has his price, Lauren. It's just a matter of how much."

"Fuck your fortune-cookie philosophy. When did you..." She couldn't bring herself to say it.

"Sell you out? I was really happy to see you at that embassy reception but before the night was over, William Palfrey made a second job offer—although a little more ambitious than yours. I used to define happiness in simple terms. But I realized that while the world around me had grown up, I was still—"

"A bastard," she snapped. "So this time it took you eight minutes to betray me. I suppose that's an improvement on your last record when you took eighteen months to do it; not only me, but all those people who considered you a family member, people like Hagip and Isabel."

He poured the bottle of Tylenols into the pitcher and stirred it, watching them dissolve. "In eight years, I've made it to the editorial office. Without connections, it's as far as I'll go at any newspaper. It took me eight minutes to realize that, Lauren, and even that was too fucking long. I don't want to spend the rest of my life bowing to senior assholes. I want to be in control, at the boardroom level. Of course, I also want to be able to keep my house since my fucking ex-wife almost pushed me into bankruptcy."

"Serves you right for marrying a lawyer," she said. She thought about spitting him in the face but her mouth felt filled with cotton-puffs. "I didn't know Palfrey owned a newspaper."

"He will soon. Reverend Moon has been very disappointed with the financial performance of the Times. We've been up for sale for some time. I learned something very interesting at that embassy reception, other than the fact that you still had a soft spot in your heart for me. Mr. Palfrey's the new owner. And, low and behold, my new boss offers me a promotion that I've only dreamed about...." He shrugged, smiling at her.

"Why did you wait this long to kill me? Why carry on the charade of helping me...?"

"Plan, dear Lauren, not charade. You wondered yourself why you're still alive since you believe they suspected you had this." He tapped the canvas bag next to him.

"They weren't sure," she mumbled, trying not to show she strained to break her bonds. She just couldn't sit and let him force the shit down her throat. She realized that she gave him the idea. She said often enough that's what she feared—to be found in her house, in her bed, dead of an overdose, an apparent suicide.

"Oh, they were sure all right. But once you started to carry on like Nancy Drew, they decided to use you—to flush out the third child, the bearer of the last tattooed map, if she was still alive."

"What for? Palfrey already found the two sites where Hitler stashed his stolen loot. What does he need the third site for? Hasn't he enough fucking money to buy a hundred lackeys like you and Carmella?"

"The theft of this," he nudged the canvas bag, "showed Mr. Palfrey how vulnerable he still is. Not only were there a ton of people out there who knew the story of the Siberian Oracle, but also somewhere out there was a child, now a senior citizen, tattooed with Hitler's treasure map. And she'd be well versed in that lurid tale of the Siberian Oracle. The last threat has to be eliminated." He grimaced. "Pity that it had to come to this. But you were always full of noble notions like going to the police, giving them the bullion and the patches. That simply can't happen."

"What about you, John? You know the lurid tale of the Oracle. How safe are you going to feel, in Palfrey's employ no less?"

For a second his eyes narrowed, but he smirked. "Psychology won't work here, Lauren. This cocktail," he stirred in the bottle of sleeping pills and for a while watched them dissolve before continuing, "will certainly perform a public service. It's your prescription. The kid at the pharmacy was so bored he didn't even bother reading the name on the label. Try to think happy thoughts. It might help."

She lowered her head to hide her tears.

"It won't hurt, Lauren. You'll just feel drowsy and fall asleep and then nothing. Tomorrow, Dr. Errington will find you dead at home, in your bed—a suicide—which won't be surprising considering you've turned your back on life five years ago."

"You fucking bastard," she pushed the words out, trying to stifle her sobs.

"Come on, Lauren. I brought you back to life for a few days. I showed you what it's like to be wanted and loved. Can't say I didn't—"

Something metal hit against the wood. She jerked her head. John leaned sideways. For a second or two he remained in a tilted position. Then slowly, he fell over and hit the floor.

"Are you all right, ma'am?" Kingsley's voice rang out. She thought she was hallucinating.

More insistently. "Ma'am?"

"Yes, yes. Can you help me...?" But she already felt her bonds loosening where he untied her.

Her head spun as she tried to stand up. Once again, Kingsley helped her to sit, but on the edge of the table this time. He faced her.

"Is there anything in your house that you might want to take with you, ma'am?" he asked. "Other than this, that is." He picked up the green canvas bag as if it was filled with feathers.

"Are you going to torch the house?" she asked, rubbing her wrists.

"No, ma'am. That would be arson," he said. He cracked a smile, but his face quickly returned to its usual severity. "Is there anything you'd like to take with you?" he repeated.

"My thesis." She motioned at the black nylon bag in the living room.

He went to get it. "What about your computer?"

"Most of my thesis is on it but I've backed up everything onto my external and my thumb drive. Both are in the bag. Why are you asking me this?"

"We're leaving, ma'am. I have orders to bring you in."

"In where? I'm not going back to Carmella's house." Once again her suspicions flared.

"No, ma'am. We're going to Pallisades."

"Oh. And what about him?" she motioned at the figure slumped on her kitchen floor.

"Do you care what happens to Mr. John McPhend, ma'am?"

She stared at the body, noticing a little trickle of blood on the floor from the head wound. Kingsley must have hit him with a cast iron frying pan. "I don't care at all what happens to him. I only hesitated because I wanted to be as fair as he was. I'm ready. Let's go."

Chapter 32

ALL THROUGH THE seventy-mile drive back to Greenwich, Lauren didn't ask Kingsley anything. She felt that had he wanted to talk to her, he'd not have opened the rear door and waited until she got inside the Lincoln. He made it clear he was the chauffeur who knew precisely where to drive his passenger and talk was unnecessary.

She didn't fear going back to the talk show hostess' fortress-estate. Gussie Wyndham was arrogant, loud, and rude, but even as she threatened them with a lawsuit, Lauren got the impression that the ultra-wealthy entertainer would never cause hardships to those she judged merely silly or misguided. Kingsley put the canvas bag on the passenger seat beside him. The fact that he took possession of the bag so matter-of-factly didn't worry her either. Carmella may have employed Kingsley, but tonight he acted with a military dryness she hadn't seen in him before. Working for Carmella as a bodyguard and chauffeur may have been his cover. Was Palfrey already under investigation by some government agency?

Gussie Wyndham would probably have some answers.

"Doesn't it seem to you like you never left this magnificent place?" Gussie Wyndham welcomed her with those words, once again opening the door herself when Kingsley walked her up the stone apron.

"It looks smaller at night," Lauren said, stepping inside.

The talk show host's laughter rang rich behind her. "Come." Gussie grabbed her arm, pulling her in a different this time. "Let's have a snack in the garden room."

Lauren protested that she wasn't hungry and came only because she needed answers. Her hostess literally dragged her across what seemed like acres of polished floors, galleries, and beautifully furnished rooms before they arrived in a glassed-in patio room. It dripped with foliage, and in spite of the soaring windows, it felt almost tropically warm.

Gussie forced her to sit down at a table already set with trays of sandwiches, cheese, fruits, and colorful pates, and made a throaty, displeased sound. "Where the hell is the wine?"

"Coming, for Heaven's sake. Calm down. I only have two hands," a voice said. Lauren spun around.

"Sit down, sit down." Gussie pushed Lauren back when she tried to rise. "What's the matter with you? You look like you'd seen a ghost." She motioned at the far side of the table. "Put the wine and the glasses there so there'll be place left for coffee. You drink coffee, don't you?" She peered down at her.

"What is she doing here?" Lauren asked, moistening her lips.

"Oh, you mean Carmella?" The old lady snapped her fingers and threw an irritated look at Carmella. "I said to the side, not on the edge where I'm sure someone will knock it off."

Carmella put down the wine bottle and the glasses and braced her hands on her hips. "Mother, why did you give your staff the night off? I'm tired from the drive, and you live in a Grand Central Station which means I'm tired by the time I find a washroom, never mind by the time I find my way back."

"Mother?" Lauren said as if learning a new language. Gussie must have heard her.

"Yes, that rude middle-aged woman over there is my daughter...what's the matter with you? Why are you looking around? Are you expecting a platoon of mercenaries to start jumping through the roof?"

"Is William Palfrey your guest tonight too?" she asked, feeling fatigue seep into her limbs. Her eyes wanted to close. She found she didn't care if she felt a noose slip around her neck.

"That sack of shit? Hell, no. What would make you ask that, child?" She felt Gussie's breath on her cheek and opened her eyes. "Are you all right?"

"I don't understand," Lauren whispered.

"Has anyone seen my spectacles? I seem to have misplaced them," another voice, less familiar but well remembered made Lauren snap her head around.

"Dr. Teffler?" She pushed Gussie's hand away and ran toward him, stopping just before she ran into him. "You're all right." She looked at Carmella and back at the doctor.

"I know you don't understand, Lauren. So let's sit down, have some food because frankly I'm starved, and mother can start explaining. She's the entertainment celebrity. Let her entertain us," Carmella said in a voice that left no room for arguments. Lauren blinked, took a sip of wine and settled down to listen.

THE VON FLEMMING family helped Analise track down her sister in America. Willhelmine von Bayern worked as a nanny for an affluent textile merchant's family in Newburgh. In 1932, she met Friedrich Pfaller through her Lutheran church group. Pfaller hailed from Hamburg, Pennsylvania and came to visit his cousin in the nearby Beacon. She married him and moved to Hamburg where Pfaller had just taken over his recently deceased father's butcher shop. Two years later, their only child, William Clement was born. In 1939, with Hitler's invasion of Poland and France, and England declaring war on Germany, the American public's sentiments about German immigrants in US underwent an about face. Friedrich Pfaller changed his name to Fred Palfrey. His wife became Myrna Palfrey. A year later, Palfrey sold his butcher shop in Hamburg, and to further distance himself from the local German community, moved his family to Pittsburgh where he opened a meat market. Later on, he added a bakery next door.

Myrna Palfrey readily identified herself as Willhelmine von Bayern to the Red Cross workers, searching for her with the help of the local church groups.

By Christmas time 1944, Analise von Bayern and her three little charges sat at the kitchen table in the Palfrey household, enjoying the plate of steaming sausages and potatoes. Ten-year-old Billy Palfrey sat on his father's right.

"I was four years old. I don't remember all that well what went on that Christmas," Gussie said, taking a thoughtful sip of her California Chablis, "but come springtime, *Tantchen* Liesel cried almost every day. She told us that we had to find another place to live. There were too many mouths to feed for Fred Palfrey, who had a belly that cast a shadow on the ground. Myrna introduced her sister to Samuel van Buren. He was part Dutch, part German, and reeked of fish. He had a fish market about a block down from Palfrey's meat-and-bakery deli. We moved into the flat above the fish market, and a year later, Analise gave birth to a boy. He died three months later of scarlet fever. Samuel got drunk, beat up his wife, and threatened to throw out her three bastards if she didn't produce him a robustly healthy son and heir. The following September, we were enrolled in Sharon Elementary, next door to St. Matthews Lutheran Church. Samuel's fish business faltered, and he started to drink. When he was drunk, fists and dishes flew at anything, anyone."

BY THE TIME the triplets turned nine years old, Analise suffered two miscarriages, and her abusive husband progressed to gambling. A month before the triplets' tenth birthday, Samuel died of septic shock. A rusty fishhook pierced his hand, and he scoffed at having the *scratch* attended.

Once the creditors were paid, Analise took the money left from the sale of the fish market and bid good-bye to her sister. Myrna, too, had suffered one miscarriage before her son was born and two afterward. Her health had already been undermined by the time her porcine husband wanted his business to prosper and she had to work eighteen hours a day, baking bread and pastries.

"I remember Billy Palfrey at sixteen very well," Gussie said. She rubbed her forehead as if the friction would make the memories flow faster. "He was beefy like his father and a bully. He wasn't stupid, just lazy. At sixteen, he was still in grade eight. We were three years behind him."

Analise sat down her triplets and told them that they should no longer call her *tantchen* or auntie, but *mutter* because the mother and her three children were about to start a new life, somewhere where the air smelled fresh and fish would be soaked in milk before breaded or fried. Someone from the church congregation told her that there was a large German settlement in South Dakota.

Gussie sighed. Obviously memories still had the power to make her sad. "What those church folks didn't know was that those Germans came originally from Russia. They were predominantly Catholic. Nevertheless, luck seemed to ride with us. We arrived in Pierre and found lodgings with a Swiss-German family, the Meyers." Gussie paused and started to rub the edge of the wine glass with her fingertip, setting it to resonate. The faint humming sound seemed to be the right music to complement the march of her memories.

The Meyers helped Analise to find a maid's job at the nearby Trinity Hotel. She enrolled the triplets in a local elementary school. A few months later, Analise received a letter from her sister in Pittsburgh. Myrna feared she was dying.

"I don't want to sound callous here," Gussie said, pausing in her tale to take a sip of wine. "But in the next four years, mother

Liesel received at least four such letters. And each time Mother would cry when she had to take all her savings to get a bus or train ticket to Pittsburgh. We're talking fifties here. The minimum wage was cents, not dollars. A hotel maid had to rely on her tips far more than her meager pay. It was during one of these emergency trips to Pittsburgh to comfort Myrna that Mother told her the story of the *Siberian Oracle* and about our true origin, how we came to be."

WHEN JOSEF MEYER'S wife died, he asked Analise to marry him. He was twenty years her senior, but a thirty-five-year-old hotel maid in mid-fifties America still needed what most women needed in the course of history: financial security and stability for her family.

"I was fifteen when mother married Joe. He was all right, but I didn't like him. Piet and Anike didn't seem to mind. The three of us did look like siblings, but we had very different temperaments. Piet was laid back, easily influenced, a follower. Anike was vain, forever the Barbie doll. All she wanted was to make it as a cheerleader at our high school. I just wanted to make-out with Juan behind the church wall and not have a curfew. Six months after mother married Joe, Juan climbed the tree underneath my bedroom window. He caught the beat-up suitcase I'd packed with my clothes and helped me to climb down. I was fifteen years old and pregnant. Not something you'd want to be in South Dakota in 1957. We made it to California, mostly hopping freight trains and hitchhiking. Juan found his brotherhood, a Latino street gang in South Los Angeles. I came to my senses and contacted a Red Cross mission. One of the workers put me up with her family."

Analise came to L.A. and stayed with Trudie until the baby was born, in St. Mary and Angels of Mercy Hospital. The young attending doctor arranged for the baby's adoption to a good family of Mexican origin to make it easier on the little girl who was part Mexican.

"Perez," Gussie said, "that's all Doctor Calvin Greer Wyndham would tell me. He figured it was a common-enough family name, not easily traceable. Mother took me home. Joe patted me on the head and said everyone made mistakes, but some lucky people learned from their mistakes and he hoped I would too. Anike paraded for me her new hoop skirt with a fuzzy bunny rabbit embroidered on the hem. She made me come to her cheerleading practice to see all her latest moves. Piet showed me the school newspaper, with two of his anti-war articles since he took over as its editor, and for a while life seemed to flow in a peaceful groove. In May of 1960, Fred Palfrey called mother. Myrna was really dying this time. Mother left for Pittsburgh. She came back a month later after the funeral. One evening, Joe went to play cards at his friend's house. Mother made the three of us sit down, her face so creased with worry she looked sixty, not forty."

Dying Myrna begged forgiveness of her younger sister since she swore on the bleeding wounds of Jesus Christ not to tell anyone about the triplets' origin or the tale of the Siberian Oracle. But her son, Billy, was doing so poorly in business. He wasn't like his father. At twenty-six, he still couldn't tell where the sirloin came from and from where he should cut the flank steak. He would never make a good butcher and working in a leather factory was hard....

"It's been decades and I still remember Mother's face when she told us. It was chalk-white. She panicked," Gussie said. "Billy Palfrey sidled up to her at the wake and started to pump her for information about the Hitler's treasure and whether the maps were really drawn into his cousins' skins. She told him that his mother must have already been delirious, speaking of such fancies and not to dwell on foolish things."

Chapter 33

MYRNA PALFREY MAY have worried about her son's future and his inability to learn an honest trade that called for long hours and hard work, but Analise realized in an instant how much damage her sister did by disclosing what she told her. She'd meant to comfort a dying woman by telling her about her own life in Germany. She told her about the year she spent with an SS officer's family in Frankfurt, learning to be a proper nanny. She spent another six months with a hundred other young women in a camp near Stuttgart, learning to empty herself of all the Christian dogmas and unhealthy religious contamination because Hitler declared all religions to be contemptible devices of those who wished to enslave freethinkers.

And finally, she told her about her *assignment* at the Perigord Chateau in southern France and Heinrich Mueller, the young laboratory technician who said she should have been named Agnes because she looked as beautiful as the white roses that name his mother used to cultivate in their garden back in Arnsberg. Heinrich had found many secret passages in the chateau. They allowed him to move undetected and listen in on the briefings going on in the rooms. He told her what the three children entrusted to her care carried tattooed into their backs. The visible words, *Das Sibirische Orakel* were Fuhrer's whimsy. But tiny white pin dots, a result of some acid-bleaching process, spelled out the names of three sites where Hitler stored his looted treasure. Chateau Dax, once a beautiful classic sixteenth century chateau built north of the border town Tardes, by Marquis Escalimont for his Spanish mistress, Estrella, was now little more than a noble ruin. However, the nearby farmhouse that contained the entrance into a cave complex where the caretakers and staff used to cultivate mushrooms, was intact. The cave was no longer used to grow mushrooms but to store crates filled with jewels and precious stones, along with many fine works of art *appropriated* by Hitler's henchmen from all over Europe.

The name of the second site was *Bonnac-Sur-Lot*. It was an old abandoned gold mine, a fitting place to hide the specially minted gold bullion decorated with Hitler's imperial crest in anticipation of his coronation as the Emperor of the World. The name of the third site could only be obtained if the first two etchings were superimposed upon the third one. The combination of the word-patterns on the two gave rise to a new unique dot cluster that spelled out the location.

"I'm sure that the cryptographer who had advised Hitler on such excellent concealment of his treasure didn't live to celebrate his success," Gussie said, making a face. "Mother told us that we were in danger. She stopped short of spelling out that her own nephew would be the root of it. Anike had a stenographer's job in a local insurance company. Piet worked for the newspaper. Neither took mother's warning seriously. I worked as a gofer for George and Stella Muldrich. The couple hosted Sunday morning's radio show in Pierre, giving mostly gardening and cooking advice. A year later, Anike got bored sitting on her boss's knee while he rubbed his face in her tits. She announced that she was going to Hollywood to become an actress. Her friend from work, Linda Lincoln, would come also, so Mother shouldn't worry."

ANALISE THOUGHT CALIFORNIA a godless place but certainly large enough to hide one six-foot blonde, blue-eyed beauty from South Dakota. Hollywood was filled with hopeful starlets waitressing while waiting for the fame to find them. A year later, Piet announced that he was going to San Francisco. Analise saddened like any mother whose children are leaving the nest but thought he'd be out of harm's way.

"One day, I approached George Muldrich and suggested that maybe if he brought gardening and cooking experts on his Sunday show, he might get better ratings," Gussie said. "He called me a silly girl who had tons to learn about what would make a radio show more successful and threw me out. A month later, he brought his first gardening expert on the show. The station's phones kept ringing off the hook. I took out my sandwich from my brown paper lunch bag. I went to the washroom, shit into the bag, wrapped it up, and put it in the pocket of George's suit jacket, the one I always had to help him put on just before the show. Once he had it on, I faced him slapped my hand against his chest and took a deep breath. I smelled shit. That's when I knew destiny had greater things in store for me."

After the "stinky stunt," Trudie Meyers was fired. She told her mother she'd resigned because Anike wanted her to come out to California, to see the coast, and smell the fresh sea-air. She arrived in Hollywood and found that her sister had returned to using the name van Buren because it sounded more like a name a star might use.

"That's why no one connected us when Anike was murdered," Gussie said.

Trudie Meyers also found a waitressing job. She settled in a small house in Los Angeles with four other girls, all of them hopeful actresses. Two weeks later, she went to the St. Mary and the Mercy Angels Hospital in south L.A. She wanted to find the whereabouts of the doctor who delivered her daughter some years ago. Much to her surprise she found Dr. Calvin Greer Wyndham still on staff.

"He didn't recognize me," Gussie said. "When he delivered my little girl, I was a scrawny fifteen-year-old, and he was a twenty-seven-year-old intern with a social conscience. I learned that he routinely attended hardship cases like mine. I asked him whether he would—if I managed to get my own radio show—come to guest and spend an hour answering questions from young women who might find themselves pregnant with no resources, no family. He looked at me like I dropped in from Mars but said, sure, he'd do it—if I ever managed to get my own radio show. A year later, serving drinks at a posh Hollywood golf club, I met Sherwin Saltzberg. The studio mogul had just bought a very ritzy car dealership for his girlfriend. Apparently, the sex kitten went to pick out her pink Caddy and the management treated her like she had no brains. She went home to her sugar daddy and complained how rude the staff was to her. Sherwin promptly bought the dealership and summarily fired everyone. He left his little kitten with a lot full of fancy cars and no one to sell them. I saw my chance."

Trudie Meyers, on the spur of the moment, introduced herself as Gertrude Johansen. She felt it sounded more serious, professional. She proceeded to offer her services to not only hire a whole new staff for Miss Ruby's new dealership, but take charge of advertising the excellent product—on the radio—and maybe even television, but first she'd have a series of radio commercials, characterized by snappy jingles that Miss Ruby, an aspiring singer, might perhaps even sing herself.

Three months later, Gertrude Johansen hosted her first radio talk show. It was aimed at women who might be thinking about liberating themselves from the stereotyping and perhaps take their place by their husbands' sides as partners, not chattels. And partners, naturally, would participate in large family decisions, such as a purchase of a family car. Her show brought not only great business to Ruby's Ritzy Automobiles, but offers of expansion for the show.

"Greer Wyndham didn't recognize me even after he came on my show," she said. "I had to take him out for dinner and drink and point-blank tell him who I was before the light of recognition lit up in his eyes. He was single because he said no one wanted to marry a poor doctor and that's all he'd ever be, so we started dating. I wrote home to Analise and told her about Greer. She phoned and said she was happy for me but she worried about me, Anike, and Piet."

Anike wasn't a Shakespearean actress, or a singer like Doris Day. Gertrude had no way to bring her on her radio show. She promised that once she broke into television, she'd reach out and drag her sister in.

"I remember it was about nine months after Kennedy's assassination. The newspaper headlines bled with every word that ever conveyed pain and suffering. *Time Magazine*, however, wrote about the New York Fair. I hadn't finished reading the issue when Greer bought me the new one, featuring on its cover the America's newest entrepreneur, wines and spirits millionaire, William C. Palfrey, age thirty. Finally, Mother's warnings made an impact. I called Anike. She was out somewhere with a bunch of hopefuls, doing rounds of casting couches. I called Piet. He must have been stoned out of his mind. He kept chanting some mantra shit. I called Mother. She said Joe caught some pranksters setting fire in the garbage bins behind the house in the alley. The fire didn't do much damage to the house but the shed was gone. I was twenty-four years old, I drove a white Caddy, lived in an apartment with a spectacular view of the Pacific, and had my own radio show and I was scared to death. Greer must have seen it."

GERTRUDE JOHANSEN TOOK Calvin Greer Wyndham for a midnight walk along the beach. By sunrise, he knew everything

Analise ever told her triplets. Wyndham made inquiries and found that the America's newest millionaire, who joined the ranks of self-made millionaires before age thirty, had help from his French wife. Marie-Chantal Escalimont's family owned the one hundred and fifty acres of fine Bordeaux Vineland surrounding the newly-restored Chateau Dax. It was the flagship of the Ste. Mireille winery. The huge success of the new vintner allowed him to make bold bids for three distilleries in receivership back home in USA. After that, success just seemed to wreath William Palfrey from one enterprise to another. To show his gratitude to the French government, he also purchased a site of an old abandoned gold mine near Bonnac-Sur-Lot. He immediately set to restore the heritage site with intentions to return it to the French people as a tourist attraction. In less than three years, the beefy son of the butcher from Pittsburgh not only married a descendant of French aristocracy but also used her family's good name and holdings to raise the St. Mireille name once again into global ranks of purveyors of fine wines and spirits.

"It was the sixties, for crying out loud," Gussie continued. "People were still in awe of the ballpoint pen, and Xerox had not yet become a household name. But Billy Palfrey becomes a millionaire overnight, through hard work. That's what he told the reporter who wrote up the Time's article."

Dr. Wyndham suggested Gertrude have the deadly patch with the tattoo surgically removed. He knew several colleagues, plastic surgeons, who'd do the work discreetly though certainly not for free. Anike agreed to have hers removed, too, if Trudie paid for it. She wanted to wear revealing bathing suits and expose her back for the camera.

A week before Anike's plastic surgery, she was found dead in her flat, strangled and with a patch of skin missing from her back. Greer convinced Trudie not to reveal to the police that she was the dead girl's sister because it meant she'd be revealing her whereabouts to William Palfrey. He drove her to San Francisco because Trudie couldn't get hold of Piet. By the time they managed to convince the Sutter Street Commune members that they were not undercover policemen, seeking to bust their member for drugs, Piet's body was found with a patch of skin missing from his back. Greer Wyndham took Trudie to Las Vegas. He married her in a pink-and-white chapel. The name on the marriage certificate read: Augusta Marie Green, born in Goldmine Junction California, November 6, 1940.

On her next radio show, Gertrude Johansen announced that she became Mrs. C. Greer Wyndham and from now on would like to be called Gussie Wyndham, not exactly a stage name but definitely with a fresher ring to it.

MOTHER ANALISE, SENSING that after the murders of her two siblings Trudie needed to fade into anonymity, severed all contact with her remaining daughter, but Greer Wyndham found a way to check on his mother-in-law from time to time. He let Gussie know how she was doing. In 1970, the small house in Pierre, where Joe and Analise lived, burned down. The fire, thought to have started when Joe Meyers, a smoker, had fallen asleep in front of TV with a burning cigarette in his hand. It claimed his life. His wife, Analise, was rushed to the hospital, suffering from burns and smoke-inhalation. She died a week later of complications stemming from her injuries.

"I was already a TV celebrity on the West Coast, and my husband was offered a research position in an East Coast hospital. What would be more natural than for us to move to New York," Gussie said. "And what better place than New York to hide someone who had "died" in a hospital in South Dakota. I didn't believe for a moment that Joe had fallen asleep with a burning cigarette in his hand. Greer talked to the doctors in Pierre. Analise suffered burns but also a bump on the back of her head that the doctors didn't think a result of a fall. She was struck from behind. For a while, Analise lived with us in Manhattan. But I saw that New York crowds frightened her. We bought a house in New Jersey; a little more modest than my Pallisades home but definitely large enough to warrant hiring a staff of six to look after it. Analise liked to dress as one of the service staff. She said it brought back memories of working all those years as a hotel maid. The staff thought her little eccentric but definitely a harmless old lady. She was only fifty years old."

Gussie Wyndham didn't broach the subject of wanting to find the child she gave up for adoption as a fifteen-year-old. Her husband knew that's what she always meant to do. He started the search on his own. He succeeded in locating Jose and Alma Perez in 1980, when a change in administrative record keeping at St. Mary and Angels of Mercy Hospital necessitated opening certain sealed files in order to make them ready for input into the new computerized database system. They still lived in Pomona, but their eldest daughter, twenty-five-year-old Carmella, lived on the East Coast. She had just become a freshly minted PhD and accepted a position as an Associate Professor in Chemistry at North Carolina State.

"I kept track of her for ten years." Gussie nodded at her daughter, who sat with her head lowered but inclined in a way that showed she listened and hadn't missed a single word of her mother's historical review. "But I didn't make contact. She was doing fancy research for Pem Pharmaceuticals and kept writing papers that even Greer had difficulty understanding and he was a brilliant doctor. I didn't want to ruin her momentum, especially since she kept sidestepping all relationships. In 1990, she married a Wall Street broker. The marriage fell apart after three months. I decided to test the waters."

Gussie Wyndham hired a lawyer to discreetly approach the newly appointed member of the National Science Board in New York. Carmella wanted to meet her biological mother, but they both knew that it would be in Carmella's best interest to keep it low-key, even secret.

Chapter 34

"I DIDN'T THINK IT would hurt my career, one way or another, if the public learned I made contact with my biological mother who was a talk show host, Carmella said." I knew I was adopted and never felt that part had to be kept secret." Carmella picked up the story effortlessly like a good actress, "But mother felt otherwise. It took a while before she told me her real reason for wanting to keep her identity secret. After I received an appointment to the Office of Science and Technology, I started to make discreet inquiries about the source of William Palfrey's wealth. He never tried to hide his roots either, but once I started to check his entrepreneurial beginnings that saw him a million-aire by age thirty, the picture grew fuzzy.

"Supposedly he used his French wife's aristocratic connections to launch his winery business. However, Marie-Chantal Escalimont and her family were penniless. The vineyards have not seen growth in centuries. They lived in a rustic shed; the part of the farmhouse that has not collapsed and lay in ruins. The chateau was an even worse mess. The story came alive once

Analise started to unravel it for me bit by bit whenever she had a lucid spell. Ten years ago, she already showed early signs of Alzheimer's. In '96, I left the science advisory post. I used all those powerful political connections to become a corporate woman."

IT WASN'T DIFFICULT for an ex-presidential Science Advisor to get the directorship of the Argosy National Laboratory or to become a board member of half a dozen prestigious companies and corporations. But it was difficult to obtain even a shred of proof that Palfrey had built his empire on Hitler's stolen gold.

"I contacted someone in the Justice Department," Carmella said. "The Inspector General, to be exact. The DOJ has a mandate to investigate individuals or organizations that are suspected of ethical, financial, or criminal misconduct. It surprised me to find out that DOJ has been uneasy about Palfrey for some time."

In 1992, Federal Marine Terminals at Port of Richmond, the operator that provides exclusive stevedoring services and full range of warehousing, export packaging, and inland transfer and distribution, had a labor strike. The management tried to bring in contracted labor force. A minor war erupted on the docks. Guns weren't discharged but bats and crowbars did a lot of damage to unloaded cargo, some of it already re-packed in distribution containers. Two such metal containers were heavily damaged when a crane operator dropped a load of raw iron rails on them. Their cargo had to be pried from between the crushed sides. The police, already on the scene, were called to stand witness as the workers extracted crates that, according to the freighter's manifest, contained French wines. However, after a dozen rolled-up canvases spilled on to the dock from a crate, the police called for reinforcements. They contacted the FBI. In a matter of hours, the strikers and contract labor were summarily locked out, pending what the FBI thought was a smuggling operation. The wine crates bore the insignia of Chateau Dax Ste.

Mireille winery, on the west French coast, just north of the Spanish border. The freighter, *"Pierre St. Martin,"* was registered at its homeport, Marseille.

The FBI opened the rest of the wine crates, a total of fifty. Thirty crates were packed with legally exported wine, twenty carried only a token bottle or two and the rest of space was filled with gold artifacts, gold bars without a refinery logo, and priceless masterpieces. The FBI lab determined that the gold was freshly smelted. Whoever did the job was a hack because no two bars weighed the same and some were badly misshapen.

The seventeen rolled up canvases went to the Smithsonian. The experts determined that they were all originals; most well-known but all thought to have been lost either during WWII or in the course of centuries. It was difficult to trace which paintings had been lost for generations and which had been lost to Hitler's looting. The FBI spent weeks going through the 1945 Roberts' Commission archives and found three paintings listed as stolen by the Nazis. The estate of Baron Sigmund Bochner, a Munich diamond merchant, filed a list of looted artwork with ownership documents supplied by Gerald Bochner, the great-nephew and the only surviving member of the Bochner family. Relatively small oil on canvas, *Frater Angelo*, one of the early works by the great Renaissance artist, Raphael, had been in the Bochner family for two hundred years.

What was it doing in a French import wine crate, on a Richmond port's dock in 1992? The two other artworks found on the list of looted Holocaust assets had been submitted by their owner's family members back in 1945. Today, only distant relatives remained and the issue rested with the estate lawyers.

THE FBI FIRST sent out careful feelers about the import product of one of the America's richest men. However, Palfrey's intelligence community must have been as sharp as the FBI. Palfrey approached the FBI with documented and notarized information that neither his staff at Chateaux Dax winery nor his US staff had knowledge of this particular wine consignment. But if someone in his organization, whether on the French or US side was smuggling stolen art and artifacts, the FBI and any other agency involved had his full cooperation to flush out the criminals.

"What the FBI back in '92 didn't have was the information that mother and Analise have—that the Raphael painting and the other masterpieces came from one of Hitler's secret hiding places, Chateau Dax, which just happens to be the flagship winery of Palfrey Distilleries," Carmella said. "I told the Justice Department about the *Siberian Oracle* without involving mother. I left the issue of the third child's location unknown. The murders of Anike and Piet were historical events, easily obtained from the L.A. Times and San Francisco Examiner. When Ralston Blumenthal translated the von Flemmings' journal, he knew it would be dangerous to keep such a book on the premises. Analise remembered von Flemmings and telling them her story. I contacted Ralston and he had no objections surrendering the journal to the Justice Department. His mother knew nothing about it. He wanted to keep her out of it to protect her." Carmella lowered her head.

"It wasn't your fault," Gussie spoke up. "It's no use to beat yourself up for things out of your control. You did your duty, alerting those who have the mandate to investigate such things that a criminal has been building his empire with things stolen from people, families who went to gas chambers."

"I don't understand something," Lauren spoke up. "Why would Palfrey hang onto the original gold bar and the two patches of human skin? From what Mrs. Wyndham here said, he found the two sites where Hitler's raiders hid the stolen art and valuables from what his mother told him. Why kill Anike and Piet?"

"Child," Gussie said, "a man like William Palfrey, who never had to work hard to get what he has, will never have enough. You know what they say. When you make your first hundred bucks, you're already planning to make the first thousand. And when you make your first million, you're already stretching your greedy fingers after your first billion. Palfrey had to get rid of Anike and Piet because they could incriminate him. Or more precisely what was tattooed into their backs. He had them killed and the patches of skin stripped off their backs to remove all traces of the *Siberian Oracle,* leading to his flagship enterprise. And once he had the two treasure maps he needed the third one to find the last site of the hidden treasure. That's why he kept the skin patches."

"But why did he keep the gold bar? Why not smelt it like he must have been doing to all the Hitler's gold he found?" Lauren persisted.

"You can't just load a freighter with gold bullion and ship it over to US," Carmella said, lifting her head. "Palfrey has been smelting Hitler's gold bars for years, bringing them over carefully in his wine crates, few at a time. If not for the labor strike in '92 at the Richmond docks, he'd still be doing it. There had to be a great amount of gold hidden in that mushroom cave at Chateau Dax farmhouse and probably a lot still remains."

"I understand that," Lauren said, "but why would Palfrey risk bringing with him to a hotel suite the bag with the gold bar and the two patches of skin?"

"Because whoever told him he knew the identity of the third child and about the existence of the map on that child's back, wanted to see proof that Mr. Palfrey had the other two pieces of the puzzle that would ultimately lead him to the final site," Carmella said.

"Are you saying that Gomez worked for you?" she whispered, because the possibility just occurred to her in light of what she'd heard.

Carmella shook her head. "Not for me, for our Justice Department."

"And he double-crossed...?"

"No, Lauren. Two years ago—after nearly eight years of trying to put together a case against Palfrey and failing miserably because we had absolutely no tangible proof whatsoever—we decided to force Palfrey's hand."

REAL OSWALDO GOMEZ was replaced with an FBI agent, who looked so much like the kid that even the Carlyle management didn't notice anything different. Bellhops aren't noticed all that much by management or guests. It took two years to set up routes such that once Palfrey received a message from Mr. X, claiming knowledge of the Siberian Oracle and the whereabouts of the third child, his intelligence community wasn't able to trace it to its source. Mr. X and Palfrey were to meet during the two-week function in August at the Carlyle. Palfrey was instructed to bring tangible proof that he had found the sites of hidden loot.

"And that's what the FBI agent Gomez was to steal," Lauren said, beginning to understand.

"Not steal, merely document possession by Mr. William Palfrey. Once he finished, agents would spring from the woodwork, identifying themselves so the sting operation would be legally valid."

"I don't understand. What happened? Gomez stole the bag and came to Winthrop," Lauren shook her head.

"Agent Delgado who posed as Gomez for two years is dead. His body was found in the river, a victim of drowning. At this point, it's only a guess but another bellhop must have followed Delgado to the suite. We don't know what happened. I doubt Mr. Palfrey will voluntarily tell us. Delgado was supposed to signal to the agents at the hotel to come forward in their official capacity. If he failed to do it, their orders were to fade and withdraw," Carmella said.

THE BELLHOP, DIEGO Berroto, not only took the bag with the gold and skin patches but also Gomez driver's license and ran. He must have been hiding within his Cuban community for a month it took him to surface in Hartford.

"At this point we're only guessing that Berroto noticed quickly enough that people followed him—and they weren't the police," Carmella said. "It must have given him an inflated idea of the gold bar's worth. That's why he hung onto it for so long. People who work for Palfrey removing obstacles aren't amateurs. They dispose of them in a way that either looks natural or incriminates one or two elements in their fold that are no longer desirable."

"They wanted to remove Errington," she began to understand, smiling but caught herself and grimaced. "I'm sorry. I didn't mean to...."

Carmella interrupted her. "You have every right to smile. Errington set you up to carry out what he was instructed to do— set up Berroto-Gomez. Why should you not feel righteous to learn he got what he deserved?"

"But why would he want to get rid of Errington?" She couldn't see how someone like her boss would be threatening to Palfrey.

Carmella poured herself another glass of wine. "Probably because Dr. Errington became greedy and started making demands to raise his profile and a degree of involvement in the college's affairs. You don't push people like Palfrey without paying the price. "

"Who killed the boy whose body was found in my office?"

"Probably Errington. He must have panicked when he didn't find on him what he was ordered to obtain and called 911, a little too early since you were probably meant to find the dead body. I don't know how that scenario was supposed to go or whether what happened was even supposed to happen. I doubt Dr. Errington would be forthcoming if we asked him. But I'm fairly sure that if Errington would have found the bag, he'd be gone by now; maybe an extended sabbatical to some exotic country, maybe a promotion—I don't know. What I do know is that wherever he'd go, soon enough he'd meet with a fatal accident. That's why Kingsley was behind you, in the shadows, every step of the way."

"Does he work for the Justice Department too?" Lauren asked.

"Amongst other things," Carmella smiled. "But no matter what he does, he does it so well that he has a trunk full of decorations.

Once I saw Palfrey talking to Mr. McPhend at the embassy reception, I knew you were in danger. A man like William Palfrey hardly ever talks to the press, unless he has something to offer them, like a promotion, or a coveted job. Kingsley told me you and John went up to Cragg's Lake. I knew right away Palfrey still pursued his obsession to find the third child but no longer to get the last treasure map. He knew he had to give up that dream because now he needed to protect the dream he'd already realized."

"So it was Kingsley who picked up Dr. Teffler that day after he told John and me about the Siberian Oracle." Lauren motioned at the retired curator who'd sat all through the round-table with a bowed head, an attentive listener.

"I didn't feel comfortable leaving you alone with Mr. McPhend but I figured that as long as there were still issues for the two of you to investigate, you'd be all right."

"Mitch and Jenny?"

"They're all right," Carmella raised the glass to her and took a sip. "Mr. Plow got a speeding ticket in his hometown, got very nasty about it, and his girlfriend came to his assistance. The police had no choice but to put them in jail to cool down. They called what sounded to me like a ton of Mitch's kinfolk to escort their native son and his girlfriend back to the depths of the bayou country."

Lauren smiled. "Was that a staged scenario?"

Carmella inclined her head. "Now, why would you think that? Isn't Mr. Plow a reckless driver?"

"Mitch drives slower than the campus trams," she murmured, smiling.

Chapter 35

"CARMELLA," GUSSIE SPOKE up. "Even with the von Flemmings' journal, does the Justice Department have enough to proceed against Palfrey? I don't see how you can connect the gold bar and the two patches to him. The names on them...hell, a good lawyer can convince a judge that it's just coincidence."

"Dr. Teffler?" Carmella looked at the curator.

"I've spent thirty-five years storing and archiving historical information," he said. "I suppose it's my nature that wouldn't let me destroy those negatives that Glathos brought me. I don't see how Palfrey can talk his way out of that situation. A Middle Eastern billionaire won't take it lightly if Palfrey claims that the Murillo belonged to him and the sheik was trying to sell it to him. Especially in today's highly charged political atmosphere, it would be unwise for Palfrey to lay the blame on the Arab oil magnate. I'm not suggesting the sheik would resort to terrorism but any business enterprise that relies on oil would be soon devastated, particularly Palfrey's foreign holdings. If he claims he didn't know Murillo was part of artwork looted by Hitler's henchmen, he'd be asked where he got it—which art dealer sold it to him. I'm sure Palfrey wouldn't want to answer that question.

"But even if he buys a scapegoat, an art dealer willing to spend years in prison, the Justice Department has the von Flemming's journal where it clearly states that one of the sites where Hitler stored his looted treasure is Chateau Dax farmhouse. And there is Mrs. Wyndham," he nodded at Gussie, "a famous talk show host with an excellent reputation. She can connect Palfrey to *Siberian Oracle* like no one can."

"I'd like to keep mother out of it." Carmella frowned.

"Oh, honey," Gussie tapped her fingernail against the glass. "I don't mind for the story to come out. I had no control over who I am and how I was born. That part never bothered me. My biological father was Hitler's SS officer and my mother was a German patriot who did what she did partly because she had no choice and partly because she was too young to understand the true nature of such glory. The woman I call mother is up in Cragg's Lake Sanatorium. She did what none of the other Adlerinas at Chateau Perigord dared to do: she saved three children. I am Gertrude von Bayern, because that's the name that figures on the official documents the von Flemmings obtained for Analise. I have no problem telling the people of this country, my audience, about my roots. If anything, I wish I hadn't had the map tattooed into my back removed. I could take off my clothes on my show for everyone to see the branding mark, a testament to Hitler's insanity."

Kingsley walked in dressed in green fatigues and a black parka, holding the green canvas bag in his hand like an oversize wallet.

"I'm leaving, ma'am," he inclined his head at Carmella. "The chopper's waiting for me in the parking lot. It's been a pleasure working with you."

"Likewise, Major Kingsley," she nodded, smiling. "And I believe that we have enough evidence to commence proceedings against Mr. Palfrey."

"Major Kingsley," Lauren spoke up. "Thank you for saving my life."

He cracked a smile. "I'm sorry I let it go that far, ma'am. I actually arrived in Rocky Hill ahead of you and Mr. McPhend but it took me a while to find your house. I couldn't see the house numbers. Once I saw your Grand Am pull into the laneway I located it. Tell your landlord to install outside lights."

"Even better," Carmella said. "Get the hell out of Rocky Hill and Winthrop."

Epilogue

S HE ALREADY HAD Terney's coffee waiting for him by the time he arrived at Sagalyn's Coffee Shop.

"Two creams and two sugars," she said.

"There's nothing wrong with your memory," he said and sat down.

"I'm sorry—" she started, but he cut her off.

"No more apologies. You spent five hours in my office apologizing. I'm surprised we managed to get through the deposition. If I wanted to hear more apologies, I'd have handcuffed you to my desk. I'm off duty now. I only want to hear the right things."

"Dr. Errington has left on a two-year sabbatical. He's gone to Brazil, I think. Linda won't divulge details but she told me that he's going to document environmental crimes in the rainforest country and write an award-winning paper for the next international environmental conference."

"Good. I hear there are a lot of snakes in a rainforest. I hope one of them will do the job for me. Without finding any prints on the crime scene, I couldn't even bring him in for questioning. Can't say he's not clever, that's for sure."

She chuckled. "Mitch is transferring back to Louisiana State. Jenny's going with him. She really liked his folks and the bayou life."

"Good. I hope he learns to drive responsibly."

This time she shook her head and laughed. "Carmella said the FBI's working with Interpol. And the Homeland Security in both countries is cooperating as well. The Chateau Dax and the goldmine at Bonnac-Sur-Lot are padlocked. Palfrey's under indictment, while the Justice Department is conducting full review of his enterprises and financial holdings. Congressman Palfrey is planning to relinquish his seat in the House. He tried very hard but no matter what he does, he just can't distance himself from his father."

"American people can be fooled some of the time, but it would have to be a complete idiot to believe that Clement Palfrey knew nothing about his father's source of wealth. And even if he really knew nothing, lesser scandals than this one have sunk many a politician. I'm still waiting to hear more right things."

"I'm going home to Rockland, for Christmas," she said and saw him frown.

"I'm not sure that's a good thing."

"I think it is. Spending holidays with Becky and Brian is just what I need. After Christmas, I'm going to Sebago Lake for a few days. Pete Whittle, my mother's friend, lives there with his kinfolk. Mom and I used to spend every Christmas in Sebago Lake and Pete would take us out on the lake, find a safe spot, and we'd put down our wooden stools, lower the line into the hole in the ice, and spend hours ice-fishing."

"Sounds very cold." He grimaced.

"We wore survival suits. Cold wasn't an issue."

"Did you catch your supper every day?"

"That wasn't an issue either. Just sitting there and occasionally glancing at Mount Washington in the distance was enough to recharge our spiritual batteries. Carmella's joining us too. She said she always wanted to see just how long she can stare at raw, unspoiled vistas, and believe me, the country around Sebago Lake is unspoiled—other than holes drilled in ice."

"I'm still waiting to hear more good things."

"Nicholas School of the Environmental Sciences at Duke has offered me a healthy grant, and I don't even have to change my thesis topic."

He smiled. "Now, that's a damn good thing to hear."

"Yes, Lieutenant. I thought so too."

THE END

www.ingramcontent.com/pod-product-compliance
Lightning Source LLC
Chambersburg PA
CBHW030913120626
46554CB00001B/138